THE PASSING OF
PARLIAMENT

THE PASSING OF PARLIAMENT

by

PROFESSOR G. W. KEETON

M.A · LL.D

Professor of English Law
University College · London

Principal and Treasurer, the
London Institute of World Affairs

LONDON
ERNEST BENN LIMITED

First Published 1952

Distributed in U.S.A. by

John de Graff, Inc.

64 West 23rd Street
New York 10, N. Y.

Published by Ernest Benn Limited
Bouverie House · Fleet Street · London · EC4
Printed in Great Britain by
C. Tinling & Co. Ltd · Liverpool London and Prescot

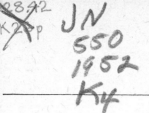

Contents

Acknowledgements

THIS VOLUME is in form an expansion of a number of articles contributed in recent years to various periodicals. I should therefore like to acknowledge the courtesy of the editors for permission to reproduce them from the pages of *Current Legal Problems*, *The Nineteenth Century*, *The Westminster Bank Review*, and *The South African Law Journal*.

G. W. KEETON

Chapter 1

The Twilight of the Common Law

IT is now more than twenty years since Lord Hewart, then Lord Chief Justice, opened a new phase of the campaign against the 'petty despots of Whitehall' by a spirited attack in his *New Despotism*. Quick gains apparently followed this legal offensive. If a Lord Chief Justice had entered the fray, then it was possible—nay, probable—that something was seriously wrong. For a time, the encroachments of bureaucracy were front-page news. Alarm spread from the Temple to Fleet Street, and the Government was sufficiently impressed to set up the Committee on Ministers' Powers in October, 1929. It was a strong Committee, for in addition to three Conservative ex-Ministers and three Labour Members of Parliament, it included three well-known King's Counsel and three leading solicitors, and, in addition, Sir John Anderson, Sir Claud Schuster and Sir Warren Fisher, and, finally, Professor Laski and Sir William Holdsworth. Thus the Committee could properly lay claim to strength, breadth of view, and familiarity with the theoretical and practical implications of delegated legislation. Its proceedings, publicly conducted, showed an anxiety to probe beneath the forms of day-to-day activity in order to lay bare the causes of modern bureaucratic encroachments. The public was reassured by its evident sincerity and ability, and when the report of the Committee appeared, with a glowing tribute to the integrity of the civil service and with recommendations for various alterations of detail, but no proposals for important constitutional change, the public heaved a sigh of relief and forgot the whole question.

Indeed, few reports have assembled so much wisdom whilst proving so completely useless, as the Report of the Committee on Ministers' Powers. Except amongst students of admin-

A*

istrative law (one is tempted to say historians of administrative law) its recommendations are forgotten, even by lawyers and administrators, and in no important respect did the report influence, much less delay, the onrush of administrative power, and the supersession of the ordinary forms of law which is today taking place. The extent to which the general conditions of the problem have changed is shown by the fact that so able a lawyer as Lord Hewart could still write of administrative law and administrative tribunals as an impudent usurpation. Today, not only are both taken for granted, but already it is possible to detect the first suggestions that the ordinary courts have exhausted their usefulness in the era of rapid change through which we are passing. The future will unquestionably see more experiments (ominous though they may be) such as the furnished rent tribunals. From there to people's courts is not so very far, especially if one reflects how far we have travelled in the past twenty years.

Nevertheless, there exists today a major problem which troubles all who are concerned with the problem of justice in the modern State. Most lawyers would admit today that the machinery of the ordinary courts functions under increasing strain. Our rules of evidence are complicated and arbitrary; our procedure is slow and expensive. Moreover, there can be no certainty that this cumbrous and expensive machinery will, in the end, dispense justice to those who invoke it. In the course of a thoughtful analysis of the defects of modern legal procedure in the British Commonwealth, no less an authority than Sir Frederic Eggleston, a former Attorney-General of Victoria and now Australian Ambassador to the United States, said recently:

'In addressing the Medico-Legal Society of Melbourne in which there were leading judges, barristers and solicitors, I stated that the truth of verdicts in trials was really accidental and that only in one case out of four could it be said that verdicts were the due result of scientific processes. I worked this out as follows: in fifty per cent. of the cases tried the verdict was probably correct on the principle of probability. Either the plaintiff or defendant was right and chance would produce a correct verdict in half the cases. In the other cases the legal process might have the effect of bringing about the right result in one case out of two. I expected to be castigated for this statement, but to my intense surprise it was not disputed and judges and advocates all supported it.'[1]

Evidently, therefore, the lawyer in his attack on administrative justice, must not assume that his own system is infallible. It may well be that the administrator has as strong a case against him as he has against the administrator.

On the other hand it is idle to deny that the existing safeguards of private right in administrative tribunals are inadequate, and that increasingly wide delegations of power at times give officials a dangerous immunity from control. In *Blackpool Corporation* v. *Locker*[2] the Court of Appeal condemned in the plainest terms one of the most serious abuses of authority which has occurred in recent times. A local authority requisitioned a house which was unoccupied but which contained the owner's furniture. It purported to act under powers delegated by the Minister of Health. This act of requisition was contested by the owner, who subsequently showed that he had bought the house for his own occupation, and when he asked for the actual terms of the Ministry of Health's circulars (which were the sole foundation of the local authority's claim to requisition) both the local authority and the regional officers of the Ministry refused to communicate them for nearly six months. Indeed, it was only in consequence of the pertinacity of the owner's solicitor that the two public authorities were at length compelled to give way—when it appeared that the corporation in fact possessed no authority at all under the circulars to requisition the houses! Clearly, cases such as this raise questions going to the root of our political association. They reveal a contempt for legal process which is comparable with that of an official in a totalitarian State, or with that of a public officer in the France of 1792. So far these cases have attracted little publicity, because the processes by which property is today removed from private ownership are complex and they are not apt material for newspaper paragraphs. Nevertheless, if the attitude revealed in this case is allowed to develop

[1] 'Legal Development in a Modern Community' in *Interpretations of Modern Legal Philosophies*, p. 181.

[2] [1948], 1 K.B. 439.

unchallenged, the entire constitutional structure of this country will be undermined. In the case under consideration, Lord Justice Scott (who served as Chairman of the Committee on Ministers' Powers) observed:

'There is one quite general question . . . of supreme importance to the continuance of the rule of law under the British constitution, namely, the right of the public affected to know what that law is. That right was denied to the defendant in the present case. The maxim that ignorance of the law does not excuse any subject represents the working hypothesis on which the rule of law rests in British democracy. That maxim applies in legal theory just as much to written as to unwritten law, *i.e.*, to statute law as much as to common law or equity. But the very justification for that basic maxim is that the whole of our law, written or unwritten, is accessible to the public— in the sense, of course, that, at any rate, its legal advisers have access to it, at any moment, as of right. When a government bill is brought before Parliament in a form which, even in regard to merely executive or administrative matters, gives a wide or unlimited discretion to a minister, and objection is made, the answer is sometimes given that the minister may be trusted by the House to use his powers with a wise and reasonable discretion. The answer may be perfectly *bona fide*; but *tempora mutantur*, and another minister or another government may use the unlimited powers indiscreetly or oppressively. If that happens, the only remedy practically open to the aggrieved citizen is action in Parliament to which alone the minister is responsible. But the Act when passed may contain delegated powers to a minister of the Crown to legislate, and the minister may within his powers make rules or orders which constitute binding legislation. Again, the aggrieved has no legal remedy against the legislative act of the minister; he is bound by the terms of the delegated legislation. But in both types of legislation, Parliamentary and delegated, the aggrieved citizen at least knows, or his lawyers can tell him, just what his rights and duties and restrictions are under the new law; because each kind of statutory law is at once published by the King's Printer—whether as Acts of Parliament or as statutory instruments. On the other hand, if the power delegated to the minister is to make sub-delegated legislation and he exercises it, there is no duty on him, either by statute or at common law, to publish his sub-delegated legislation; and John Citizen may remain in complete ignorance of what rights over him and his property have been secretly conferred by the minister on some authority or other, and what residual rights have been left to himself. For practical purposes, the rule of law, of which the nation is so justly proud, breaks down.'

It should not be thought that the powers conferred by delegated and sub-delegated legislation are limited to control or confiscation of property. They may, and have been, extended to the personal freedom of the citizen, for example, in the direction of labour. As yet, their potentialities in this direction are imperfectly appreciated, but an illustration from my own personal experience may serve to illustrate them. During the recent war a friend of mine was charged with a breach of the Defence of the Realm Regulations in being unlawfully on a railway siding (where he had gone in pursuit of his small child, aged three). I was reliably informed that it was only my friend's absence from home at the time of the summons that prevented his arrest. Neither he nor I was at that time aware that the regulation was drafted in such comprehensive terms, and we were unable to secure a copy of the Defence Regulations from the local bookseller. It occurred to me, however, that there would be a copy of them at the nearest police station, which I accordingly visited. On asking to see a copy of the regulations I was informed that *it was not in the public interest that they should be revealed!* In this case the regulations were actually published, and I secured a copy from London, but if they had been unpublished sub-delegated legislation, my friend would have been in a plight as bad as (or worse than) that of the plaintiff in *Blackpool Corporation* v. *Locker*. As one might expect, it is in Nazi Germany and in the U.S.S.R. that the potentialities of this legislative device have been exploited to the uttermost limit.

Lord Hewart's book was not the only contribution to the discussion of this major problem of constitutional law to appear twenty years ago, although it naturally attracted the most popular attention. It was anticipated by the first edition of Professor W. A. Robson's acute and stimulating study *Justice and Administrative Law* (the third edition of which appeared in 1951), whilst Dr. Port's *Administrative Law* was published almost contemporaneously with Lord Hewart's. Unhappily, Dr. Port died shortly after its appearance, with the consequence that the researches which he there initiated into the nature and function of administrative law in foreign systems remained incomplete.

The appearance of these three important works so close together was symptomatic. They defined the nature of the problem for lawyers and others, and they indicated the views which it was possible to hold in respect of it. Not unnaturally, the force with which Lord Hewart had delivered his onslaught produced a reaction, in which the lawyers were pressed hard, but the tide once again turned temporarily in their favour with the appearance of Dr. C. K. Allen's *Bureaucracy Triumphant*, and his fuller work, *Law and Orders*, which appeared in 1945. Of Dr. Allen, Professor Robson, in the second edition of his own book, writes that he represents 'in a more refined and scholarly manner, the school of thought of which Lord Hewart was the crudest and most undiscriminating exponent.'[3]

To understand this great controversy, in which most of our constitutional lawyers and political scientists have joined in recent years, it is necessary to revert to the more settled days of the late nineteenth century, when Anson and Dicey were the high priests of orthodox constitutional theory. They inherited an outlook upon the constitution which owed something to Burke, Blackstone and Bagehot, and which saw in the English system the climax of political achievement. It was left to Dicey to formulate in general principles the assumptions upon which political association in England was founded. They were the doctrine of Parliamentary sovereignty and the Rule of Law. Parliament was omnipotent: it could do, or undo, anything, but it was in no danger of abusing its powers because it was a combination of diverse elements, linked together by an intricate system of 'checks and balances' (*pace* Bagehot), and also because Englishmen possessed, to a markedly greater degree than other peoples, a mysterious political instinct. Moreover, their innate sense of fair play was expressed in legal terms in the Rule of Law, which meant that everyone, from highest to lowest (except the sovereign himself) must answer for his acts before the ordinary courts, according to the ordinary law of the land. There were no official, or administrative, courts in England, deciding disputes between the administration and the ordinary citizen, because there was no official class or bureaucracy.

[3] P. 367.

Everyone, from Cabinet Minister to the meanest clerk in a government office, remained a citizen, and preserved as far as possible, his amateur status in relation to government.

This was satisfying doctrine for a society which was still predominantly aristocratic, rural and individualist; and a note of condescension, almost of contempt, characterises Dicey's exposition of continental constitutions, which contain 'constitutional guarantees' which break down in times of emergency, and which breed increasing numbers of industrious middle-class officials who require the protection of special administrative codes applied in administrative tribunals.

All Dicey's critics have noticed, however, that his complacency is much less marked in the last editions of *Constitutional Law* to be prepared by him in the period just before the first World War. The close of Victoria's reign had witnessed, even in England, the first cautious steps towards the collectivist State. With the assumption of new social responsibilities by the State came new types of official, armed with new power. Steadily, too, the pace of legislation quickened, and as its scope became more comprehensive the practice of delegating legislative power grew. In the last half-century, there has been a shift in the governmental centre of gravity from the floor of the House of Commons to the offices of the great departments of state, where in reality policy is framed. Parliament becomes year by year less of a governing council and more of a censor of executive acts. Even in the sphere of legislation its function is increasingly to define the orbit of legislative activity upon a topic, leaving the detailed working out of the programme to the appropriate department, which, not infrequently, possesses the power to amend the Act by which legislative power is conferred upon it. Dicey's own treatise, *Law and Opinion in England*, shows that he was aware of the general trend of the changes which were taking place in our constitutional structure. It is possible that before his death he would have conceded that an unwritten constitution is not necessarily superior to a written one. His *Constitutional Law* in successive editions had shown a strange inability to recognise that the peculiar strength and stability of the American system owes something to the constitutional compact which is embodied in the American constitution. Had he written his lectures thirty years later it is possible that he would have had a good deal more to say on this point. In any event, in the edition of his *Constitutional Law* which appeared before the first World War, he sounds a note of alarm. The Rule of Law is under attack. It is no longer true that we have no administrative law in England. We have a good deal of it, and it is urgently necessary to set limits to its encroachments.

Whatever might have been the result of the growing awareness of the classical constitutional lawyers of the stealthy inroads of administrative power upon Parliamentary sovereignty had there been no war, the conclusion of the first World War ushered in a new phase of development, for during four and a half years of war Parliament had sanctioned successive extensions of administrative power without precedent since the execution of Charles I. Once the emergency had passed, however, lawyers who had been trained in the school of Anson and Dicey, and who now occupied leading positions within their profession, waited confidently for a return to the pre-war system. Administrative power did not decline, however; it continued to grow very rapidly, and appetite grew with what it fed upon. Indeed, the temper of the times had changed. The era of controls and compulsory powers had opened.

Accordingly, the appearance of the works of Lord Hewart, Dr. Port, and Dr. Robson (as he then was) within the space of a few months was significant. They indicated that we were face to face with one of the great issues in the history of our political evolution. The reaction of each of the three writers was significant. In spite of Professor Robson's strictures, Lord Hewart's book is of major importance. It represents the anxiety of the head of the historic courts of common law at a new threat to the supremacy of law. The terms in which Lord Hewart writes recall (no doubt intentionally) the terms used by Coke, one of the greatest of Lord Hewart's predecessors, in defending Parliamentary sovereignty and the rule of law. Dr. Port's approach is quite a different one. He wishes to discover how far English experience has any counterpart abroad. He finds that it has—not only on the Continent, but in the United States.

Apparently, therefore, even a written constitution could not save us from administrative encroachment. It is, in fact, a product of the modern social consciousness. But Dr. Port points out the significant fact that the Continental nations whose constitutions had been damned with faint praise by Dicey, had established regular systems of administrative law, applied in administrative courts, and in so doing, had more effectively protected the subject against arbitrary official action than the English system had so far been able to do. This somewhat surprising conclusion received weighty confirmation from another distinguished constitutional lawyer, Professor J. H. Morgan, K.C., in a little work which is not sufficiently widely known.

Professor Robson's work has again a different method of approach. Whilst by no means ignoring the importance and implications of increasingly wide grants of legislative power by Parliament to executive departments, he is primarily concerned with the alleged conflict between law and administration in the decision of cases between subjects and the state. A court of law, it is said, exists to decide private rights; a department of state exists to promote a policy. Yet judicial decisions are manifestly the expression of judicial conceptions of social policy, and it is rarely possible to point to policy decisions which ignore private rights. What is needed, therefore, says Professor Robson, is the extension of the main elements of the judicial process to decisions upon private rights within the departments. Summing up one phase of his argument, Professor Robson says:

'What we advocate, therefore, is that all administrative tribunals, and other bodies performing judicial functions, should be required invariably to describe the reasons on which their decisions are founded. The reasons, like the decisions, may be good or they may be bad, the premises from which the argument starts may be true or false, the inferences unwarranted, and cause confused with effect; but the obligation to evolve a chain of reasoning which must stand the strain of criticism and discussion, is desirable from the point of view of promoting a sense of the judicial spirit in the adjudicator no less than in importing certainty into the body of the law.'

Professor Robson's development of this thesis leads him to the conclusion that private rights would be better pro-

tected by a regular system of administrative courts acting
in accordance with the principles he has discussed than by
a perpetuation and extension of our present administrative
chaos. Unfortunately, this view was decisively rejected by
the Committee on Ministers' Powers, which does not seem
to have grasped its implications, and since the publication
of its report the situation has deteriorated a good deal further.
Indeed, the Committee seems to have laboured under the
delusion that an eloquent and well-merited tribute to the
integrity of the civil service, coupled with a few procedural
amendments, disposed of this great issue. Its report restored
to the public a sense of security, which had been badly shaken
by Lord Hewart's book, and which subsequent events have
proved to be false.

The three books which have been discussed above are
by no means the whole literature upon this question to
appear in recent years. Indeed, to a greater or lesser degree
every work upon Constitutional Law and most works upon
Jurisprudence now have something to say upon it. The attitude of Dr. C. K. Allen has already been mentioned. It
remains to add the names of Sir Ivor Jennings and Professor
Laski to those who are by no means dismayed by recent
developments but who would nevertheless wish to see the
present administrative chaos replaced by some coherent
system. At this point the reader will no doubt perceive an
interesting circumstance. Professor Robson and Professor
Laski, Sir Ivor Jennings and Dr. Port either hold or have
held important teaching posts at the London School of
Economics and Political Science, and in spite of important
differences in point of view between them, they may all
be grouped together as exponents of a particular type of
political thought. Their adversaries can also be grouped
together. Amongst the most distinguished of them are Dr.
C. K. Allen, the late Lord Hewart, and the late Sir William
Holdsworth. This is not accidental. Those who regard
modern developments with equanimity have done so because
they have recognised the growth of administrative power as
an instrument of planning in a period of rapid social change.
As yet, the possibilities of administrative power have by no
means been fully explored. Sir Stafford Cripps and Professor

Laski pointed out in the inter-war period that revolutionary changes might have to be brought about by a general delegation of power by Parliament to the executive. This is, in fact, no more than happens in war-time. It also happened in Germany between 1930 and 1939. The delegation of still wider powers of legislation to the departments would necessarily involve also the establishment of new adminstrative tribunals, working independently of the ordinary courts. Already this process has gone very far in England. If ministerial conduct is to be scrutinised it is no longer by the ordinary courts, but by an *ad hoc* Tribunal of Inquiry. If rents of furnished houses are thought to be excessive, no one suggests that magistrates' courts may establish fair rents. Special rent tribunals are set up. From here to special marketing tribunals, and special tribunals for motor-car accidents is no more than a step—and then what is left of the common law, or, for that matter, of private right?

This is, as it were, the problem behind the problem; and when Holdsworth, Lord Hewart and Dr. Allen attacked the extension of administrative powers of legislation and adjudication, it was with the knowledge that each successive delegation for the purpose of developing a policy and each delegation of powers of adjudication to administrative tribunals represented a fresh victory for policy over private right. The whole conception of the orbit and enforceability of a private right differs fundamentally today from what it meant sixty or seventy years ago. A private right may, without exaggeration, be defined as an area of personal freedom which exists only so long as it does not impede the development of a social policy by a public organ. When it does, compulsory powers of acquisition or of personal direction, coupled with departmental legislation and adjudication will effectively compass its destruction. It is only very exceptionally today that the hunted citizen can escape from the comprehensive meshes of this spider's web into the somewhat Olympian calm of the ordinary courts—and when he does it is frequently to be told that, however regrettable it may be, the court has no power to interfere with the inexorable advance of departmental policy.

Behind this constitutional conflict between law and administration it is evident that there exists a still more fundamental problem. The days of individualism have ended, for the time being at any rate. Everywhere, to a greater or a lesser degree, the collectivist state is triumphant. There are, it is clear, many possible forms of collectivism, but they all use certain clearly recognisable techniques to develop their policies. We are all aware which way the tide is running. How far do we wish it to run? Do we wish it to batter down the few remaining barriers between the executive and the citizen? Are we really satisfied that official policy is necessarily a satisfactory substitute for private right? The consideration of these questions passes far beyond the province of the constitutional lawyer; beyond, indeed, the province of the jurist or the political scientist. Nevertheless, it will only be when these fundamental questions have been answered that we shall be able to define the purpose, function, and orbit of administrative law and administrative justice in the modern State.

The Road to Moscow

I

THOSE who frequent the cinema will be familiar with the exploits of two American comedians, both world-famous, who periodically combine in a succession of films, each describing their adventures together on the road to some great city. The technique is in every case the same. The two comedians set out with no clear idea where they are going, or how they are going to get there. At times they appear to be travelling anywhere except to their nominal destination. There are innumerable digressions and irrelevancies, and then, unexpectedly, in the last hundred feet of film or so, there they are in the city after all! So far, however, there is one great city towards which Messrs. Hope and Crosby have not directed their wandering feet. As yet, there has been no 'Road to Moscow'. Possibly that is because their technique in this instance has been anticipated by developments in these islands since 1945. Without set purpose and with many hesitations and digressions, our feet have stumbled some significant part of the way along the road to Moscow. Whether we shall eventually arrive, yet remains to be seen.

If we ask ourselves what are the outstanding political characteristics of the Soviet system, we should conclude that they are three: (1) a one-party organisation in which, although there is a wide power of criticism within the party, no external opposition is tolerated; (2) an all-powerful executive, which can put into effect the programme decided upon by the party, without substantial impediment or modification, especially that which might emanate from an independent Parliament, and (3) an economy which is moulded within the framework of a comprehensive plan, and in which all the more significant activities are government monopolies, subservient only to executive control.

So far, it is clear, we have not yet arrived in Moscow. We do not yet have the one-party state. Today, the executive is not quite all-powerful, although it is beyond question that it has increased very considerably in power during the past quarter of a century, and that it exists increasingly for the purpose of putting into effect a pre-determined plan. As far as the third characteristic is concerned, very considerable development, indeed has occurred. Successive measures of nationalisation have brought about the establishment of huge state-monopolies, subordinate to the executive, and over which Parliament exercises only a tenous scrutiny through the medium of questions to the Minister, within whose sphere the state monopoly operates.

Thus, a recent writer of eminence concludes her analysis of recent constitutional developments in Great Britain with the following weighty warning:

'The trend of modern constitutional development towards a concentration of legislative, administrative, and judicial powers in the hands of the Executive has already gone a long way towards upsetting the balance of powers as it obtained in the nineteenth century. The democratic method of law-making by a representative assembly is being superseded in many fields by the autocratic method of governmental legislation. Though this legislation is delegated and controlled by Parliament, it can no longer be described as subordinate as it is usually equipped with the force of law. Owing to the wide discretionary powers conferred by the instruments of authority, it also enjoys to a great extent immunity from judicial control. The Government is thus being instituted as a second legislature and the ordinance changed into a law. Whatever are the reasons for these changes, it would be futile to minimize the dangers which result from the present lack of constitutional balance. These dangers are real dangers, despite the fact that they are so far not of an actual, but of a potential danger only. Though it is true that up to the present no British Government has made full use of all the powers which confident Parliaments have bestowed upon it, these powers exist and their very existence may—in changed circumstances—constitute a serious threat to the democratic foundations of the British Constitution.'[1]

It may, perhaps, be argued that these developments, the cumulative effect of which upon our constitutional structure is very considerable, have no necessary connexion with

[1] M. A. Sieghart. *Government by Decree.* pp. 147-8.

Moscow; that indeed, they are part of an inevitable change in the nature and functions of government to meet changed twentieth-century conditions. Such a hypothesis, however, conceals the underlying truth—that it is change *in a particular direction* and *in the light of a particular theory* which has occurred. Other types of change are possible. The change which has occurred has led directly to the aggrandisement of the State and the Executive and, as a necessary consequence, to diminution of the status and freedom of action of its component individuals. As yet, the Soviet system illustrates this development in its most extreme form, but the political and economic structure of this country now affords a fairly-well developed example of the same type. The most ominous feature of the development is that modern techniques of social control make it possible to organise slave-states on a scale never before contemplated. The machinery already exists. What to a considerable degree conceals its significance in Great Britain is that the system of two-party government is deep-rooted in our political consciousness. If it were not, then the extent to which our political machinery resembles that of Soviet Russia would be more clearly apparent. So long as a plurality of parties does exist, then although Parliament and the courts can be, and in fact are, frequently by-passed, they cannot be ignored.

2. *The Growth of the Machinery of Despotism*

Dicey's *Introduction to the Law of the Constitution* is still the most illuminating exposition of the nineteenth-century constitutional system which we possess. In that volume, his primary purpose is to discuss the factors which have given one constitutional life stability, especially when contrasted with the successive constitutional experiments of the major states of the continent. He concludes that the twin pillars upon which our system rests are the sovereignty of Parliament and the supremacy of the common law, administered in the ordinary courts independent of the executive, over everyone within the realm, whether public official or private citizen. This is, indeed, precisely what one would expect, for these were the twin principles for which the great constitutional struggle, beginning with the accession of James I and ending with the flight of James II, was fought. The first two Stuarts had denied the sovereignty of Parliament, asserting their own freedom of action, by assertion of the prerogative. As a necessary consequence, they sought to make the judiciary subservient to their policy, and when they failed completely to overawe the judiciary, they were led to rely increasingly upon courts, such as the Star Chamber, which were in origin offshoots of the King's Council, and which did not regard themselves as bound by the rules of common law. The Star Chamber, says F. Maitland, was "a court of politicians enforcing a policy, not a court of judges administering the law".[2] Inevitably, the royal policy provoked opposition from Parliament and from the common lawyers, and the late Sir William Holdsworth, in a memorable Creighton Lecture,[3] has shown how the alliance of Parliamentarians and common lawyers, first brought about the overthrow of royal pretensions, and then preserved the essential constitutional tradition of the country against a succession of reforming cranks. When the struggle was at length complete, Parliamentary sovereignty stood unchallenged, whilst the common lawyers also reaped their reward in the abolition of the prerogative courts which had challenged the supremacy of the common law. The result was that for nearly two centuries, there was an almost complete absence from England of anything resembling executive absolutism, and with it a system of administrative law operating outside the jurisdiction of the ordinary courts. The subject was free to do as he pleased, except in so far as he was forbidden by the ordinary rules of the common law. In England, that is to say, there existed no class of men, officials or others, who were privileged in having their acts placed beyond the reach of the ordinary courts. It was this fact which appealed so strongly to foreigners who, like Voltaire and Montesquieu, contrasted the English system with that prevailing on the continent in their day. Moreover, during the same period, changes in the law were not only enacted by, but initiated and decided in, Parliament.

---

[2] *Constitutional History*, p. 263.
[3] *The Influence of the Legal Profession on the Growth of the English Constitution. Essays in Law and History*, p 71.

This system was peculiarly well adapted for the Englishmen of the eighteenth and nineteenth centuries, and it stood the test of successive strains. The period from 1688 until 1815 was one of prolonged and bitter wars, during which Great Britain survived two Jacobite insurrections, numerous threats of invasion, and, during the Revolutionary war with France, two naval mutinies and an Irish rebellion simultaneously. During the Napoleonic wars, Great Britain for a time stood alone against a continent which had been united under an aggressive military dictator. It cannot be contended, therefore, that the structure built at the close of the seventeenth century was apt for periods of peace but not for times of stress. It emerged in 1815 substantially unchanged from twenty-two years of war with France, during which a widespread attempt had been made to overturn our constitutional system by means of what today we should term 'fifth-column' activities, which had been met by emergency measures which passed with the restoration of peace. Of necessity at such a period, ministers were sometimes compelled to act very boldly indeed, but they acted in general within the limits traced out in the constitutional settlement a century earlier, and where they were compelled to overstep these limits, they asked Parliament for an indemnity. If the successive phases of the War of 1793-1815 are examined, it will be found that there arose exactly the problems which were faced again in the wars of 1914-18 and 1939-45.

On the other hand, in time of peace, this system had peculiar advantages. It gave the individual citizen that security and self-reliance in which he could prosecute his affairs without risk of arbitrary interference. The accepted function of the state was to foster and preserve those conditions in which the individual could achieve the greatest self-realisation. By modern standards, this is possibly not an ideal conception. It left too much to individual initiative. It was, however, that individual initiative, and not state enterprise, which built the British dominions overseas, and which brought the British flag and British commerce to every port in the world. France, it should be remembered, had tried the method of state-enterprise as an instrument of empire-building in the seventeenth and eighteenth centuries, but the French colonies overseas had remained struggling communities, incapable of survival against increasing British pressure. It was only after the fall of French power in North America, and with it the system of paternalism which that power fostered, that the foundations of the modern prosperity of French Canada were laid.

In the second half of the nineteenth century, however, a change in outlook slowly took possession of government. This can be traced directly to the progressive extension of the franchise during the century. Such a vast transfer of political power brought with it the necessity for developing new objectives in domestic policy. To foster a steadily-rising standard of living by means of a continuous expansion of trade was not enough. There must be more direct and tangible benefits for those whose votes now dominated elections. Accordingly, policy changed steadily from social reform to social revolution. It was not sufficient that conditions should be improved. They must be changed. Simultaneously, the function of taxation changed. Instead of being a means whereby the necessary funds for essential State services should be raised, taxation itself became an instrument of social change. It became an annual redistribution of wealth, and a means whereby an ever-increasing range of benefits could be secured to the lower income groups. By the turn of the century, this fundamental change was already well under way. For example, Sir Michael Hicks Beach, as Chancellor of the Exchequer, in his Budget statement in 1899 said:

'I daresay I am old-fashioned in my ideas, but I look with alarm on the tendency of the present day, quite irrespective of political opinion—a tendency which is perhaps more rife on this side of the House than on that—to look to the Exchequer and the central Government for superintendence, for assistance, for inspection, and for control in all kinds of departments of life, in all kinds of relations between individuals, in which, in the old days, the Government of the country was never deemed capable of action at all.'[4]

That short statement placed the extent of the change in the political outlook in a nutshell. Sir Michael Hicks Beach, however, was the last of the old line of Chancellors, bred

[4] V. Hicks Beach. *Life of Sir Michael Hicks Beach*, Vol. II, pp. 95-96.

in the school of Sir Robert Peel, and his appeal met with little support, even from fellow-members of the Cabinet. The Press clamoured for a 'broader basis of taxation', some organs for defence and others for increased social services. Two years later the Chancellor was still fruitlessly pleading with his colleagues, and in a letter to Joseph Chamberlain, on October 2nd, 1901, he writes:

'I do not ask for a reduction of our present burthens. That is impossible without a reaction, which, as you say, has not yet visibly begun. But I do ask for a cessation, so far as may be possible, of their increase; and certainly for a much less rate of increase than has prevailed in the past six years. It is true that our present burthens, in peace time, are very light—considering the increase in population and wealth—as compared with those borne by our ancestors 100 years ago. But they were then engaged in a life and death struggle with France; the cases do not admit of comparison. It may also be that our people at large (not payers of direct taxation) are more lightly taxed than the people of other European countries now. But one of the main causes of the increase of the wealth and comfort of our population in the last 50 years, far greater than in any other European nation, has been the lightness of our taxation; and if our peace taxation is to grow largely, as it must if our present rate of expenditure continues, wealth and comfort will be so diminished as to cause grave danger to our social system.'[5]

Hicks Beach completely failed to convince his colleagues, however, and on his resignation, the race of saving Chancellors was extinct. Every subsequent Chancellor has been a spending Chancellor, even if the pace of expenditure has not remained constant. The consequences on our economy are plain to see, whilst even today, half a century after Hicks Beach's unheeded appeal, the cry is still for more armaments and more social services, with more administrative control over every phase of the national economy.

The development of social services, with their new techniques of social control, produced a crop of new problems for Parliament. To define the social regulation of millions of lives, or of important branches of industry, in terms of legislation is never easy. Statutes became longer and more complex, as successive volumes of late nineteenth century statutes will show. Even so, the machinery of control needed to be

[5] *Ibid.,* pp. 157-158.

more complex than an Act of Parliament permitted. Control is always experimental, and it needs progressive modification, if its objects are to be achieved. Hence, there arose the practice of defining the broad objects of social change in a statute, leaving the department charged with its administration to devise the necessary regulations for its enforcement. Such regulations, in origin at least, were subordinate to the statute to which they owed their origin. They were, moreover, subject to Parliamentary scrutiny and repeal. Thus, it came about that Maitland, writing so long ago as the middle-eighties could say :

> 'We are becoming a much-governed nation, governed by all manner of councils and boards and officers, central and local, high and low, exercising the powers which have been committed to them by modern statutes.'[6]

Already before the end of the nineteenth century, the process of submitting all this departmental legislative activity to Parliamentary control was causing anxiety, but two successive Parliamentary Counsel, Sir Henry Jenkyns and Lord Thring, were able to offer reassurance by reaching the conclusion that it was a great advantage to be able to save Parliamentary time by leaving the details to the departments, leaving a greater amount of time for matters of more general concern, whilst any attempt to by-pass Parliamentary scrutiny could be checked by the process of laying draft orders before the House.[7] Neither distinguished counsel, however, attempted to explain who was going to exercise this check, if Parliamentary time was increasingly consumed with 'more serious questions'. Today, the annual output of subordinate legislation is nine times the annual output of statutes. These latter usually fit two fat and closely-printed volumes. How the private member is to grapple with the substance and implications of departmental legislation has never been satisfactorily explained. In recent years, a special Parliamentary Committee has been established to scrutinise it, but even this cannot cope effectively with the avalanche of regulations; rules, orders and other departmental material which ceaselessly pours forth.

[6] *Constitutional History*, p. 417.
[7] C. K. Allen. *Laws and Orders*, p. 28.

3. Are the Departments Sovereign?

Dicey pointed out that one main consequence of the sovereignty of Parliament was that Parliament was legislatively omnipotent; that is to say, that it could make or unmake any law it pleased, and that there existed no rival legislative body which could make laws which overrode those of Parliament or which could not be forced to yield to the force of a Parliamentary statute. This, indeed, was one of the main points of contention between Parliament and the first Stuarts. Both James I and Charles I claimed that they had power to make binding laws independently of Parliament. The Revolution of 1688 ended such claims by the monarch. Today, however, the departments have for all practical purposes established an independent legislative power.

The steps by which this position has been established, notwithstanding the jealousy of Parliament, and the reassurances of Lord Thring and his predecessor, are plain and continuous. The Reform Bill of 1832 liberated Parliament from the legislative inhibitions of the eighteenth century. Thereafter, legislation was used increasingly as the instrument for social change. Of necessity, this could not be completely comprehended within the clauses of statutes, so that little by little the practice grew of setting out the main features of the proposed change in the statute itself, and at the same time Parliament conferred on the appropriate government department power to make regulations having statutory force, within the terms of the statute. At first, the potentialities of this innovation passed unnoticed. Even so acute a critic as Dicey observed, with some complacency:

> 'Unless the temper of Parliament should materially change, attempts to give delegated powers in unduly wide terms, or to extend them beyond matters of minor importance, or to strain their exercise, would produce a reaction which would have a mischievous and embarrassing effect on the form of Parliamentary legislation.'

Whether Dicey means by this that excessive delegation would lead to the abolition of delegation altogether, which would be a bad thing, or whether he means it would upset the balance of the constitution is not altogether clear. The fact remains that the temper of Parliament has changed and with remarkable rapidity. All Parliaments this century have conceded to the departments power to legislate in increasingly wide terms, and their readiness to do so has no doubt been increased by inevitable growth of executive power during two world wars.

The constitutional lawyers are not to be condemned, however, for failing to perceive the sinister possibilities of the new instrument which Parliament had created. Until the end of the nineteenth century, the pressure of public business was not so great that important measures had to be rushed through Parliament by a pliant majority, without adequate debate, as they not infrequently are today. Moreover, until the Parliament Act of 1911, the House of Lords acted as an effective brake upon hasty legislation, especially if the social changes which it embodied were far-reaching. Altogether apart from these legislative limitations, however, there were two other factors which operated to keep the departments within bounds. They were the operation of the *ultra vires* doctrine, and the possibility of testing the effect of the regulations themselves in the ordinary courts. These two judicial checks were often associated in appeals to the courts, but they were in substance quite distinct.

The *ultra vires* doctrine was one further and necessary consequence of Parliamentary sovereignty. If the authority of a statute was unchallengeable, it followed that all regulations made in pursuance of it must be limited by the circumstance that they must be within the terms of the competence conferred on the department, and further, they must not contravene the statute itself. If it were alleged, therefore, that a Minister's regulation, made under a statute, had exceeded the competence conferred on the minister, this was a matter which must be tested before the courts. In this way, the courts became the guardians of the constitution, on behalf of Parliament, to ensure that its sovereign authority was not infringed. Moreover, when an official act was done, either under the statute or the regulations, any person who was adversely affected by that act could appeal to the ordinary courts, exactly as he could if the act had been committed by a private citizen. This, as we have seen, is the essence of the rule of law. Departments, however, have habitually considered it inappropriate, either that they should be subject to the control of a sovereign Parliament or that they should be answerable in the ordinary courts, as all other citizens are, for what they do. Accordingly, in many statutes they have taken powers to make regulations and orders which, *by the mere fact of being made*, are conclusive evidence that they are within the terms of the statute conferring the power to make them. They have even gone further, and taken powers to vary, by departmental regulation, the terms of the statute itself; and finally, they have taken the precaution of excluding all appeals to the ordinary courts by subjects who are aggrieved by the exercise of departmental despotism. It is in vain that successive judges in the courts have drawn attention to the fact that such powers completely upset the balance of the constitution, and that they have stressed the very grave threat to individual freedom that these powers constitute. Inasmuch as the Press cannot report every arbitrary invasion of the subject's rights, and inasmuch of what the department does is done behind the closed doors of the ministry, the ordinary citizen is unfortunately only too prone to regard what is being done as of no direct interest to him, until some particularly audacious onslaught, as for example, a planning order under the Town and Country Planning Act, compelling him to remove some treasured, but amateur erection from his garden, compels him to take notice how far this deprivation of liberty has already gone. It raises, moreover, an even more fundamental question. If Departments can today legislate beyond the reach of Parliament, and if, as they do constantly, they exclude the jurisdiction of the ordinary courts, substituting for it the jurisdiction of their own departmental tribunals, is it not clear that they have effectively excluded the rule of law and the control of Parliament from increasingly wide areas of the subject's social existence? If this is so, is it not clear that 'the rule of law' and 'the sovereignty of Parliament' have both become polite, and increasingly meaningless fictions?

The procedure by means of which the departments take powers to amend the constitutive Act, *or any other Act*, is usually included in what is known as the "Henry VIII clause", significantly named, not only from the most powerful English king, but also from the Statute of Proclamations which conferred upon Henry, alone of English sovereigns, the power to make proclamations with full legislative force. Since, where this clause exists, there is no possibility of attacking it in any court, appeals to the ordinary courts upon the effects of this clause are practically non-existent, and when the effect of this clause was discussed by the Committee on Ministers' Powers, several witnesses remarked that although they greatly disliked it, they were not aware of any abuse. The very nature of these observations, however, recalls the arguments used in the Soviet Union to defend the Soviet conception of democracy, viz. that there is little or no opposition to it. When anything which a Minister does can be embodied in statutory form, then abuse is naturally impossible, for the sufficient reason that opposition can never be effective. We have, in fact, reached the threshold of tyranny. I may, for example, regard an order of the Minister of Town and Country Planning as contrary to the principles of natural justice, as made in violation of every principle of the common law, and as destructive of my livelihood, but there is nothing I can do about it in the ordinary courts. My protests will be considered by administrative authority throughout, in accordance with administrative practice. In Great Britain, we do not even have, as some Continental countries have, a uniform system of administrative tribunals, with a uniform procedure, or the possibility of an appeal to an administrative Court of Appeal, in which the judicial element is preponderant. The position has been grimly emphasised in recent years in the case of *Franklin* v. *Minister of Town and Country Planning*.[8] In that case, Franklin and others were occupiers of land and houses in Stevenage. On August 3, 1946, the Minister of Town and Country Planning prepared the draft Stevenage New Town (Designation) Order, 1946, under powers conferred in the New Towns Act, 1946, and on August 6, 1946, he caused this to be published, and notices to be issued as prescribed by Paragraph 2 of the First Schedule

[8] [1948] A.C. 87.

of the Act. Thereafter objections were received from numerous persons, including Franklin and others. The Minister then sent an Inspector of the Ministry to hold a public local enquiry as prescribed by Paragraph 3 of the First Schedule. The enquiry was held on October 7th and 8th, 1946, and on October 25th, the Inspector submitted his report to the Ministry. On November 11th, the Minister made an order for the creation of the New Town, as prescribed by Paragraph 4 of the First Schedule, whereupon, on December 9th, 1946, Franklin and others applied to the King's Bench Division to have the order quashed on various grounds, of which the chief were that the terms of the Act had not been complied with, in that the Minister had already declared, before the enquiry was held, that he was going to make the order, notwithstanding the opposition. The Minister, therefore (it was alleged) was biassed in his consideration of the objections raised at the enquiry. Henn Collins J. in the King's Bench Division held that the order must be quashed, since the Minister had failed to act judicially in considering the objections. If he reached any other decision, he said, he would be forced to the conclusion that the procedure of public enquiry, as prescribed by the Act, was a sham, which gave the subject 'a right to fulminate and nothing more'. Both the Court of Appeal and the House of Lords, however, decided that the order must stand. This decision was reached, not on any variation in view between them and Henn Collins J. in respect of the proceedings at the enquiry or of the conduct of the Minister, but simply on the ground that the Minister, in making the order, was acting administratively, and not judicially, so that the question of bias was irrelevant. In matters such as this, therefore, it is evident that the subject has simply a right to fulminate and nothing more, for he is far beyond the reach of any assistance from the courts.

Franklin's case does not stand alone, nor is it in any way remarkable for its facts. In 1939, for example, there was decided the case of *Robins* v. *Minister of Health*,[9] the remarkable facts of which are tersely summarised in Lord Justice MacKinnon's judgment in the case as follows:

[9] [1939] 1 K.B. 537.

B

'The appellants some years ago bought this property with the sole object of obtaining a vacant site for buildings which they wished to erect as an extension of their existing premises in the course of the development of their business. They have been prevented from carrying out that desire by reason of the operation of the Rent Restriction Acts. The corporation,[10] having power to acquire the site unhampered by those Acts, could and did declare it to be a clearance area under s. 25 of the Housing Act, 1936. The corporation could then under subsection (3) of that section secure the clearance of the area either (a) by ordering the demolition of the buildings, or (b) by purchasing the land. Considering that an order for demolition would be welcomed with alacrity by the appellants, and that there can be no doubt as to their ability to comply with it, one might have expected that an order under (a) for demolition would be made. But the corporation preferred to proceed by purchase under (b), and they eventually made a compulsory purchase order which has been confirmed by the Minister. Unless that order can be set aside by this court, they can thus pull down the buildings, although as I have said, there is no suggestion that the appellants themselves could not pull them down with equal diligence. The corporation, if they pull down the buildings and acquire the land, can sell it under sec. 30 (1)(a), or, without pulling down the buildings, they can sell the site under sec. 30 (1)(b), subject to a condition that the purchasers shall pull them down. Obviously, in either case the appellants who want to extend their existing premises, must be the most eager purchasers. In such circumstances, the possibility of using the provisions of the Act for the indirect purpose of making money out of the appellants is apparent.'

The Court of Appeal was forced to hold, nevertheless, that it had no power to help the appellants, and that the Act permitted the corporation to act in a way which, in an individual, would scarcely have been regarded as creditable.

4. The Machinery of Dictatorship

Moreover, the subject can no longer comfort himself with the reflection that it is merely the whole of his property which is today exposed to the rapacious attentions of the departments. In the war of 1914-18, Defence of the Realm Regulation 14B conferred upon the executive powers to detain *indefinitely and without trial* persons who, though British subjects, were, in the opinion of a Minister deemed to be of hostile origin and associations. If internment occurred,

[10] of Brighton.

the House of Lords decided in *Zadig's Case*,[11] there was no legal process whereby they could either be brought to trial or freed. So long as the Regulation existed, therefore, the imprisonment might well be perpetual. In the war of 1939-45, this procedure was extended under Regulation 18B of the Defence Regulations to British-born subjects of "hostile associations". In *Liversidge* v. *Anderson*,[12] the House of Lords reached the conclusion, not only that there was no legal machinery which could be invoked to assist persons so interned, but that there was no method known to law whereby the reasonableness of the Home Secretary's action could be tested. So far, such imprisonment (or, as it is normally styled, internment) has been confined to war-time only, for these oppressive Regulations have been amongst the first to be repealed, once hostilities have ceased. Nevertheless, under the Emergency Powers Act, 1920, it is provided that where a state of emergency has been proclaimed, Ministers may by Order in Council, make regulations

> 'for securing the essentials of life to the community, and those regulations may confer or impose on a Secretary of State or other Government department, or any other persons in His Majesty's service or acting on His Majesty's behalf, such powers and duties as His Majesty may deem necessary for the preservation of the peace, for securing and regulating the supply and distribution of food, water, fuel, light, and other necessities, for maintaining the means of transit or locomotion, and for any other purposes essential to the public safety and the life of the community, and may make such provisions incidental to the powers aforesaid as may appear to His Majesty to be required for making the exercise of those powers effective.'

Hitherto, Governments have shown themselves extremely reluctant to make use of powers which are wide enough to establish a rigid dictatorship by the simple expedient of proclaiming a state of emergency. Their successors, however, may not necessarily be so restrained. Should they fail to be so moderate, they will be able to cite in support of their actions the writings of Sir Stafford Cripps, who wrote in an essay entitled 'Can Socialism Come by Constitutional Methods?' in *Problems of a Socialist Government*.

[11] [1917] A.C. 260.
[12] [1942] A.C. 206.

'From the moment when the Government takes control rapid and effective action must be possible in every sphere of the national life. . . . The Government's first step will be to call Parliament together at the earliest moment and place before it an Emergency Powers Bill to be passed through all its stages on the first day. This Bill will be wide enough in its terms to allow all that will be immediately necessary to be done by ministerial orders. These orders must be incapable of challenge in the courts or in any way except in the House of Commons.'

The régimes of both Mussolini and Hitler, it will be remembered, began in exactly the same way, and inasmuch as Sir Stafford points out that all opposition to government policy is to be treated as sabotage, it is clear that the dissolution of an effective Parliamentary opposition would rank high on the list of priorities. Neither Sir Stafford nor his associates it must be conceded fulfilled the promise of these inter-war years. That, however, misses the point that the machinery exists for the use of others in whom, when the testing time comes, the liberal tradition is less firmly engrained.

There was, perhaps, a special appropriateness in the remarks of Mr. Clement Davies in the House of Commons on October 23rd, 1950, that

'it was sad to see how little interest was being taken in a matter that concerned the sovereignty of Parliament by members of all parties. During the last thirty years the tendency had been to surrender back to the executive powers that had been won from them over the centuries. There was a tendency to initiate a new judicial power, to create administrative laws, making the executive to a large extent judges in their own case. The sovereignty of Parliament was threatened. All the time we were being called on to surrender more and more of our rights and privileges to the Government of the day. This continuous erosion was far more dangerous to liberty than any attack from the other side. We were awake to that and could resist it, but the drip, drip, drip of erosion was more likely to destroy the House.'

These last remarks are worthy of careful consideration. Once powers have been conceded to the executive for a special emergency, there is deep-rooted resistance to the suggestion that they should be surrendered, even though the emergency is long past. Isasmuch as administrators have found it convenient to govern by the use of these powers, that in itself is considered to be a good enough reason for their retention. A very clear illustration of this is found in the history of identity cards. Although they have long been known in continental police States, they were unknown in the United Kingdom until the recent war. Even during the war of 1914-18 no need was felt for introducing them. However, a scheme of national registration, including the introduction of identity-cards, was included in the National Registration Act, 1939, and it was declared in the Act that it should remain in force until such date as the King by Order in Council should declare to be the date on which the emergency contemplated ended. In 1951, however, not only were identity cards not abolished; their production was being demanded by officials of all kinds on an increasing number of occasions. In *Willcock* v. *Muckle*,[13] Mr. Willcock appealed by way of case stated from a conviction before the Highgate justices for refusing to produce his identity card when called upon to do so by a uniformed constable, who had stopped Mr. Willcock whilst driving his car. Mr. Willcock contended that as the emergency contemplated in the Act had passed, the Act itself had lapsed. Neither the justices nor the Divisional Court could accept this contention, but the Lord Chief Justice and other members of the Divisional Court expressed in the clearest possible terms their dislike of the existing official practice. Although the justices had been compelled to record a conviction, they had nevertheless granted Mr. Willcock an absolute discharge, and the Divisional Court congratulated them upon their action. In the words of Lord Goddard,

'Because the police might have powers it did not follow that they should exercise them on all occasions as a matter of course. It was obvious that at the present time the police as a matter of routine demanded the production of identity cards whenever they stopped a motorist for any offence. It was one thing if they were searching for a stolen car or for particular motorists engaged in committing crime; but to demand the production of an identity card from all and sundry—for instance, from a woman leaving her car outside a shop longer than she should —was wholly unreasonable. The Act was passed as a measure

[13] [1951] W.N. 381.

of security and not for the other purposes for which identity cards were now sometimes sought to be used. To use Acts of Parliament passed in war-time for particular purposes now that war had ceased tended to turn law-abiding subjects into law breakers, which was most undesirable, and the good relations between the police and the public would be likely to suffer from it.'

The House of Lords, in a debate shortly afterwards, very strongly condemned the retention of identity cards, and passed a resolution calling for their abolition by a vote of 54 to 28. Members of all three parties strongly condemned the practice of requiring their production, and Lord Goddard put the matter in the clearest possible fashion when he said that he objected to an Act which was passed for security purposes being used merely for administrative convenience, and he added that his experience was that identity cards were not protection at all against post office savings banks frauds. Lord Amwell and other Labour members of the House were equally emphatic that liberty was preferable to "streamlined administrative efficiency" (which assumes that efficiency is produced by the multiplication of irksome restrictions).

5. Administrative Tribunals

It has been pointed out that in increasingly wide areas of social regulation, the departments have completely ousted the jurisdiction of the courts, substituting for it a system of administrative justice, within the control of the appropriate department. The layman, however, is probably largely ignorant of what tribunals exist, or how they function. That is because, although the supreme judiciary of this country must function in public, administrative tribunals may frequently sit in private. Moreover, the citizen who brings his case before them may or may not be entitled to legal representation, and he may or may not be entitled to see the report of the tribunal upon his case. More serious still, there is no guarantee that his administrative judge has any familiarity with legal principle at all, whilst the association of the normal forms of justice with the proceedings of the tribunal may be of the slenderest. A startling illustration of the extent to which neglect (or even contempt) for the ordinary forms of justice has proceeded is afforded by the Landlord and Tenant (Rent Control) Act, 1949, and the regulations made thereunder. These have established rent tribunals comprising laymen, to determine the appropriate rents for houses and flats referred to them. Such tribunals need receive no evidence, nor is there argument in the accepted sense, before them. The tribunal can, if it wishes, inspect the premises, and often does so. Otherwise, the proceedings appear to the lawyer to be simply arbitrary, and in the recent case of *R.* v. *Brighton and Area Rent Tribunal*[14] the King's Bench Division decided that even if the tribunal had decided of its own knowledge, and not from evidence submitted by the tenants, the ordinary courts were unable to give redress to a landlord whose rents were reduced by the tribunal. Moreover, such decisions, once made, are subject to no appeal. They are, in fact, reasonably close counterparts to the decisions upon private law made by law tribunals in the Soviet Union. The main difference is that in the Soviet Union, the People's Judges who preside over the courts delineating private rights are elected directly by the people, whereas the staffs of the Rent Tribunals are appointed by the Minister of Health in consultation with the local authority.

All who have written on administrative tribunals in Great Britain have emphasised the chaos, lack of unifying principles of adjudication which exist, as well as the serious drawback which is furnished by the absence of any administrative court of appeal. Unfortunately, since the introduction of coherence and system into this jungle of jurisdictions would necessarily reduce the degree to which the departments control the tribunals which they create, an early removal of the principal obnoxious features is scarcely to be expected.

6. Public Corporations

There remains for consideration the constitutional position of the great public corporations which have been created to conduct nationalised industries. The term public corporation is, in reality, a complete misnomer. It impliedly suggests something representative. In fact, however, these great

14 [1950] K.B. 410.

organisations, although for legal purposes they have been given the capacity of suing and being sued as legal entities, have no constituent human members, as commercial companies or local government authorities, have. In reality, they are vast state monopolies, closely resembling those which exist in the Soviet Union, and created to carry out an overall economic plan. In this country, the legislation governing the establishment of these vast State monopolies has followed the same general plan. The Act itself defines the structure, organisation and functions of the monopoly, as well as the powers of the Minister in respect of it. The monopoly itself is then given a wide discretion as to the manner in which it will discharge its functions, and the Minister is given extremely wide legislative competence on all matters affecting the nationalised industry. To the Minister also is entrusted the power of determining the general policy of the State monopoly. To this extent, the Minister becomes responsible to Parliament for the affairs of the monopoly, but where the monopoly is acting within the terms of its own discretion, it would seem that it is no more responsible to Parliament than any private enterprise is. As yet, the limits of effective Parliamentary control have not been determined. Whilst there was fairly wide agreement among members in the House of Commons at the end of December 1950 that the existing discretions of managing boards should be retained, the proposal of a Select Committee of the House to conduct inquiries into the activities of the monopolies was rejected by the Government, although Mr. Morrison welcomed the suggestion of periodic reviews of their work, at approximate intervals of seven years, along the lines of those held in respect of the B.B.C.

Within the monopolies themselves, these boards are required to have machinery for joint consultation with the workers. In the words of Mr. Morrison:

'This element of industrial democracy was one of the important new chapters in democracy. Suggestions put forward by the workpeople ought to be carefully examined. It was not good enough when the management forgot them, or merely said "No". The workers' representatives should strive to acquire a sense of responsibility and to educate themselves so as to get as near as possible to a basis of intellectual equality with the management side, because otherwise the thing would fail and there would be a sense of frustration on the workers' part.'

Whatever may be the intrinsic merits of these observations, it is undeniable that they are an excellent expression of the machinery of the great Soviet State enterprises, which have shown great solicitude for the establishment of machinery for exactly the purposes described by Mr. Morrison. The operation of this machinery would repay careful study, and would perhaps go some way towards elucidating the stresses and strains to which the British State monopolies are periodically subject. Soviet experience could even furnish useful information upon the problem of centralisation *versus* greater local or sectional autonomy which is one of the main topics discussed in Commons debates on nationalised industries.

7. *Conclusion*

Today, in Great Britain we live on the edge of dictatorship. Transition would be easy, swift, and it could be accomplished with complete legality. Already, so many steps have been taken in this direction, due to the completeness of power possessed by the Government of the day, and the absence of any real check such as the terms of a written constitution or the existence of an effective second chamber, that those still to be taken are small in comparison. Moreover, in view of the urgency of our needs in the sphere of rearmament, no mitigation of the existing system is to be expected, but rather an intensification of it. Today, virtually our only remaining constitutional safeguard is the habit of tolerance and the existence of a powerful political opposition, both of which owe their existence to the Revolution of 1688. If both these safeguards disappeared, our constitutional machinery would forthwith become the instrument of a totalitarian despotism.

B*

Chapter 3

The Stuarts and the Constitution

T HE accession of James VI of Scotland to the throne
of England in 1603 marked the opening of a struggle
between Crown and Parliament which continued,
with occasional intervals, until the flight of his grandson,
James II, in 1688. The Stuarts were unlucky, not only in
their Scottish background, but in the period of their accession. The history of Scotland for many years previously had
been turbulent. James had succeeded to the Scottish throne
in infancy, on the deposition of his mother, Mary, Queen
of Scots. Plots for her restoration to the Scottish throne, and
for the murder of her cousin, Elizabeth, ended only with
Mary's execution at Fotheringay in 1572. The murder of
Mary's second husband, and James' father, the unhappy
Darnley, in 1567 had been the direct cause of Mary's
abdication. Her father, James V, had died prematurely in
1542 after an unsuccessful border war, leaving his infant
daughter as queen of a divided Kingdom. He had succeeded
to the throne as an infant in 1513, following the death of
his father, James IV, in the disastrous defeat at Flodden in
1513. Thus it had happened that throughout the sixteenth
century, whilst England had enjoyed strong centralised
government under the popular Tudors, Scotland had witnessed the succession of three infants in succession, and
during the long regencies which these events had neces-
sitated, her great nobles had struggled for power, intriguing
continuously with the English court. Moreover, Scotland
herself had suffered a succession of English invasions. It is
therefore not surprising that the Stuarts, when they reached
manhood, were eager to reassert royal prerogatives that had
been usurped during their minorities, and also, since in
Scotland there was no counterpart to the centralised justice

of the Common Law courts, their methods of asserting royal power were upon occasion very direct.

In contrast, England during the sixteenth century had been governed by a succession of powerful sovereigns, to whom only Edward VI stands as an exception. The country as a whole had accepted the forcefulness of the Tudors without protest, since it had wearied of the long-drawn out Civil War between the Houses of York and Lancaster. The Tudors, moreover, were careful to clothe their strong personal rule with the forms of Parliamentary government, and Parliament itself was hesitant to press its privileges to their furthest extent. Even so, however, the long period of domestic tranquillity during Elizabeth's reign coupled with the feeling of international security which followed the defeat of the Armada, gradually induced a more independent spirit in the later Parliaments of the sixteenth century. Already before 1603, some of the issues which divided the nation in the reign of Charles I had been raised, but they had not been settled. The transition from the medieval to the modern world had left the limits of the respective spheres of Crown and Parliament undefined, and much tact and patience would have been in any event necessary to reach a satisfactory compromise. Unhappily, the Stuarts possessed neither quality, and the constitutional struggles of the period between the death of Queen Elizabeth and the outbreak of the Civil War frequently give the impression that there was more legal substance in the Crown's case than is generally believed, but that the sovereign himself was incapable of putting his case upon the firmest legal ground. Whatever might be the letter of the law, the spirit of the times had changed, and expediency, if no higher motive, warranted a compromise.

Basically, the issues dividing the nation on the outbreak of the Civil War were two, and they are precisely the two which have provoked increasing concern at the present day. The first was the question whether the King possessed a legislative power, independent of Parliamentary control. The second was whether the ordinary law of the land—the historic Common Law of England—governed all causes and all men, or whether, on the contrary, the King, by virtue of the royal prerogative, had power to create new courts, dispensing 'administrative justice'.

It will be apparent that the two issues are very closely connected. An asserted royal power of legislation would fall to the ground, if the ordinary courts of the realm refused to recognise it. On the other hand, it could become an instrument of royal despotism, if the King established courts in which his commands, issued independently of Parliament, could be enforced. Further, if the King could legislate independently of Parliament it followed, that he could levy taxes in this way. Accordingly, if these claims were conceded, the King would be well on the way towards governing independently of Parliament, and outside the framework of the ordinary law of the land.

It was the most serious handicap under which the Stuarts laboured that they came to the English throne without adequate appreciation of the course of English constitutional development. In Scotland, the royal authority had fluctuated violently from reign to reign. Under an infant or an adult of weak character, the greater nobles might achieve a *de facto* independence, as they had done in England during the reign of Henry VI. A strong King, on the other hand, by a series of forceful interventions, might bring his baronage temporarily to submission. Unfortunately, in Scotland there was no counterpart to the wealthy and increasingly important middle class, which proved to be such a stabilising factor in Tudor England. It was the tragedy of the Stuarts that they sought to employ against that powerful and politically-conscious middle class the force which their ancestors had in Scotland directed against a lawless, and at times, treacherous baronage.

It must at once be conceded that even as late as 1603, the extent of the Crown's power to legislate independently of Parliament was still uncertain. The Tudors had legislated extensively by proclamation, but they had often (but not invariably) taken the precaution to secure prior Parliamentary sanction. In the Middle Ages, both Parliamentary statutes and Royal ordinances had been recognised as possessing full legislative force, although there was a vaguely-understood convention that Royal ordinances related to matters either of temporary interest or of a specialised nature. In any event, however, the successive religious settlements by statute between 1535 and 1603 had done much to emphasise the importance of embodying great changes in statutory form, and what Parliament was reluctant to concede to the Tudors it would emphatically refuse to the Stuarts. Hence, in the *Case of Proclamations*[1] in 1610, the judges resolved

> 'that the King by his proclamation cannot create any offence which was not an offence before, for then he may alter the law of the land by his proclamation in a high point . . . but the King for the prevention of offences may by proclamation admonish his subjects that they keep the laws, and do not offend them; upon punishment to be inflicted by the law. Lastly, if the offence be not punishable in the Star Chamber, the prohibition of it by proclamation cannot make it punishable there.'

This was the legal death-warrant of the King's independent legislative power, and the fact that Charles I had ignored this judicial decision was one of the grounds for his eventual overthrow. Moreover, four years before the *Case of Proclamations*, the Court of Exchequer had decided in *Bates' Case*[2] that the King had no power by proclamation, independent of Parliament, to levy customs duties. By bringing these matters to a head early in his reign, the first Stuart provoked decisions which established clear limits to powers which before that time had been uncertain in extent. These decisions in effect denied that the Crown had legislative power independent of Parliament, and in this way they conceded to Parliament a legislative omnipotence which has survived to our own day.

There were similar uncertainties in respect of the jurisdiction of what were known as the "prerogative courts". The Common Law of the land was administered in the three Common Law Courts of King's Bench, Common Pleas and Exchequer, which had been established shortly after the Norman Conquest. The bulk of the criminal work was discharged either before the magistrates or before the Common Law judges at Assizes. In later Plantagenet times, however, the machinery of the criminal law had not worked

[1] (1610) 126 Rep. 74.
[2] (1606) Lane 22.

well, and in particular, the Justices of the Peace had failed in their task of preserving public order. This was one of the principal reasons which led to the establishment of the prerogative Court of Star Chamber. There is some evidence that such a Court, as an offshoot of the Council, functioned in the reign of Edward IV. A statute of 1487, however, assigned certain matters, including infractions of the peace, and the supervision of the work of the magistrates, to it. During the reigns of the first two Stuarts, there remained in this way an unsettled controversy whether the Star Chamber was limited in its jurisdiction to the matters specified in the statute of 1487, or whether it had a general criminal jurisdiction apart from the statute. The Crown's case was that its jurisdiction was general, and in particular, that it could inflict heavy penalties upon those who had ignored royal proclamations. During the reign of Charles I, this claim was pushed to the furthest possible limits. Already in the reign of James I, the King had sought to overawe the legal profession by instituting proceedings against barristers who appeared for persons charged with offences in pre-rogative courts. In 1607, James had sought to intimidate Nicholas Fuller, a Bencher of Gray's Inn and formerly a member of the House of Commons, in this way. Fuller was fined £200 and imprisoned by the High Commission Court (the ecclesiastical counterpart to the Star Chamber) for defending two Puritans before it. In 1613, James White-locke, another barrister-member, was imprisoned by the Star Chamber for giving advice to a client in opposition to the royal policy. In the following reign, the Crown went a good deal further and in the eleven years between 1629 and the assembly of the Long Parliament in 1640, during which the King ruled without a Parliament, the Star Chamber became the judicial instrument through which the royal despotism was enforced. As an eminent constitutional historian puts it:

'In lieu of Acts of Parliament, royal proclamations, more numerous and oppressive than those which excited so much opposition under James I, were issued from time to time and declared to have the force of laws. The Common Law judges, with a few honourable exceptions, upheld by their decisions

THE STUARTS AND THE CONSTITUTION 39

the acts of the King; whilst the courts of Star Chamber and High Commission, by extending their authority and exercising a vigilant and severe coercive jurisdiction whenever the slightest opposition was manifested against the civil tyranny of the king or the ecclesiastical tyranny of Laud,[3] maintained for some years what may not be unfairly designated as a reign of terror.'[4]

In the long run, the challenge of the first two Stuarts was to the liberties of the entire nation, but two groups were in the forefront of the struggle. For Parliament, the issue was no less than the question whether its legislative authority was to be curtailed, and eventually ignored. For the common lawyers, the issue was whether the ancient and customary laws of the realm, as they had been evolved continuously from the time of the Norman Conquest were to continue to shape and control the rights of citizens, or whether their lives and liberties should be delivered over to the jurisdiction of the prerogative courts. The Common Lawyer, therefore, sought to bring about the curtailment of the jurisdiction, and ultimately the abolition of the pre-rogative courts, and he demanded the appointment of a judiciary which was independent of royal influence, and which enjoyed security of tenure. He rejected the conception that the orbit of the Common Law could be restricted by royal proclamations. In all these issues, he found full support from the majority of members of the House of Commons. Thus it came about that when the Long Parliament met in 1640, the abolition of the Star Chamber and the Court of High Commission, and the end of all royal claims to legislate independently of Parliament occupied a prominent place on the list of grievances demanding an immediate remedy. In 1641, the Star Chamber, the High Commission Court and the criminal jurisdiction of the Council were all abolished; and with the execution of Charles I in 1649, the first chapter in the great constitutional struggle of the seventeenth century closed.

Even so, however, the period 1660-1685 saw many of the main issues raised again. Judges still held office only during the King's pleasure. The claim of James II to dispense with

[3] Archbishop of Canterbury.
[4] Taswell-Langmead, *Constitutional History*. Tenth Edn. Ed. Plucknett, p. 425.

laws in favour of particular persons (mainly Roman Catholics), and to suspend their operation entirely was in reality a revival of the claim of the Crown to independent legislative power, which was further illustrated by the issue of proclamations with asserted legislative force. The old Court of High Commission was in substance revived under the title of the 'Court of Commissioners for Ecclesiastical Causes'. No doubt if the reign had lasted longer some counterpart to the Star Chamber would have been similarly established. Once again, however, the country would have none of it, and with the flight of James II, and the accession of William III, the long seventeenth century struggle at last ended with a complete victory for Parliament and the Common Lawyers.

The Revolution of 1688—Macaulay's 'glorious revolution'—is one of those great landmarks in constitutional history which is at once an end and a fresh beginning. It marked the end of all pretensions to personal government by the King in England. In the legal sense, Parliament, and not the King, was sovereign. Parliament had unlimited legislative power, and the King had no power to legislate except in pursuance of Parliamentary authorisation. Moreover, the ordinary Common Law of the realm governed all men. There was no special body of law applicable to public officers; nor did they enjoy any special immunities. Again, no subject could be proceeded against or imprisoned, or in any way punished, except for some offence known to the ordinary law. 'Star Chamber justice' was a thing of the past. Even 'general warrants' to seize persons unnamed were declared illegal by the Court of King's Bench in *Leach* v. *Money* in 1765,[5] whilst the Courts have declared that no official may plead 'act of state' when sued by a subject or friendly alien for an unlawful act.[6] Thus, in the fullest sense, the Parliamentarians and the Common Lawyers were victorious, and it was the nature of that alliance which gave our constitution, unwritten, and relying to such a considerable degree upon the Common Law rights of individual subjects, its peculiar character in the next two

---

[5] (1765) 3 Burr. 1692, 1742.
[6] *Johnstone* v. *Pedlar*, [1921] 2 A.C. 262.

centuries. So long as that alliance was all-powerful, personal liberty and Parliamentary sovereignty were alike secure.

The triumph of the Parliamentary party also decided one further question. The Stuarts had been most formidable when they had powerful ministers to execute their policy. Hence, the seventeenth century saw a succession of Parliamentary attacks upon great royal servants. Strafford and Laud perished by Acts of Attainder in the reign of Charles I. Danby was successfully impeached, but escaped by pleading a royal pardon in the reign of Charles II. Plainly one aspect of this great constitutional struggle is the attempt by Parliament to ensure that Ministers of State are ultimately responsible to Parliament for the policies they execute. In this struggle, the weapon of impeachment, which is discussed more fully in the next chapter, was formidable, but clumsy. Full harmony between the legislature and the executive was not restored until it had become accepted practice that, although the King selects his ministers, they remain in office only so long as they retain the confidence of Parliament, and particularly of the House of Commons. This was a gradual process, which was not completed until the beginning of the nineteenth century. It led to the evolution of the Cabinet, whose members were at once the leaders of the dominant Parliamentary party and the heads of the great Departments of State. Ultimately, too, this development fostered the growth of party government, and that regular alternation in office of the great parties which has remained such a striking feature of English life. This alternation of parties has in turn fostered still another important development—the growth of a civil service of high traditions and abilities, which is impartially at the service of whatever party is for the time being in office. Such a development has won world-wide praise, and, indeed, it has many wholly admirable features. In our own day, however, it has produced new, and unexpected developments. The relentless growth in size and function of the Departments of State, and the relatively high level in calibre of those who staff them, coupled with the steady decline in importance and function of Members of Parliament, has led to a gradual transfer of power and influence from the floor of the House of Commons to the private rooms of permanent civil servants. Even a Minister of State no longer controls his department as he did in the nineteenth century. The vast growth and increasing complexity of public business places him to a greater degree at the mercy of his expert advisers than his predecessors in Queen Victoria's reign were, more especially as he must spend a good deal of his time in Parliamentary debates, in committees of many kinds, and in explaining the policy of himself and his party to the country at large. In fact, if not in form, Parliament has conceded to every one of the great Departments of State wide powers of autonomous legislation. At some point, as in the seventeenth century struggle, it will awake to find its legislative supremacy challenged, and possibly overthrown. This will have been achieved, not by any violent onslaught, not even by the practical realisation of any political theory, but by the progressive and unceasing withdrawal of an increasing number of matters from Parliamentary debate for Departmental decision, on the ground that Parliamentary time must be used to greatest effect, and that Parliamentary debates must therefore concentrate upon questions of 'general principle', leaving the implementation of such principles to the departments.

From this point of view, therefore, the seventeenth century struggle is today of major significance. The Stuarts, it will have been noticed, never denied the legislative power of Parliament. They simply claimed a concurrent power, and if the great constitutional cases of the seventeenth century are perused, it will be found that this concurrent power was claimed in the interests of national safety (as in the *Case of Ship-money*)[7] or because the matters legislated upon were of trivial and varying importance. These are the grounds upon which, in recent years, the successive invasions of private right by departmental activity have been defended. In the *Case of Ship-money*, it was unquestioned even by the Parliamentary lawyers that the country needed ships. The scepticism to the royal claims which they uttered was due to the very real doubt whether the money which Charles sought to raise was going to be used for the purpose of

[7] *R. v. Hampden* (1637) 3 St. Tr. 825.

building ships. Rather was it to be used to strengthen royal tyranny still further. The doubt which many citizens feel today is whether continued encroachments upon individual liberty really advance public welfare or promote national security, or whether they are not simply stepping-stones to a state of affairs in which all resistance to official policy is futile and perilous.

Chapter 4

The Passing of Impeachment

ONE great chapter of English constitutional history records the struggle between Crown and Parliament for the control of the executive. During the course of that struggle two procedures for the control of political acts by high officials were elaborated—impeachment and acts of attainder. Historically, they were used for different purposes, though it would seem that such differentiation is not inherent in the nature of the remedies. Impeachment was the weapon fashioned and employed by Parliament to secure punishment for grave abuses committed by men who were in reality, as well as in name, the King's servants. Acts of attainder, on the other hand, were employed by the Tudors, and particularly by Henry VIII, to get rid of ministers who obstructed the royal will, although such acts had also been used during the Wars of the Roses to bring about the destruction of political opponents, and they were used again in the eighteenth century against the Jacobites.[1] It was, moreover, by act of attainder that Strafford, the great minister of Charles I, perished in 1641, and a similar procedure was employed against Archbishop Laud in 1645, although on this occasion the Royal Assent was not given, because of the existence of the Civil War. An act of attainder affords the most striking example known to English law of the omnipotence of Parliament. It is, in fact, homicide by statute, for Cromwell, Henry VIII's Chancellor, obtained an opinion from the judges that Parliament might properly proceed to pass such an Act without preliminary judicial proceedings. Ironically, Cromwell himself was one of the first persons to lose his life in this way.[2]

[1] See Maitland, *Constitutional History*, pp. 246, 317-318.
[2] Taswell-Langmead, *Constitutional History* (10th ed. Plucknett), pp. 261-262.

Surveying the occasions on which acts of attainder have been used to destroy public men, it may be said that they can be divided into three distinct classes: (1) Acts of political revenge, e.g. of Lancastrians against Yorkists, or of Yorkists against Lancastrians, or of Parliamentarians against the ministers of Charles I; (2) Acts of royal despotism. These are confined to the reign of Henry VIII;[3] (3) Acts of political expediency, e.g. the acts of attainder against the Jacobites, the procedure here being employed because of the unsettled state of the country, and the uncertainty of securing a conviction for treason from a jury. All three classes of case may therefore be regarded as abnormal, and the first two have the character of political persecution. Moreover, all acts of attainder are examples of the legislative process. They have neither the form nor the substance of judicial procedure, and their revival in modern times could only be imagined during or at the close of a civil war.

Impeachment, however, has a longer history, and raises more difficult problems. The first clear example occurs in 1376, the last in 1805. Between these dates, impeachments were in no sense continuous. They occur in waves, the first being in the closing years of the reign of Edward III, and during the reign of his grandson and successor, with a few in Lancastrian times, the last being that of the Duke of Suffolk in 1449. Thereafter, there is an interval until 1621, when Mitchell, Mompesson, Bacon and others were impeached to be followed by the impeachment of the Lord High Treasurer, the Earl of Middlesex, in 1624; by that of Buckingham in 1626; and by that of Dr. Mainwaring in 1628. Once again there is an interval, until the meeting of the Long Parliament in 1640. In the first two years of its existence there was a fresh crop—the largest in any single period in English history. There were several others between the Restoration and the accession of William III; and a few additional cases occurred in 1715, the accused being

---

[3] Cf. Taswell-Langmead, *op. cit.*, p. 320: 'The act of attainder asserted the same irresponsible despotism over the individual as the acts of suppression had done over ecclesiastical corporations, and both of them denied the profoundest conviction of the Middle Ages, namely, that the liberty of the subject rested upon the inviolability of his person and his property within the limits of due process of law'.

Jacobites implicated in the Rebellion of the Old Pretender. In 1746 Lord Lovat was impeached for high treason. Thereafter, impeachment tends to fall into disuse, the last two cases being those of Warren Hastings, at the end of the eighteenth century—a case which dragged on for seven years, before the great Indian administrator was acquitted; and finally, that of Lord Melville in 1805. Thereafter, impeachments have ceased to be brought in England, though there have been occasional hints that they might be revived.

For what may a person be impeached? The trials show that either a peer or a commoner may be impeached for high treason, for felonies, and for high political misdemeanours.[4] The latter is an elastic term which has never been defined. Thus, Dr. Roger Mainwaring, was impeached in 1628 for three political sermons (two of which had been preached before the King), which had been published under the title of 'Religion and Allegiance'. The trend of these sermons was to exalt the royal authority, and to maintain that those who refused to pay taxes imposed by royal command and without parliamentary authority, offended against the Law of God and the King's Prerogative, and were guilty of impiety and rebellion. For these adventurous views Dr. Mainwaring was condemned by the Lords to imprisonment during the pleasure of the House, to pay a fine of £1,000, to be suspended for three years from the ministry, and to be incapable of holding any ecclesiastical or civil office. However, the King pardoned him forthwith, and subsequently he was appointed Bishop of St. David's.[5] Even charges of high treason, however, were often little more than cloaks for political attacks. Thus, although twenty-eight articles were exhibited against Strafford, when impeached for high treason in 1640, they proved so flimsy that it early became apparent that the impeachment would fail. It was accordingly dropped, and Strafford forfeited his life under an even more arbitrary act of attainder.[6] The charges against Laud, who was impeached in 1641, were still more remote from the legal conception of treason, even as judicially

---

[4] Anson, *Constitutional Law*, 5th ed., Vol. 1, pp. 384-388; Ridges, *Constitutional Law* (ed. Keith), pp. 215-217.

[5] Taswell-Langmead, *op. cit.*, pp. 591-592.

[6] *Ibid.*, pp. 592-593.

extended, and once again the judicial proceedings were abandoned in favour of an act of attainder.[7]

The incidence of impeachments is extremely interesting. The evolution of the process in the last years of Edward III's long reign was the product of a popular movement (which enjoyed the sympathy of the Black Prince) to free the old King from the corrupt advisers and favourites who surrounded him. In 1376, the 'Good Parliament' which met for the first time in that year, impeached two peers, Latimer and Nevill, and four commoners, who were farmers of customs and of various monopolies. There were many charges in the impeachment, but the three principal ones are interesting. They were (1) that the accused had advised and procured the removal of the Staple from Calais, contrary to statute; (2) that they had lent money to the King at excessive rates of interest; (3) that they had bought up cheaply old debts due from the Crown, and had subsequently paid themselves in full from the Royal Treasury. The accused were in due course found guilty after a full consideration of the charges and the defences offered, the principal punishment inflicted being imprisonment for varying periods. Thus, on the occasion of the first use of this powerful constitutional weapon, we find that it is employed essentially for political, rather than for legal shortcomings, and this impression is confirmed by a perusal of the political history of the period. Both Stubbs and Taswell-Langmead in their constitutional histories[8] emphasise the fact that the impeachments were in reality the opening and most important moves in a political campaign, the object of which was to destroy the monopoly of administration which had been secured by John of Gaunt, Duke of Lancaster, during the illness of the Black Prince and the dotage of Edward III. Thus, at a period long before responsible government was evolved, there was introduced into the English constitution the principle of legal responsibility for political acts, which could be invoked at any time by a party which came to power on a wave of popular enthusiasm, which a newly-

[7] *Ibid.*, p. 593.
[8] Stubbs, *Constitutional History*, Vol 2, pp. 430-434; Taswell-Langmead, *op. cit.*, pp. 184-185.

elected Parliament in times of political stress will normally reflect. This lesson was driven home during the reigns of Edward III's successors. Richard II attempted to rule in defiance of popular opinion, as expressed in Parliament, and his ministers paid the penalty. Thus, in 1386, the Commons impeached Michael de la Pole, Earl of Suffolk, and Lord Chancellor, and procured his removal from office, coupled with a fine and imprisonment.[9]

So far, impeachment, though judicial in form, appears rather as a move in a political campaign than as a genuinely judicial proceeding. If a minister carries out the King's policy in defiance of the prevailing sentiment in Parliament, he will be accused, forced from office, and compelled to pay a fine for his termerity. The actual charges do not appear to be taken too seriously, and are regarded rather as pegs upon which to hang political attacks. This character was never entirely lost. Indeed, it reappears in the fullest and most complete form in the trial of Warren Hastings at the end of the eighteenth century, when the leaders of the parliamentary attack upon him, and especially Burke, Fox and Sheridan, used the flimsiest charges of corruption as a pretext for attacking the entire achievement of Hastings in India, as well as the system under which India was governed, and the English ministries under whom that system had grown up. So employed, impeachment appears as the extreme weapon of a victorious faction, used against an administration whom it regards as having governed oppressively. 'Oppressively', however, is a term which is incapable of exact definition, at any rate in such a context. Modern historians agree that the long ministry of Walpole, at the beginning of the eighteenth century, was the period in which political toleration first took deep root, and in which Government learned to make its existence as unobtrusive as possible. Yet when Walpole was at length driven from office in 1742, there was a very real possibility that he would be impeached. Indeed, his biographer suggests that he spent considerable sums of money in bribes to avoid it.[10]

[9] Taswell-Langmead, *op. cit.*, pp. 190-191; Stubbs, *op. cit.*, Vol. 2, pp. 474-475.

[10] John (Viscount) Morley, *Life of Walpole* (Twelve English Statesmen Series).

In the end all thoughts of impeachment were abandoned, and this, as much as anything, proved the decisive moment in modern English constitutional history. Had Walpole been successfully impeached, it is possible that, notwithstanding the evolution of theories of ministerial responsibility to Parliament, every Prime Minister, on defeat in the House, would have run the risk of impeachment, especially if issues of any moment had been decided during his tenure of office. Yet the abandonment of this weapon is most strikingly illustrated by the failure to impeach Lord North for the loss of the American Colonies, more especially as Lord North approximated more closely to the position of King's instrument (and as such is comparable with Michael de la Pole, the first Duke of Buckingham and the Earl of Strafford) than any other Prime Minister since the Revolution of 1688. It is by no means without significance that the American Colonies, after the close of the War of Independence, retained impeachment as a part of their constitutional machinery. Even today, it is a weapon which may be used against an unpopular or inept State Governor, and it has more than once been threatened against a President himself. It was a very real possibility against Lincoln's successor, General Ulysses Grant, whose desire to benefit his friends at the charge of the nation sometimes outran his discretion.[11]

Whilst the first cases of impeachment were intended to establish the constitutional principle that the Ministers of the Crown must answer to Parliament for their policy, a second group of impeachments in the reign of Richard II pointed ominously to possible future developments. In 1397 Richard made a strong attempt to destroy the fetters which his barons had placed upon him, and he secured the return of the House of Commons subservient to his wishes. Forthwith, the newly-returned Parliament impeached the

---

[11] J. L. De Lolme in his essay on *The Constitution of England* describes impeachment as 'an admirable expedient, which, by removing and punishing corrupt ministers, affords an immediate remedy for the evils of the State, and strongly marks out the bounds within which power ought to be confined; which takes away the scandal of guilt and authority united, and calms the people by a great and awful act of justice: an expedient, in this respect especially, so highly useful, that it is to the want of the like that Machiavel attributes the "ruin of his republic"' (ed. Hallam, p. 181). But American experience has been no happier than our own.

leaders of the baronial opposition. These included the Archbishop of Canterbury; the King's uncle, the Duke of Gloucester; and the Earl of Arundel. Of these, the Archbishop was
banished, Arundel was condemned and beheaded, and the
Duke of Gloucester was found murdered at Calais before
the charges against him could be investigated. In spite of
this a sentence against him was recorded.[12] Thus, in the space
of ten years, the Commons had impeached the chief instruments of royal despotism, and then, at the behest of a temporarily triumphant King, had proceeded to destroy the
chief authors of the limitations upon the royal authority.
The lesson is thus made terribly clear that, if once constitutional restraints are thrown aside, the inevitable swing
of the political pendulum will in turn destroy the leaders
of both parties. During the faction fights between the Houses
of York and Lancaster, these consequences followed inevitably upon a temporary change of dynasty. However, by
this time, the protagonists had tired even of the forms of
judicial process. So, after the impeachment of the Duke of
Suffolk, Michael de la Pole's grandson, in 1449, impeachment was abandoned for the more summary act of attainder.
Once again the monarchy learned the lesson which this
change implied, and the Tudor despots relied upon the
act of attainder, permitting impeachment to lapse for 171
years—a period longer than that which has elapsed since
the impeachment of Lord Melville in 1805.

With the exception of the impeachment of the Jacobite
lords in 1715 and 1746, and of the impeachments of Warren
Hastings and Lord Melville, every impeachment of a great
political figure since the revival of this constitutional device
in 1621 had been intended to bring home to the Ministers
of the Crown the lesson of ministerial responsibility to
Parliament. Since 1714, as we have seen, no impeachment
on this ground has been preferred, the reason usually given
being that since the accession of the Hanoverians, this
lesson has been finally learned. Thus, Maitland, writing
in the far-off days of the nineteenth century, says:

'It seems highly improbable that recourse will again be had
to this ancient weapon unless we have a time of revolution

[12] Taswell-Langmead, *op. cit.*, pp. 196-197; Stubbs, Vol. 2, pp. 495-496.

before us. If a statesman has really committed a crime then he can be tried like any other criminal; if he has been guilty of some mis-doing that is not a crime, it seems far better that it should go unpunished than that new law should be invented for the occasion, and that by a tribunal of politicians and partisans; for such misdoings disgrace and loss of office are nowadays sufficient punishments'.[13]

This is, however, the political philosophy of a settled and progressive age, and it is noteworthy that Maitland, with characteristic caution, excepts a period of revolution.

There is great wisdom in this exception, for the hypothesis that impeachment has fallen into disuse because of ministerial responsibility for political acts to Parliament seems inadequate as an explanation; otherwise, impeachment would have been used to curb the increasing extra-parliamentary power of the Cabinet, or to punish a minister such as Lord North, who was only maintained in office by constant royal pressure, and whose policy in North America was repudiated and denounced by most of the great statesmen of the day. The real explanation for the disuse of impeachment is to be found in the Revolution Settlement of 1688, and it is well exemplified in the political discussions which accompanied the fall of Walpole in 1742. Articles of impeachment were prepared but were not proceeded with. A bill of pains and penalties was next drawn up, but it was abandoned because it was realised that there was no chance that it would pass the House of Lords. Finally, the incoming Ministry appointed a secret committee to examine into the last ten years of Walpole's administration, but it failed to report anything of substance. One after another the possible punitive measures had broken down, and the reason may perhaps be found in a significant paragraph in John Morley's biography:[14] When Walpole went to the levee, the King (says Morley),

'could not conceal his delight at seeing again the friend and author of so many good counsels, and the new ministers were in agony lest the King should call him into the closet. They all, however, kept that fair countenance which often among political men hides such dismal emotions. They came and spoke to him, and he had a long and jovial talk with Chesterfield. Nobody seemed to bear anybody else malice. The Duke

[13] *Constitutional History*, p. 477.
[14] P. 246.

of Newcastle gave his colleagues a dinner one Sunday at Clare-
mont; the servants got drunk and the coachman tumbled off
the box on the way back. They were not far from Richmond,
and the innkeeper told them that perhaps Lord Orford would
lend them his coachmen. So Walpole's coachman drove
Pulteney, Carteret, and Limerick home. Carteret at a levee
came up to thank him, the Duke of Newcastle standing by.
"Oh, my lord," said Walpole, "whenever the duke is near
overturning you, you have nothing to do but send for me, and
I'll save you." '

Newcastle, Chesterfield, Pulteney, Carteret and Limerick
were all Whigs, as Walpole himself was, but they were the
leaders of the coalition that overthrew him. The Revolution
of 1688 had decided that the Whigs were to enjoy a monopoly
of government for the next eighty years. Politics were therefore reduced to a game of manoeuvre between rival Whig
groups. A group might be in office today, and in opposition
tomorrow. Selected as they were from a single small class,
there were clear limits to the action which they could initiate
against one another. Further, the Revolution of 1688 had
established a parliamentary settlement which lasted in all
essentials until the middle of the nineteenth century. Constitutional principles were no longer in dispute, but merely
particular aspects of political action. On these, there might
be many possible variations of opinion, but they were not
matters for which gentlemen could lose life, fortune or reputation. Warren Hastings, however, was impeached for a
major constitutional principle. His trial was a clumsy method
of making the Government of India subservient to Parliament, and it is therefore in line with the great impeachments of the seventeenth century. The last impeachment of
all, that of Lord Melville in 1805, was on the other hand
simply for maladministration whilst a Minister of the Crown.
As such, it was something of an anachronism, and was
ineffective. Melville was a personal friend of the Younger
Pitt, then Prime Minister, and the decision to impeach was
made upon the Speaker's casting vote. Melville was eventually acquitted, and the verdict of history seems to be that
the proceedings were misconceived, and that they were in
reality a veiled political attack upon Pitt himself. At any
rate, Pitt felt the attack very deeply. 'Some have ascribed

his death to Ulm', says Lord Rosebery,[15] 'and some to Austerlitz; but if the mortal wound was triple, the first stab was the fall of Dundas'. Of the impeachments of Warren Hasings and Melville, May says: 'The former was not a minister of the Crown, and he was accused of offences committed beyond the reach of parliamentary control; and the offences charged against the latter had no relation to his political duties as a responsible minister'.[16]

The Revolution of 1688 established in these islands the liberal State founded on political toleration. Its lifeblood has been the acceptance of certain fundamental principles underlying our political organisation, the 'agreement to differ' together with the acceptance of a clear delimitation between the spheres of private and State action. There is no warrant in English constitutional history, at any stage of our political development, for the tolerance of intolerance, whether the intolerance was that of militant Catholicism or that of advocates of arbitrary power. It was only when the lesson had been learned at the cost of long and bitter struggles and great loss of life, that milder habits became possible. This dates from the fall of Walpole—the time when England's long commercial and maritime supremacy were becoming firmly established. It was natural for the constitutional historians of the late nineteenth century to assume that these social conditions would continue indefinitely. Instead, our commercial supremacy has gone, our colonial empire is going, and for the first time since the Revolution of 1688, political doctrines based on intolerance of opposing views are being industriously propagated. These are new conditions, giving rise to political problems different in nature from those which have existed during the past two centuries. Nor is this all. The progressive abandonment of extraordinary judicial methods of coercion for political acts was, as we have seen, made possible by the acceptance of the conception of the liberal State, with its comparatively few points of contact with the individual. Today, the liberal State is passing away, in favour of a planned society. This is not the place to consider whether, in spite of emphatic assertions to the contrary,

[15] *Life of Pitt*, p. 251.
[16] *Constitutional History*, Vol. 2, p. 93.

anything more than the empty shell of liberty can exist in a planned society, but it is already apparent that the responsibility of government for policies affecting every aspect of individual activity is higher in a planned society than it was in a liberal State.

The increased responsibilities which have been assumed by servants of the Crown in recent years may have in the future important implications in the sphere of constitutional law. We have seen how the extraordinary remedies of the constitution fell into disuse when government became restricted to a choice of alternative courses of action within an agreed political and social framework. That framework today is passing away. It has been in course of liquidation during the past half century. Today, in Great Britain, there is more disagreement over the bases of political action than there has been for two and a half centuries. This may involve a heavier degree of ultimate responsibility for mistakes which may involve any one or every one of us in ruin. This does not inevitably follow, and it may not be desirable, but so long as human nature—even British human nature—remains what it is, it is at any rate a possibility which cannot be completely discarded.

Chapter 5

The Transformation of Parliament

THE history of modern political society is in large measure the history of the struggle of the ordinary citizen to exercise some influence upon government—and of his repeated failures to achieve that modest ambition. All governments control the governed. They vary widely in the extent to which they make that control manifest. Some, as in Nazi Germany or Soviet Russia, manufacture an elaborate ideology, synthetically producing various 'communal' objectives, expressed in general terms, for which the mass of the people are quite arbitrarily assumed to be striving. Behind this collection of generalities, an organised minority forcibly assumes power, and then ruthlessly perpetuates its own ascendancy. In the Western world, the process of control is subtler in consequence of the existence of opposing political parties, each professing different ends. Such a system, however, could not work at all unless there was agreement underlying the policies of all parties to work the political machine in the traditional way. It is because the Communists reject such a fundamental assumption that they cannot be regarded as a normal political party. They are, in fact, a disruptive element in any non-Communist State. Even with this qualification, however, it must be conceded that the term 'democracy' as used to describe Western political society, has practically nothing in common with Greek democracy, and that it bears little resemblance to philosophic expositions of the meaning of the term. From the beginning of the nineteenth century, it has been assumed that political democracy is synonymous with the exercise of the vote by the adult population, male and (later) female. Hence the successive extensions of the franchise during the nineteenth century. These, however, have necessarily involved the increasing insignificance of the individual elector. Since individual votes are so numerous that they are almost valueless, and it is only in the mass that they achieve significance, each extension of the franchise has increased the power of the major political parties. They have relentlessly driven out independent representatives and have destroyed smaller parties, and they exercise a predominant influence in the selection of candidates. When the candidate is returned to Parliament, he finds himself controlled by the party system, without the support of which he cannot hope to be returned in a future election. Accordingly, it follows that those who control the machine of the principal political party are the persons who exercise political power in a Western democracy. In Great Britain, those persons are also the leaders of the party within the House of Commons, and therefore they can force legislation through Parliament. Again, they are the political heads of the Executive, and in this capacity they frame policy, and enforce its execution. Moreover, by the development of departmental legislation and administrative tribunals, much of what they do is beyond the reach of the courts or even the scrutiny of Parliament. Great Britain today illustrates the dictatorial powers of a Cabinet in extreme form for, unlike the United States, Great Britain possesses no effective Second Chamber. Further, again unlike the United States, it possesses no written constitution. Any constitutional change whatever can be achieved within the lifetime of a normal Parliament, in little more than eighteen months by the use of a majority in the House of Commons, and the machinery of the Parliament Act. Perhaps even more serious, however, is the fact that Parliament can, and does, give away such wide powers to the departments without the possibility of such abdication of authority being challenged as unconstitutional. It may also be added that the position of stalemate which was established at the General Elections of 1950 and 1951 is the only one in which the wishes of the ordinary citizen can be expected to be directly and constantly in the mind of either of the major political parties, although it may be agreed that indirectly his influence upon the formation of party programmes may still be extensive.

It will be valuable in this chapter to attempt a sketch of the process by means of which the present insignificance of the private citizen has been achieved.

In a remarkable book, *The Crowd*, written nearly sixty years ago, a French writer, G. le Bon, called attention to some observations of Herbert Spencer in *The Man Versus the State*, in which the English philosopher observes of recent tendencies in government in England:

'Legislation since this period has followed the course I pointed out. Rapidly multiplying dictatorial measures have continually tended to restrict individual liberties, and this in two ways. Regulations have been established every year in greater number, imposing a constraint on the citizen in matters in which his acts were formerly completely free, and forcing him to accomplish acts which he was formerly at liberty to accomplish or not to accomplish at will. At the same time heavier and heavier public, and especially local, burdens have still further restricted his liberty by diminishing the portion of his profits he can spend as he chooses, and by augmenting the portion which is taken from him to be spent according to the good pleasure of the public authorities.'

On this, le Bon comments:[1]

'This progressive restriction of liberties shows itself in every country in a special shape which Herbert Spencer has not pointed out; it is that the passing of these innumerable series of legislative measures, all of them in a general way of a restrictive order, conduces necessarily to augment the number, the power, and the influence of the functionaries charged with their application. These functionaries tend in this way to become the veritable masters of civilised countries. Their power is all the greater owing to the fact that, amidst the incessant transfer of authority, the administrative caste is alone in being untouched by these changes, is alone in possessing irresponsibility, impersonality, and perpetuity. There is no more oppressive despotism than that which presents itself under this triple form."

These observations were written before the close of the nineteenth century, when the usurpation of power by government departments was then in its early stages. They have an even more ominous significance today, when we are witnessing the accumulating difficulties of Parliamentary democracy. Even in Great Britain, Parliament no longer governs. It criticises,

[1] P. 203.

c

and sometimes checks government, and by an adverse vote, it can dismiss a ministry. Owing to the intensity of the Party system, however, such a right has become almost as formal as the royal veto. It was a reality so long as it was still possible to assume that Members of Parliament might be influenced in their votes by debates in the House of Commons. Today, the vote is pre-determined before the debate begins, and the absurdities of the present system were repeatedly illustrated after the General Election of 1950, when each of the principal parties went to extreme lengths to bring into the division lobbies members who were hastily extracted from hospitals and nursing-homes and who, except for the mechanical act of voting, were otherwise too ill to take any intelligent part in the proceedings.

If we examine the century and a quarter which has elapsed since the agitation leading to the first Reform Bill of 1832 reached considerable proportions, we can only conclude that the movement to invest the adult population of these islands with political significance has been substantially a failure. Voting was an act of some personal significance when electorates extended to a few hundreds, but the political significance of the vote has diminished with each extension of the franchise. So also has the importance of the Member of Parliament. Moreover, by an apparently inexorable political law as the adult population has, by successive Franchise Acts, acquired the vote, the powers of Parliament have steadily declined before the rapidly expanding activities of the Departments. So, in our own day, the seventeenth century battle between Parliament and Common Law on one side, and the Executive on the other, is being fought again, but this time the struggle shows every indication of being decided in favour of the despotism of the Executive.

It has often been remarked that the Parliament of the eighteenth century not only legislated, but governed. Departmental staffs in the modern sense did not yet exist. In any event they did not possess the qualifications, ability or status to advise and control their Parliamentary chiefs effectively. The control of central over local government was a development reserved for the nineteenth and twentieth centuries. In the absence of the telephone and telegraph and a popular press, foreign affairs were matters for leisurely discussion between diplomatic representatives, invested with wide powers, behind closed doors. During Walpole's long tenure of office at the beginning of the century, the watchword of government was *Quieta non movere*, and although not all of his successors could remain as inactive as he, on account of wars with France, the aim of all governments was nevertheless to interfere with the ordinary citizen as little as possible.

It followed, therefore, that debates in Parliament for the most part reflected either the personal views of the speaker, or those of the small group to which he belonged. Parties in the modern sense did not yet exist. There were, instead, numerous small cliques, each with their aristocratic chiefs. Such a political structure was the antithesis of modern conceptions of democracy. It depended for its continuation upon a static franchise in which Privilege could exercise a preponderant influence, yet which was not so rigid and exclusive that it was impervious to gusts of popular feeling. Both the Elder and Younger Pitt, for example, looked rather to the nation at large, than to a Parliamentary majority for the power to execute their policies, and had not the French Revolution supervened, it is probable that the Younger Pitt would have made Parliamentary Reform follow the successful conclusion of his policy of commercial expansion.

By that time the wars of the French Revolution and Napoleonic Period had finished, however, the manufacturing and commercial middle classes of England had increased very considerably in wealth and importance, at the expense of the territorial aristocracy. We were on the threshhold of a new age, in which railways, inventions, and limited liability companies would play an increasingly important part. Such a transfer of economic power must therefore ultimately be reflected in Parliamentary representation, and once the fears evoked by Jacobinism had died away, the way was clear for the general enfranchisement of the substantial middle class. This was all the first Reform Bill accomplished. Less than half a million new voters were added to the country's electoral roll. Nevertheless, the Duke of Wellington was right when he hailed the first Reform

Bill as the first stage of a flood which would eventually submerge the Constitution. Once the claim of the prosperous half-million had been conceded, there could be no final halting-place before the goal of adult suffrage, male and female, had been reached. Nor is this all. Once it is conceded that the counting of heads, irrespective of what is inside them, is the criterion by virtue of which a choice is made between opposing policies, then it follows that a second chamber is an obstacle to progress. Accordingly, during the past forty years, the House of Lords has been progressively deprived of all power to halt, or even effectively to delay, the onward march of Collectivism. Today, Great Britain is governed by a Party whose chiefs, whilst commanding a majority in the House of Commons, possess dictatorial powers, which are subject only to the limitation that if that Parliamentary majority is lost, they must give way to those who have successfully opposed them.

It is therefore patent that the primary aim of modern government must be to retain a Parliamentary majority. This can best be achieved by maintaining, and where possible, extending, Parliamentary discipline. In the past two and a half centuries, the position of the Member of Parliament has passed through successive and well-defined phases. In the eighteenth century, except where he represented one of a few constituencies with wide franchises, he was a placeman, voting and speaking as the owner of the seat bade him. After the first Reform Bill, the member for a time enjoyed more independence of thought and action than he had done before, or has done since. The number of electors were small, they belonged to the politically mature middle-classes, and they were immune from susceptibility to corruption. Party organisation was still loose, and the expense of elections was less than it had been before (when electors often required to be corrupted) or have become today, when large-scale campaigns in constituencies are essential. If the political history of the nineteenth century is examined it will be found that on great issues, such as Catholic Emancipation, the Repeal of the Corn Laws, or the Don Pacifico incident, a decisive number of votes in the House was capable of being turned in the course of the debate. At this period therefore, the individual views of Members of Parliament were still of significance in government. Today, this is no longer true. The forum in which the views of the individual member can be expressed with the expectation that they will have some influence on policy is the party meeting, or better still, the party's annual conference. In the House, the member's duty is plain. If he wishes to remain a member, he must vote as the Party Whip tells him.

Within limits, such party discipline is by no means a bad thing. It prevents almost completely the creation of splinter parties, and it also prevents the development of government by a coalition of groups, which has at important points in recent history, paralysed effective rule in France. Moreover, it has given party leaders an authority within their party organisation which not infrequently has enabled them to look beyond mere party advantage to the needs of the country as a whole. Even when so much has been conceded, however, the tendency of the party system to become an increasingly powerful and rigid mechanism must be regarded with anxiety. Its effect is to emphasise the extraordinary concentration of power in the hands of the leaders of the party forming the government of the day which now exists in Great Britain. On the morrow of a General Election in which a comfortable majority has been secured, the government is, internally at least, virtually omnipotent. There are no limits to the legislative changes which can be initiated, and there is now no possibility that the House of Lords can delay them beyond the space of twelve months. Control over the members of the party itself is absolute; so also is control over the machinery of the great Departments of State, which themselves must be regarded as fairly complete governmental systems. If it be argued that, wide though these powers are, they are limited by the existence of public opinion, it must also be added that public opinion itself can be very widely influenced by the government of the day. Just as the extension of the franchise has diminished the significance both of elector and member, so also has the spread of popular education and the universality of the habit of newspaper reading reduced the significance of public opinion. Even more serious inroads upon its importance have been made in recent years by the diminution in the size of newspapers, in consequence of which all newspapers now have imposed upon them a task of selection in the matter of news, which it is virtually impossible to exercise without bias. If at any time the Press were subject to any kind of State control, the powers of the government of the day would thereby become almost absolute.

The regimentation of Members of Parliament has coincided with their increasing insignificance. Virtually the whole of Parliamentary time available for legislation is now monopolised by the Government. Bills promoted by private members which eventually reach the statute-book have the scarcity value of freaks. Even so, they can usually be explained on the ground that they achieve some reform which many admit to be desirable, but which cannot be adopted as part of the programme of any party, for fear of losing votes. Such, for example, was Sir Alan Herbert's Divorce and Matrimonial Causes Act of 1937. Nor is this all. Government measures tend to become bulkier and increasingly technical. This is not surprising, for many of them are concerned with complicated social issues, and they are prepared by large and skilled staffs in the Departments. The private member therefore often lacks both the time and the skill to make an effective contribution to the discussion of the measure. He contents himself with discussing the general questions of policy, as he conceives them, which are involved in the proposals. Only in this way is it possible to explain the frequent and serious inroads of individual freedom embodied in modern Acts, which slip through Parliament, often virtually undiscussed. It is true that the establishment of the Select Committee on Statutory Rules and Orders has in recent years extended the knowledge of the private member of this point, but even so, discussions on the concession of additional powers to the executive frequently lack conviction. The private member fears that he is fighting a losing battle with Departments. If he is a supporter of the Government of the day, he is usually unable to counter the stock argument that, after mature consideration, the powers claimed have been deemed to be necessary, and will not be abused. The criticism of members of other parties will be suspect on the ground that it is merely partisan—and in the end, in the great majority of cases, the powers claimed will be conceded.

No doubt it is the consciousness of the decline in the importance of the individual member which has made the House of Commons, in recent years, so tender in respect of its collective powers and dignities. Allegations of breach of privilege have been pushed further than at any time since the great constitutional controversies of the seventeenth century. This attitude itself, if persisted in, is a further symptom of a dictatorial tendency. As *The Times* observed in a leading article on August 1st, 1951,

'during the two Parliaments since 1945—and particularly during the past year—more and more members of the House of Commons have sought to use privilege as a weapon by which to restrict the free discussion of political issues. . . . This is no new danger. During the seventeenth century privilege was a valuable weapon to employ against an interfering monarch; during the eighteenth century, when this need for it no longer existed, it was nevertheless still used—and used unreasonably—against the Press and the public. . . . Parliamentary government means government by a majority, and there is always the danger that the majority may be oppressive. Significantly it is Labour members of Parliament who since their party was returned with a majority in 1945 have been most active in bringing complaints of breach of privilege against members of the general public. The threat to liberty may not at the moment seem great, but this does not lessen the need for vigilance. As has been apparent during the past year, sensitivity to public criticism is an infectious disease: one complaint of breach of privilege encourages another. "It is undesirable", said the Committee of Privileges earlier this year, "to restrict the freedom of discussion unduly". Members of Parliament should recall these words before they seek refuge from the harsh winds of public criticism behind the "obsolete claims" of Parliamentary privilege.'

Chapter 6

The Menace of Delegated Legislation

IN order to understand what is meant by delegated legislation, and to define some of the principal problems created by it, it is necessary to revert to the sovereignty of Parliament, which received unchallenged acceptance as the basis of our modern constitution, at the close of the great seventeenth century struggle. The essence of Parliamentary sovereignty is: (1) that Parliament (i.e. King, Lords and Commons) can pass laws on any topic whatever; (2) that such laws, if passed, cannot be challenged, or held invalid, in any Court; (3) that no other body has similar legislative powers. No other body, that is to say, has power to pass compulsory rules binding on the community as a whole, and changing the existing law, unless it derives its authority ultimately from Parliament itself.

Each of these three principles had been challenged by the Stuarts, who had sought to suspend the operation of particular statues passed by Parliament, and who had also claimed power to enact laws themselves, independently of Parliament. For both contentions of the Stuarts there was some warrant in past history. It is difficult to determine exactly what constituted a statute in the Middle Ages. Sometimes the King legislated with the advice and consent of Lords and Commons. Sometimes, on the other hand, he made laws with the advice of his Council only. Laws made in Council were often known as Ordinances, and there was a vague suggestion that such laws were normally of a temporary, local, or special character (e.g. they might apply to some particular trade or profession), but there was no formal rule about this, and one or two of the best-known medieval statutes were passed in the Council, and not in Parliament.

Moreover, prior to the Reformation there was a suggestion, which was repeated in some of our earliest legal text-books, that an enactment, whether statute or ordinance, which ran counter to the principles of the Common Law, was void. No one seems to have paid serious attention to such a principle in practice, however.

As Parliament steadily developed its corporate existence and extended its powers, several important changes occurred. In the first place Parliament, and especially the Commons, secured greater control over the *form* of legislation. The actual draft of the proposed measure was usually prepared by members of one or other House of Parliament. The King's function progressively dwindled to the point where he either accepted or rejected the measure put before him. Further, Parliament consistently sought to establish the principle that the Crown's legislative power could only be exercised subject to ultimate Parliamentary control. No one doubted, however, that the royal legislative power existed. The Tudors made frequent use of it, but it is significant that the most powerful Tudor of all, Henry VIII, took the precaution of securing the passage of the Statute of Proclamations through Parliament in 1539. These exceptional statutory powers did not extend beyond Henry's own reign, however, for the Statute of Proclamations was repealed at the beginning of the reign of his successor. It was, therefore, not until the second half of the nineteenth century that the almost limitless possibilities of delegated, subordinate legislation became apparent. The convenience of the device first became fully appreciated when the dominating trend in legislation turned from reform to social reorganisation. This change owed a good deal to the spread of Benthamite ideas as the century progressed. Bentham, and following him John Austin, had regarded statute law as the principal, and most developed form of law, and it was therefore natural that legislation should come to be regarded as the most expedious means of bringing about the changes which were required. Parliament, the constitutional lawyers were apt to say, could do everything except make a man a woman, and in the past three-quarters of a century, it has fully lived up to this claim.

C*

Bringing about far-reaching social changes by way of legislation in turn produced a crop of Parliamentary problems. Bills themselves became longer and more technical, as they sought to embody ideas which had not previously been expressed in statutory form. Moreover, they were bitterly contested by those who were adversely affected by them. More and more Parliamentary time was occupied by the process of putting them on the statute-book, and, as was shown in the last chapter, in the long run, the clash of interests which legislation of this kind produced was directly responsible for the prolonged struggle over the powers of the House of Lords, which ended only with the virtual destruction of an effective second chamber in 1948. It was in this environment that modern delegated legislation became once more a normal instrument of government. Once Parliament had adopted the general principles underlying an important measure of social change, the task of applying those principles in their every-day impact upon ordinary citizens devolved upon the Departments, which were progressively enlarged, and strengthened, by the recruitment of technical staffs, to discharge tasks which steadily increased in volume and importance. Moreover, since it was the Departments which accumulated the expert knowledge upon the manner in which a piece of social legislation was working, it was appropriate that there should be committed to the Department, not only the power to make detailed regulations in the first place, but also to amend them from time to time, as problems arising from the administration of the Act emerged.

This is the basis of government by the Executive Departments, which has now become an accepted, and increasingly important, part of our political system. It will at once be apparent, however, that its development has raised a major constitutional problem. In reality, the bulk of the legislation by which today the conduct of the citizen is controlled is made, not by Parliament, but by government officials inside the Departments. These officials are in no sense responsible to the electorate for what they do. They are civil servants, enjoying security of tenure during good behaviour, and they work remote from the light of public criticism. They are, in fact, experts, doing a skilled job. What then is, or should be, their relationship to the elected representatives of the people in the House of Commons?

Parliament is sovereign and omnipotent, and the legislative power of the Departments is delegated and subordinate. That means that it is derived from Parliament, which defines the limits within which the Departments can legislate. That is the point of departure, although it will be shown that the modern legislative power of the Departments has long ago emancipated itself from the principle that departmental legislation, like other forms of subordinate legislation, is subject to the *ultra vires* rule. This implies that if a Department, in the exercise of its rule-making power, passes beyond the limits set by Parliament, a citizen affected by it, can claim that the rule is of no legal validity. If he succeeds in establishing that the rule is *ultra vires* the power of the Department to make it, the Court will hold it null and void.

In the light of this constitutional rule, it would appear that Parliament can itself set limits to the legislative power of the Departments, so that there can be no challenge to its legislative supremacy. It was because this was assumed to be the position that the increase in delegated legislation in the period between 1870 and 1910 was regarded with comparative complacency. It was for Parliament to set limits to the practice, and so long as Parliament could check the legislative activity of the Departments, and had knowledge of its nature, there seemed to be little possibility either of abuse or of a fetter being imposed upon the legislative powers of Parliament.

Unfortunately, the Departments have shown the greatest ingenuity in evading the control alike of Parliament and the Courts. Before this process is analysed, however, it should be noticed that the subordinate legislation which is now under consideration may assume a variety of forms, which are not substantially different in nature and function. It may, for example, take the form of Orders in Council, which are prepared by the Department primarily concerned with the matters affected by the Order, and they are then adopted by the King in Council. This latter has long been a purely formal process. Again, the subordinate legislation may take the form of rules, prepared and promulgated directly by the Department upon the authority of the appropriate Minister, acting under statutory power. Orders vary very greatly in form. Some are in reality a detailed code, carrying out a general purpose which has been stated in general form in the parent Act; others are specific prohibitions. Some again are *provisional orders*, which do much of the work done in former times by Private Bills, others are *special orders*, which are variants of provisional orders. Again, there are rules of various kinds, and provisional rules, which are in theory made on grounds of urgency, or for some other special reason. These come into operation immediately on publication, and they continue to be effective unless and until they are rejected by Parliament. It must also be pointed out that there may today be four, and even five-tier legislation. A statute may provide that its provisions shall be implemented by Order in Council. The Orders in Council, when made, may confer upon a Minister power to make rules. When the rules are made, the Minister may have power under them to prepare a scheme, e.g. for a particular industry. Under that scheme, the Minister may have power to make an Order. All this makes for incoherence and uncertainty, especially as Departments are progressively developing a jargon of their own in framing their legislation. It is regrettable that no anthology of Departmental jargon has so far been compiled from subordinate legislation actually in force today. Almost any lawyer could contribute his quota. If one takes, for example, the Departmental legislation power of the Ministry of Education, one notices that although it is voluminous, it is for the most part well-drawn and understandable. The *Pupils Registration Regulations, 1948*,[1] however, has points of interest. It is prefaced by an explanatory note which reads as follows:

'These Regulations are made under Section 80 of the Education Act, 1944, as amended by Section 4 of the Education Act, 1948, and replace the Registration of Pupils at Schools Regulations, 1945, made under Section 80 of the Act of 1944.

[1] S.I. 1948, No. 2097.

'The principal changes are (i) the omission of the requirement forms of application by parents for the admission or
withdrawal of pupils; (ii) the inclusion of specified grounds
which must be satisfied before the name of a pupil is removed
from the registers; (iii) the extension of the Regulations to all
pupils in the school irrespective of age; and (iv) the application
of the Regulations for the first time to pupils of independent
schools.

'The purpose of the changes is to assist in securing observ-
ance of the law of school attendance.'

So the object of these regulations at last is clear. The
public will notice the courteous use of the word "assist".
They will also notice that in four years the administrative
net was thrown more widely than before. However, let
us look at one section of the Regulations themselves:

'4. The following grounds are hereby prescribed as those
on which the name of a pupil is to be deleted from the Admission Register, that is to say—

'(i) where a pupil is registered at the school in accordance
with the requirements of a School Attendance Order, that
another school is substituted for that named in the Order or
the Order is revoked on the ground that arrangements have
been made for the child to receive efficient full-time education
suitable to his age, ability, and aptitude otherwise than at
school;

'(ii) in a case not falling within sub-paragraph (i) of this
paragraph, that he has been registered as a pupil of another
school;

'(iii) in a case not falling within sub-paragraph (i) of this
paragraph, that he has ceased to attend the School at which
he is registered and his parent has satisfied the Authority
that he is receiving efficient full-time education suitable to his
age, ability and aptitude otherwise than by attendance at
school;

'(iv) except in the case of a boarder, that his ordinary residence
has been transferred to a place whence the school at which he
is registered is not accessible with reasonable facility;

'(v) that is certified by the School Medical Officer as unlikely
to be in a fit state of health to attend school before becoming
legally exempt from the obligation so to attend;

'(vi) that he has been continuously absent from school for
a period of not less than four weeks and the proprietor of the
school has failed, after reasonable enquiry, to obtain information of the cause of absence;

'(vii) that the proprietor has ascertained that the pupil has died;

'(viii) that he will cease to be of compulsory school age before the school next meets and intends to discontinue in attendance thereat; or

'(ix) in the case of a boarder, that he has ceased to be a pupil of the school:

'(a) provided that in a case not covered by sub-paragraph (i) of this paragraph, the name of a child who has under arrangements made by an Authority become a registered pupil at a special school shall not be removed from the Admission Register of that school without the consent of that Authority or, if that Authority refuse to give consent, without a direction of the Minister; or

'(b) if he is not of compulsory school age, on any of the following grounds:

'(i) that he has ceased to attend the school or, in the case of a boarder, that he has ceased to be a pupil of the school;

'(ii) that he has been continuously absent from school for a period of not less than four weeks and the proprietor of the school has failed, after reasonable enquiry, to obtain information of the cause of absence; or

'(iii) that the proprietor has ascertained that the pupil has died.'

All this to remove a name from the register; and it must be remembered that the local Authority where the school is situated has power to complicate the teacher's task still further. The following is a choice specimen from the Schedule to the Town and Country Planning (Transfer of Property and Officers and Compensation to Officers) Regulations, 1948:

'35 (i) Where a person to whom compensation is payable under these regulations for loss of employment has become or becomes entitled to a pension in respect of the employment he has lost otherwise than on losing such employment or where a person to whom compensation is payable under these regulations for loss of employment or diminution of emoluments has become or becomes entitled to a pension in respect of any employment the remuneration of which was payable out of public funds and which he had obtained in place of the employment he had lost or in place of or in addition to the employment the emoluments of which were diminished, and in calculating the amount of such pension account is taken of any service which was taken into account in calculating the compensation payable, then, if the compensation does not exceed such part of the pension as is attributable solely to that service, the compensation shall cease to be payable, and if it exceeds such part of the pension as aforesaid, it shall be reduced by an amount equal to that part.'

The regulations under the Town and Country Planning Act, 1947, it should be noticed, are rich in jargon of this sort. So are those issued under the Steel Industry National-isation Act. Thus, Statutory Instrument 1345 of 1951 contains the following little conundrum:

> ' "High-speed steel" means any alloy steel containing by weight either (a) 12 per centum or more of tungsten, or (b) both molybdenum and tungsten in respective percentages such that when the percentage of molybdenum therein is multiplied by two and added to the percentage of tungsten therein, the sum is not less than 12.'

However, even this pales into insignificance compared with this gem, culled from form 1S GRA/C119, issued under the statutory instrument just mentioned. The purpose of the form is to require a return in duplicate of stocks to the Ministry of Supply. Article 5 of this form reads:

> 'If by the usual course of business of any undertaking the usual principal periodical completion of records of business for that undertaking would be completed on some day other than the 30th day of June, 1951, being a day not earlier than the 15th day of June, 1951, nor later than the 15th day of July, 1951 (which day in respect of that undertaking is hereafter in this Order called "the private reference day") then such information as is required by or under the provisions of Article 1 of this Order to be given with reference to a specified day or period may be given as if that day or period were set back or brought forward (as the case may require) to correspond with the difference between the undertaking's private reference day and the 30th day of June, 1951.'

It is almost unbelievable that large sums of money are being paid in salaries to allow Departments to issue rubbish of this kind. Unfortunately, the tortured and incoherent language of these and other documents is indicative of the manner in which the Departments are today transacting the nation's business.

It should be added that today the Departments are by no means the only bodies to whom there has been committed the task of making subordinate legislation. Local authorities issue by-laws; so does the Railway Executive. In addition

Parliament has shown a steadily-increasing inclination to commit the rule-making power to statutory bodies, either independently, or with the approval of a Government Department. Many of these Boards function in connexion with the industry, and they are, in fact, instruments for organising and controlling industries still remaining under private ownership. It will be sufficient to give by way of illustration the Cotton Industry Board, with legislative powers derived from the Cotton Industry (Reorganisation) Act, 1939; the Catering Wages Commission, constituted under the Catering Wages Act, 1943; and the various Marketing Boards (e.g. the Milk Marketing Board) established under the Agricultural Marketing Acts. The powers conceded to these miscellaneous bodies are often very wide, ranging from the power to inflict a substantial fine, to the power to put a person trading in the industry out of business altogether. It will be shown in the next chapter that in the great majority of instances, these Boards have excluded the aggrieved citizen from access to the Courts altogether, in cases in which he is charged with an infraction of the rules issued by the Board. Dr. Allen writes of the proceedings of such Boards:

'Although the defendant may be represented, the Board is not bound by any rules of evidence. When it is remembered that the defendant may be ruined by the revocation of his licence (and if he trades without it he is liable to prosecution in the ordinary Courts), and that his judges cannot possibly be regarded as impartial, since they are themselves producers pecuniarily interested in the finance of the whole scheme, it is difficult to imagine a greater travesty of a "judicial" proceeding or one more contrary to all accepted notions of procedure and fairness. There is, it is true, appeal to an arbitrator, but the Board is not bound to accept the defendant's nominee, and in that case the Minister appoints an arbitrator who is usually a Civil Servant. To complete the picture, execution of the Board's judgments falls on the ordinary courts; they are thus made mere machinery to exact penalties with which they have no concern and which, for all they know, may be highly arbitrary.'

It has been said that the Departments have shown very great ingenuity in emancipating themselves from Parliamentary control over the subordinate legislation which they issue. The methods by which they secure such freedom will now be described. The principal device is for the draftsman to include in the Act conferring a grant of legislative power, a further power to amend the Act itself. To some extent, the existence of such a power is not open to serious objection, provided the Act is careful to define the limits within which it is exercised. No one quite knows how a complicated piece of social legislation is going to work out, and a power to modify its details may have considerable effect in promoting its smooth operation. Moreover, the vast majority of amendments into Statutes in this way relate simply to matters of detail. On the other hand, instances have been known in which the Departments have sought more extensive powers by this device than Parliament was originally prepared to concede. A further development of this device is what is known as the 'Henry VIII Clause', recalling the grant of power by Parliament to that monarch to legislate free from Parliamentary interference. By virtue of the 'Henry VIII Clause', power is conferred on the Department to modify, not only the Act from which the power is derived, but also any other Act, in order to remove difficulties, or to bring the Act more fully into operation. Serious anxiety has been frequently expressed concerning the scope of this clause, which, if widely used, would go far towards by-passing Parliament altogether, and in recent years, instances of its insertion into Statutes have been rare.

Two other devices call for comment under this head. A Statute may give a Department power to make such rules as, *in its opinion*, are necessary in order to bring the Act fully into operation. It will be seen that this is really a variation of the 'Henry VIII Clause'. If this is the position, and the rules are made, then the subject is for all practical purposes, beyond the power of the Courts to protect him. Finally, a Statute may lay down that certain conditions are to be observed by the Department in rule-making, but it may also provide that a statement by the Department that the provisions of the Act have been complied with is conclusive evidence that the requirements of the Act have been fulfilled.

One or two illustrations will be sufficient to show the effect of these devices in practice. In *Institute of Patent Agents*

v. *Lockwood*[3] the Patents, Designs and Trade Marks Acts, 1883 and 1888 conferred on the Board of Trade power to make such rules, as, in the opinion of the Board, were necessary to give effect to the provisions of the Acts governing the registration of patents agents. Such rules, when made, were to have effect as if embodied in the Act itself. One of the rules so made required every patent agent to pay an annual registration fee on pain of being removed from the register. Lockwood failed to pay, and was removed from the register. He continued to practice, and the Institute of Patent Agents sought to restrain him from describing himself as a patent agent. The House of Lords reluctantly came to the conclusion that it had no power to assist Lockwood, since the Act gave the Board of Trade power to make rules which, when made, had statutory force, in the sense that they were to be read as a part of the Act itself. This made it impossible to challenge them on the ground that they were *ultra vires*.

This decision appears to exclude the possibility of judicial enquiry into delegated legislation framed under such wide powers altogether, but the position of the Courts in respect of it was explored further in *R.* v. *Minister of Health: Ex parte Yaffé.*[4] In that case, the Liverpool Corporation had made an improvement scheme under the Housing Act, 1935, and the scheme was approved, with some modifications, by the Minister of Health under Section 40 (3) of the Act. Section 40 (5) of the Act provided that 'the Order of the Minister when made shall have effect as if enacted in this Act.' Yaffé owned two houses which were compulsorily acquired under the scheme, and he sought to have the Minister's Order confirming the scheme quashed, on the ground that at the local inquiry held by the Minister certain provisions relating to the furnishing of plans had not been complied with. The Court of Appeal took the view that, as the statutory provisions had not been complied with, the Minister's purported Order was not a valid Order at all, and therefore could not take effect under Section 40 (5). The House of Lords, however, by a majority of four to one, Lord Russell of Killowen dissenting, reversed the decision

[3] [1894] A.C. 347.
[4] [1931] A.C. 494.

of the Court of Appeal, on the ground that the Minister's Order, when made, covered any defects in the original scheme. However, the House of Lords were at pains to suggest that the terms of Section 40 (5) did not give the Minister of Health unlimited legislative power. Lord Dunedin, in his speech, says:

'The first question, and it is a very important and far-reaching one, is, therefore, as to the effect of Section 40, sub-section 5. Has it the effect of preventing any enquiry by way of *certiorari* proceedings by an order confirmed by the Minister? It is evident that it is inconceivable that the protection should extend without limit. If the Minister went out of his province altogether, if, for example, he proposed to confirm a scheme which said that all the proprietors in a scheduled area should make a *per capita* contribution of £5 to the municipal authority to be applied by them for the building of a hall, it is repugnant to common sense that the order would be protected, although, if there were an Act of Parliament to that effect, it could not be touched. The high-water-mark of inviolability of a con-firmed order is to be found in a case in this House which *necessarily* binds your Lordships. It is the case of *Institute of Patent Agents* v. *Lockwood*. . . . There is an obvious distinction between that case and this, because there Parliament itself was in control of the rules for forty days after they were passed and could have annulled them if motion were made to that effect, whereas here there is no parliamentary manner of dealing with the confirmation of the scheme by the Minister of Health. Yet, I do not think that that distinction, obvious as it is, would avail to prevent the sanction given being an untouchable sanction. I think the real clue to the solution of the problem is to be found in the opinion of Lord Herchell, L.C., who said: "No doubt there might be some conflict between a rule and a provision of the Act. Well, there is a conflict sometimes between two sections to be found in the same Act. You have to try and reconcile them as best you may. If you cannot, you have to determine which is the leading provision and which the subordinate provision, and which must give way to the other. That would be so with regard to the enact-ment and with regard to rules which are to be treated as within the enactment. In that case probably the enactment itself would be treated as the governing consideration and the rule as subordinate to it".

'What that comes to is this: The confirmation makes the scheme speak as if it was contained in an Act of Parliament, but the Act of Parliament in which it is contained is the Act which provides for the framing of the scheme, not a subsequent

Act. If, therefore, the scheme, as made, conflicts with the Act, it will have to give way to the Act. The mere confirmation will not save it. It would be otherwise if the schemes had been *per se*, embodied in a subsequent Act, for then the maxim to be applied would have been *posteriora derogant prioribus*. But as it is, if one can find that the scheme is inconsistent with the provisions of the Act which authorises the scheme, the scheme will be bad.'

The two decisions of the House of Lords reflect two differing attitudes towards the Departments. In 1894, the extent to which Departmental legislation might threaten Parliamentary sovereignty had not been perceived. In 1931, the House of Lords was anxious to preserve any controls which might still remain.

Possibly the high-water mark in the legislative audacity of the Departments was attained in *Earl FitzWilliam's Wentworth Estates Co. Ltd.* v. *Minister of Town and Country Planning.*[5] The Estate Company refused to lease a plot of land on which to build a house except for a term of 300 years at a rent of £20.10.0 a year, and subject to the condition that the tenant should pay the development charge in return for an assignment of the right to compensation for loss of development rights. The applicant for a lease refused this offer, and applied to the Central Land Board, who after unsuccessful negotiation with the company, made an order under section 43 (2) of the Town and Country Planning Act, 1947, for its compulsory purchase at existing use value. The owner objected, and the Minister, after enquiry, confirmed the order. The Company thereupon applied to have the Minister's order and confirmation quashed as *ultra vires*.

Section 43 (2) of that Act gives the Central Land Board power to acquire land compulsorily, for the purpose of carrying out their functions. These functions are described in other sections of the Act, and they include the ascertainment of development values and the fixing and collection of development charges. It will be apparent that this case in reality raises the fundamental question whether the Central Land Board has a general commission compulsorily to acquire the land of private owners, whenever such private owners have been unable to agree on terms of sale with

[5] [1951] 2 K.B. 284.

prospective purchasers. If, in fact, that is the result of the
Act of 1947, it is, in reality, if not in form, a measure of
land nationalisation which has never been discussed by
Parliament at all. It should be added that the Central Land
Board, in this case, was seeking to carry out the provisions
of a memorandum which it had circulated to landowners
and prospective purchasers under the heading: 'House 1'
in which it had stigmatised the sale of land at a price which
included building value as unfair. The Court of Appeal,
nevertheless, held that the order of the Minister was *intra
vires*, but Denning L. J. in a powerful dissenting judgment,
put forward arguments against such a course which appear
unanswerable. He said:

'My conclusion therefore is that the ultimate object of the
board and the Minister is one which is not lawful, because
it is not their function to legislate. I would willingly support
their action, if I could, because I see no reason why this landowner should make an undeserved profit out of the purchaser.
But there is a principle at stake which is far more important
than the stopping of one particular piece of profiteering.
The principle is that the legislative power in this country
resides in Parliament and not in the government departments.
If once it appears that the ultimate object of the board is
one which is not authorized by Parliament, then it is the
duty of the courts to interfere, for it is a principle of our law
that a public authority, which is entrusted with executive
powers, must exercise those powers genuinely for the purposes
for which they are conferred. They must not be used for an
ulterior object, which is not authorized by law, however
desirable that object may seem to them to be in the public
interest.

'I am greatly strengthened in this view by the judgment of
Birkett J., who said[6] quite clearly that the powers of the board
did not enable them to exercise and enforce a policy that land
should not be sold at a price greater than its existing value.
He only decided in favour of the board because he thought it
was not their *sole* purpose to enforce their policy. It was at
that point, in my opinion, that he fell into error, for, even if
it was not their sole purpose, nevertheless if it was their predominant purpose, as it clearly was, that is sufficient to
invalidate their action.

'After all is said and done it come to this: the Central Land
Board required this landowner to conform to their policy of
"sales at existing use value only", and because he refused they

[6] i.e., in this case at first instance, in the King's Bench Division.

took his land compulsorily at that value. I do not think that they had any right to do this. If it is to be the law of this country that landowners are to sell their land at existing use values only, that law should be enacted by Parliament. It is often said that Parliament can do anything, but I do not know that even Parliament can so divest itself of its functions as to leave the making of such an important enactment to a government department without any consideration of it by Parliament itself.'

The other two members of the Court of Appeal, it would seem, thought this was precisely what Parliament *had* done, and the House of Lords was of the same opinion.

Sufficient has been written to show that, under the wide forms of legislative delegation recently practised, the control of the Courts has been so greatly weakened that in the majority of cases, they can no longer assist a subject who considers himself to be aggrieved. To what extent does Parliament retain control, independently of the terms of the Acts delegating legislative power themselves? Here it must be mentioned that the procedure governing the promulgation of departmental legislation is not uniform. Some rules and orders must be laid before the House 'as soon as may be'. This means that forty days notice of them must be given. During that time a Member may ask a question, but Parliamentary procedure does not allow this to be followed by discussion and amendment. If this method is used, the rules come into operation at once. An alternative practice is that the rules shall be laid before the House, but they shall not come into force until the expiration of a specified period, which again is usually forty days. Here the suspensory condition again allows questions to be asked, but no other effective action can be taken. Again, the Act may provide that rules or orders shall lie before Parliament for a given time, during which they are exposed to the possibility of a resolution that they shall be annulled. Meanwhile, the rules are operative. If this method is used, there is the possibility of an effective debate in the House of Commons, and there have been a number of instances when rules framed too widely have been modified, following the expression of strong opinions during the debate on the prayer for annulment. Finally, it may be provided that an order shall lapse after a specified period, unless the House, or both Houses, expressly affirm it. In such a case, it may further be provided that the order shall not be effective until an affirmative resolution has been carried. This is obviously the most effective method of Parliamentary control, and opinions have been expressed that it should be employed oftener than it is.

In addition to these various forms of procedure in relation to rules and orders, the House of Commons in 1944 set up the Select Committee on Delegated Legislation, for the purpose of considering all Statutory Rules and Orders, in order to discover whether the special attention of the House should be drawn to it on any of the following grounds:

'(i) That it imposes a charge on the public revenues or contains provisions requiring payments to be made to the Exchequer or any Government department or to any local or public authority in consideration of any licence or consent, or of any services to be rendered, or prescribes the amount of any such charge or payments; (ii) that it is made in pursuance of an enactment containing specific provisions excluding it from challenge in the Courts, either at all times or after the expiration of a specified period; (iii) that it appears to make some unusual or unexpected use of the powers conferred by the Statute under which it is made; (iv) that there appears to have been unjustifiable delay in the publication of it; (v) that for any special reason, its form or purport calls for elucidation.'

The importance of such a committee, provided that its functions are effectively discharged, may perhaps be gathered from the proceedings in which it originated. In 1941, the Fire Services (Emergency Provisions) Act gave power to the Home Secretary to issue regulations amalgamating local fire services, and to create a war-time National Fire Service. The Act provided that the regulations were to be laid before Parliament 'as soon as may be', and if either House within twenty-eight days resolved that a regulation should be annulled, it should thereupon cease to be operative. Regulations were made under the Act, but three years later Mr. Morrison, as Home Secretary, revealed to the House the fact that they had never been laid before Parliament. The upshot was an Act of Indemnity freeing the Home Secretary from all liability for failure to comply with the requirements of the Act, and the debate which resulted in the creation of the Select Committee on Delegated Legislation.

Chapter 7

Administrative Tribunals at Work

IT was shown in the last chapter that the Departments have been increasingly concerned, in securing grants of legislative power from Parliament, to ensure that their exercise of it should, as far as possible, be immune from the supervision of the ordinary courts. Their exercise of legislative power, however, has also been accompanied by the exercise, in a very wide range of cases, of the judicial function. Indeed, to a very considerable degree, the two are associated in the mind of the administrator. If there is conferred on a Ministry the power to organise an industry, and to make regulations governing the conduct of that industry, then undoubtedly it will be convenient if the Ministry has power to nominate persons who can adjudicate upon alleged violations of those regulations. Again, a Ministry, in the exercise of powers conferred on it, may wish to execute a policy which adversely affects the property of a citizen. Once again, it will be convenient if the Ministry has power to nominate persons who can decide whether the person aggrieved should be compensated by the Ministry or not.

It was for these and similar reasons that, imperceptibly almost at first, there grew up the practice of conferring judicial powers upon the Departments in ever-widening terms, until today the Departments have, either formally or in practice, replaced the ordinary courts in the decision of disputes in wide fields of social obligation. This process is continuous. A few years ago, it was decided by Parliament that the wide field of Workmen's Compensation should be transferred from the ordinary courts (who had admittedly treated it with a greater degree of technicality than Parliament had originally intended) to the Ministry of National

Insurance, by the National Insurance (Industrial Injuries) Act, 1946—an Act which confers a very wide rule-making power upon the Minister. An elaborate code of procedure, largely excluding the jurisdiction of the ordinary courts, is set out in the Act, and this is supplemented and amplified by Regulations made by the Minister under the Act. Under Section 42, an Industrial Injuries Commissioner is to be appointed, together with a number of deputy commissioners. These are lawyers of ten years standing or more. The regulations under the Act provide that questions of law or special difficulty may be decided by a tribunal of three commissioners, and for questions of fact of special difficulty to be considered with the assistance of one or more specially qualified assessors. Section 43 provides that local appeal tribunals are to be set up by the Minister, one or more persons representing the employer, and a similar number of persons representing insured persons. The regulations provide that the Minister may appoint one or more doctors to sit with the tribunal, either as additional members or as assessors. Panels of persons representing employers and insured persons are set up by the Minister for different areas, and members of a local appeal tribunal are drawn from these panels.

Section 44 provides that full-time insurance officers are appointed by the Minister for the various districts. In addition, the Act provides that the Minister shall appoint medical boards of two or more doctors, one of whom serves as chairman; and the Minister also appoints medical appeal tribunals, composed of three doctors, one of whom acts as chairman.

Let us see how this machinery works in practice. A claim for benefit must in the first place be made to an insurance officer, who must consider the claim immediately. If he decides that no 'special question' arises, and that the claim should be wholly or partially allowed, then benefit is awarded. If he is not satisfied, he must either decide against the claimant or refer the case to the local appeal tribunal, as far as possible within fourteen days of the claim being submitted to him. If the award of the insurance officer is adverse, the claimant may himself appeal to the local appeal tribunal. If the insurance officer's decision is based solely on a 'special question', then it will be necessary for the claimant to obtain leave of the chairman of the appeal tribunal before the appeal can be proceeded with. From the local appeal tribunal, either the insurance officer or a claimant may appeal further within three months to the Industrial Injuries Commissioner. This further appeal can only be brought with leave either of the local appeal tribunal or of the Commissioner. In certain cases also, the trade union of which the claimant is a member may also appeal.

The 'special questions' which have been referred to are enumerated in Section 36 of the Act. Their importance lies in the fact that after the remedy by way of successive appeals has been exhausted, the Minister himself may review the decision in the case of certain 'special questions', if new facts are brought to his notice. Moreover, on some 'special questions' there is an appeal on a point of law from the Minister to the High Court, whose decision is final (i.e. there is no possibility of a further appeal to the Court of Appeal or the House of Lords).

It will be seen, therefore, that the National Insurance (Industrial Injuries) Act, 1946, establishes a complete system of administrative courts to deal with industrial injuries. Possibly also because the topic of workmen's compensation has a long and complicated history in the ordinary courts, the system established contains several noteworthy, and wholly admirable features. For example, in addition to the balance of interest in local appeal tribunals between employer and employed, it is provided that the Industrial Injuries Commissioner and his deputies shall have adequate legal experience. Moreover, there is completely adequate provision for rehearings, and there is finally the possibility of a further appeal on a point of law to the High Court. The fully-developed scheme established by this Act in an exceedingly important field of industrial law therefore meets very nearly all the criticisms which have been lodged against administrative tribunals from time to time. It does not, it is true, provide for the legal representation of the claimant, but it is at least doubtful whether this is by any means generally desirable, particularly as in case of necessity, he will be advised by a member of his trade union, who is familiar with the work of the tribunals.

The problem of administrative tribunals is one which today goes to the very roots of our constitutional system (or lack of it). The 'classic' constitutional lawyers were apt to condemn the growth of administrative tribunals simply because they merged or confused the executive with the judicial function. This view, in fact, implied an acceptance, either express or implied, of Montesquieu's theory of the separation of governmental power, which was based on a misreading of the English constitution in the eighteenth century. It would in any case, however, be difficult to argue in favour of the eternal validity of Montesquieu's hypothesis, even if it were well-founded. Different social conditions may well demand a change in constitutional machinery. The argument from the past may be, and sometimes is, an argument against all significant change.

Nevertheless, it is well to remember that there are other and deeper problems underlying the question of the exercise of judicial power by administrative departments. All government, in the last resort, depends upon the consent of the governed, and if large enough numbers of people feel a sufficiently deep sense of injustice against the existing regime, they will in the long run rebel. That is why the impartial administration of justice is one of the main ends of government, and why it may often be used to test the stability of a regime. Therefore, if a Department appears to be at once prosecutor, principal witness and judge in its own cause, a deep conviction of injustice will remain in the minds of those adversely affected by its activities. The demand for really independent judges in administrative tribunals is therefore deep-rooted and genuine. No-one doubts that the officials appointed for this purpose by the Departments are men of high ability and integrity, who seek to deal impartially with the cases which come before them. The fact remains, however, that they are Departmentally appointed, and that it is through the Department that they will secure promotion. In any event, they are in daily contact with the senior staff of the Department, and they would be superhuman if they failed to pick up something of the attitude of mind of the makers of Departmental policy through this regular contact. It is in ways such as this, and not by the cruder methods of pressure that Departments profit through the tribunals they have created.

The problem of administrative tribunals may be examined more closely still. Professor Robson, in his classic *Justice and Administrative Law* has explained in detail in what way the judicial outlook differs from that of the administrator. The two are applying completely different techniques. The function of the judge is to secure the proper enforcement of legal rights and duties. The primary function of the administrator is the execution of a policy. Over large fields of social legislation these two functions must today stand in sharp contrast. From the standpoint of the administrator, a policy once agreed upon, must be carried out. He will attempt to carry it out intelligently and with the minimum disturbance of individual rights, but from his point of view, a private right too sharply asserted against his policy is a blemish to be removed. If necessary, he will seek a grant of wider powers to secure the success of his efforts. This has been done over and over again—for example, by successive Housing Acts. The administrator's task is therefore to promote a policy; the judge's, to administer justice. The two, therefore, do not merge. When an attempt has been made to do this, the result has generally been unsuccessful. In the long run, one function has superseded the other. Thus, in the early period of its evolution, the Court of Chancery was a mixture of law court and administrative department. In the long run, however, its administrative functions were completely subordinated to its judicial activities, and eventually, the bulk of its administrative work was abandoned altogether. Wolsey, during his Chancellorship, attempted to revive some of its administrative powers, but he met with widespread resistance, and it was because the judicial character of the Chancery was clearly recognised that it escaped destruction during the Commonwealth. The Star Chamber, on the other hand, suffered a different fate. In origin, the Star Chamber had been distinctly popular. It had been regarded as the tribunal in which the sovereign would bring to justice powerful magnates, at the suit of ordinary citizens. Under the first two Stuarts, however, the functions changed, and the Star Chamber became the principal bulwark of royal absolutism. This change is strikingly summarised by Maitland. He says:

> 'There can, I think, be little doubt that the Star Chamber was useful and was felt to be useful. The criminal procedure of the ordinary courts was extremely rude; the Star Chamber probably succeeded in punishing many crimes which would otherwise have gone unpunished. But that it was a tyrannical court, that it became more and more tyrannical, and under Charles I was guilty of great infamies is still more indubitable. *It was a court of politicians enforcing a policy, not a court of judges administering the law.*'[1]

Very much the same could be said of our administrative tribunals today, making due allowance for a changed social environment. The object of a Department, in bringing into operation an important piece of social legislation is to establish by detailed regulation certain intricate patterns of social conduct. The function of the administrative tribunal is not the determination of private rights under the law, but the suppression of deviations from that pattern. Individual instances of such activity, therefore, may not infrequently appear to be oppressive, and unless the Department shows great restraint, may in fact become so. On the other hand, the scrupulous respect of the courts for acquired rights may at times appear to the Departmental administrator to be an almost deliberate frustration of his policy. Yet the enforcement of a policy frequently involves the substitution of an official's opinion of what is good for us for our own decision on this question. As Mr. R. O'Sullivan has noticed, Mr. Douglas Jay, who has occupied Ministerial office in the post-war Labour Governments, wrote in a book recently:

> 'Housewives as a whole cannot be trusted to buy all the right things, where nutrition and health are concerned. This is really no more than an extension of the principle according to which the housewife herself would not trust a child of four to select the week's purchases. For in the case of nutrition or health the gentleman in Whitehall really does know better what is good for the people themselves.'[2]

[1] *Constitutional History*, p. 263.
[2] R. O'Sullivan, K.C. 'The Making of Everyman and his Undoing" *Current Legal Problems*, 1948, pp. 67-68.

It is for this reason that the gentlemen in Whitehall have made it impossible for the housewife to buy since the war anything more than the materials for bare subsistence? Or is it perhaps, remembering the spectacular failure of the groundnuts scheme, that these modern overlords lag somewhat behind the ordinary citizen in normal business acumen? The question is one which merits further exploration.

To point out that the judicial and the administrative functions do not mix does not dispose of the problem presented by administrative tribunals, however. To object to them simply because they are novel is to advance an argument which would bar the way to all social change. After all, the Court of Chancery was in origin an administrative tribunal. So was the Court of Exchequer. Both developed into great courts for the protection of the subject's lawful rights. They did so because their judicial staffs increasingly possessed the judicial temperament, and became permeated with the respect for human personality and private rights, which is the outstanding characteristic of the Common Law. To the extent that they did so, they ceased to look at the problems which came before them administratively. Moreover, they acquired popularity with litigants because in their early years, they enjoyed a reputation for speedy and effective determination of disputes. Later, as is well known, the Chancery became a by-word for delay and expense, and a non-legal critic would be justified in pointing out that this only occurred when the domination of this great court by professional lawyers was complete. It is unfortunately true that the great respect for form and precedent which a legal training develops can, if carried to excess, defeat or delay justice, by introducing complexities which do not add to the lustre of the law. It may very well be, therefore, that insofar as disputes between Government Department and subject are concerned, where these are civil in nature, there is some disposition towards passivity at the operation of Departmental tribunals, simply because these are speedily undertaken, and because their proceedings are very largely free from technicalities. To give an example: If a road-haulage firm is denied a licence by the Ministry of Transport, it does not want to initiate litigation which, if taken to the House of Lords, may extend over three years, and which may cost many thousands of pounds. It wants a quick and final decision, and this is what is given by the Traffic Commissioners, but the firm would be more satisfied with the procedure than it is at present, if it were possible to appeal once and finally on a point of law to a court with a more judicial composition than an administrative tribunal can possibly have, and preferably to one of appellate status. Some Departments, as we have seen, make elaborate provision for appeals within the Department, but this does not dispel the deep-seated conviction of the subject who is adversely affected by Departmental action that he will not secure a completely independent adjudication until he gets outside the Department altogether.

It is necessary, in discussing administrative tribunals, to guard against the assumption that wherever their proceedings differ from those of the ordinary courts they are therefore inferior to the ordinary courts. Even the question of legal representation before administrative courts is one on which much can be said on either side. Moreover, it is one on which the practice of the Departments varies very widely. Some administrative tribunals permit such representation, and then, by imperceptible stages, the practice of the tribunal tends to approach that of the ordinary courts. Others exclude it completely, and in some a high degree of informality may exist. It is unfortunately true that wherever legal representation is allowed, costs tend to rise sharply. Moreover, too much can be made of the extent of the handicap suffered by those to whom legal representation is denied. With the passing of class distinctions, much of the fear of those in authority has also disappeared, even among children, as everyone who is familiar with the work of Juvenile Courts is well aware. Few today, therefore, are tongue-tied where their own rights or conduct are in question. Moreover, although it may perhaps be heresy for a lawyer to say it, in courts dealing with industrial relations, where a workman is represented by a fellow trade unionist, he may be as well represented in that environment as if he had employed counsel.

Again, the argument that administrative tribunals are not bound by the rules of evidence, and that members of the administrative court may be completely ignorant of them, is not one which necessarily involves a condemnation of administrative courts for this reason. Few lawyers would claim that our English rules of evidence are the perfection of human reason. They abound with technicalities and relics from earlier times. They are urgently in need of simplification and codification. They are essentially the product of a Common Law case-law system, and to apply them in their entirety to administrative disputes would be absurd. What is far more important is that administrative tribunals should adjudicate in a recognisably judicial manner. They must decide upon the evidence before them, and not from their own knowledge or supposition. They must give each side the same opportunity of being heard, and above all things, in deciding, they must have regard exclusively to the merits of the case before them, and whilst adjudicating, they must exclude from their minds the consideration of the possible effects of their decision on general administrative policy. It is probably in this last respect that administrative tribunals are most frequently found wanting, and it is because citizens frequently feel that the requirements of justice are being subordinated to questions of policy that they feel resentment against the decisions of such tribunals. They have, moreover, a great deal of evidence for such a feeling, more especially in the attitude of the Departments themselves to adjudication. Their fixed determination to exclude, wherever possible, an appeal to the ordinary courts even upon a point of law, is rooted in the determination not to allow 'purely legal factors' (i.e. a consideration of the rights of parties affected by policy) to stand in the way of the achievement of that policy. This is a matter which perhaps deserves closer examination. The achievement of broad social policies in the mid-twentieth century necessarily involves the abridgment or destruction of individual rights. Inevitably, therefore, the achievement of that policy involves a series of contests between the Departmental and individual citizens, in which the scales are initially weighted against the citizen, simply because Parliament has thought fit to confer powers upon the Department to achieve a policy. It is quite possible and competent for Parliament to confer upon the Department power to destroy private rights without compensation and without any form of preliminary inquiry in which the citizen may express his objections to what is proposed. If Parliament adopted this course consistently, then it is beyond argument that we should have ceased to be a democracy, and that our traditional form of government would have been replaced by open tyranny. So far, therefore, Parliament has rarely adopted so drastic a course. It has chosen to define the terms on which a Department may override private rights, and it has usually provided also for an enquiry of some type before rights are destroyed. Such an enquiry may have within its scope two questions: (1) whether the individual rights is to be destroyed or abridged at all; (2) whether, if it is destroyed, compensation is payable, and if so, how much. Manifestly, if such an enquiry is prejudged by the requirements of policy, then it simply supplies cover for the arbitrary execution of Departmental policy, and we have once again passed from a constitutional to an absolute regime. Even this, however, is by no means the end of the matter. Reference to the decisions in which the limits of administrative discretion have been tested in the courts will show a disposition on the part of counsel and the court to divide executive acts affecting the subject's rights into three classes: (1) judicial; (2) quasi-judicial, and (3) administrative. Where a Department exercises a judicial, or (according to most writers) a quasi-judicial function, then the forms of natural justice must be observed. This has the necessary consequence that the courts may enquire whether the administrative tribunal has, in fact, conformed to the requirements of natural justice. On the other hand, it is settled practice that no question of natural justice arises where what is done is an administrative, and not a judicial, or a quasi-judicial act. It need scarcely be added, therefore, that the whole weight of Departmental opinion is exerted to show wherever possible, that the Department has done what it has done administratively and not judicially. Their task is made easier by the fact that there is no unanimity among judges where the dividing line is to be drawn. Thus, in

D

Franklin v. *Minister of Town and Country Planning*,[3] a case
which has already been discussed in Chapter 2, Henn-
Collins J. in the King's Bench Division said that in holding
the public local enquiry required by the New Towns Act,
1946, the Minister was acting quasi-judicially, and that in
the holding of that enquiry and in confirming the ensuing
order the requirements of natural justice had not been observed. The Court of Appeal also took the view that the functions of the Minister in this matter were quasi-judicial, but
they differed from Henn-Collins J. in that they thought the
Minister had not acted improperly. The House of Lords,
on the other hand, were of opinion that the action of the
Minister in making the order for a new town at Stevenage,
following a public local enquiry, was purely administrative,
and was therefore not subject to review by the Courts at all.
Lord Thankerton, in his speech in the House of Lords, in
the final appeal, says on this topic:

'In my opinion, no judicial, or quasi-judicial, duty was
imposed on the respondent,[4] and any reference to judicial
duty, or bias, is irrelevent in the present case. The respondent's
duties under Section 1 of the Act and the First Schedules
thereto are, in my opinion, purely administrative, but the
Act prescribes certain methods of, or steps in, discharge of
that duty. It is obvious that, before making the draft order,
which must contain a definite proposal to designate the area
concerned as the site of a new town, the respondent must have
made elaborate inquiry into the matter, and have consulted
any local authorities who appear to him to be concerned, and
obviously other departments of the Government, such as the
Ministry of Health, would naturally require to be consulted.
It would seem, accordingly, that the respondent was required
to satisfy himself that it was a sound scheme before he took the
serious step of issuing a draft order. It seems clear also that
the purpose of inviting objections, and where they are not
withdrawn, of having a public inquiry, to be held by someone
other than the respondent, to whom that person reports, was
for the further information of the respondent, in order to
(ensure) the final consideration of the soundness of the scheme
of the designation; and it is important to note that the development of the site, after the order is made, is primarily the duty
of the development corporation established under Section 2
of the Act. I am of opinion that no judicial duty is laid on the

[3] [1948] A.C. 87.
[4] i.e. the Minister.

respondent in discharge of these statutory duties, and that the only question is whether he has complied with the statutory directions to appoint a person to hold the public inquiry, and to consider that person's report. On this contention of the appellants no suggestion is made that the public inquiry was not properly conducted, nor is there any criticism of the report by Mr. Morris.[5] In such a case the only ground of challenge must be either that the respondent did not in fact consider the report and the objections, of which there is here no evidence, or that his mind was so foreclosed that he gave no genuine consideraion to them, which is the case made by the appellants. Although I am unable to agree exactly with the view of the respondent's duty expressed by the learned judge, or with some of the expressions used by the Court of Appeal in regard to that matter, it does appear to me that the issue was treated in both courts as being whether the respondent had genuinely considered the objections and the report, as directed by the Act.'

Such a line of argument offers an easy way of escape for the Courts from the dilemma created by the conflict of Departmental policy and private right. Once a proceeding has been declared to be administrative, and not judicial, then the only legal question which can arise is whether the administrative forms prescribed by the Act have been followed. The effect of the judgment in the *Franklin Case* is therefore to shift the duty of control of the Department in such cases from the courts to Parliament—which has already abdicated in favour of the Department! In these circumstances, it is not altogether surprising that the subject should sometimes come to the conclusion that he is being ground between the upper and the nether millstones. The following consequences of a compulsory purchase order, made by the London County Council under the Housing Acts were reported in the *Daily Express* of August 24, 1951:

'WIDOW'S GARDEN IS "SEIZED" BY THE COUNCIL MEN'

Son struggles with police

'A widow's two sons struggled with police and bailiffs while London County Council workmen fenced off 700 ft. of the garden of her bungalow at New North Road, Hainault, Essex, yesterday.

[5] Who held the inquiry.

'The widow, 73-year-old Mrs. Florence Attridge, has resisted for nearly four years a compulsory purchase order by the L.C.C. to acquire the bungalow—where she lives alone—and an acre of garden.

'The L.C.C. offered £1,300 and said the land was needed for council houses.

'Yesterday several men arrived at the bungalow by car. One said he was a sheriff's officer, and that the others were bailiffs.

One watched

'Mrs. Attridge watched from her bedroom window as her two married sons, Claud, 49, and Laurence, 38, challenged the visitors.

'Several council officials arrived, and began to measure the garden. Said Laurence: "You are not taking from my mother yet. It is a violation of justice to deprive an old woman of her living."

'Mrs. Attridge—her husband was a docker—supplements her old-age pension by hiring her garden to summer campers.

'Laurence caught hold of the tape, and struggled with the bailiffs. A police sergeant and two constables intervened, and there was a further struggle.

100 watched

'By this time more than 100 people were looking on and Mrs. Attridge's four-year-old grand-daughter Marion stood sobbing in the garden.

'Claud Attridge tried to remove a pole hammered into the garden, and Laurence again struggled with the police.

'He was taken into custody. His mother, with a red dressing-gown over her nightdress, ran into the garden.

"You thieves, robbing an old woman," she shouted.

'A lorry arrived with fencing, and workmen, surrounded by officials and police, fenced off 700 ft., leaving Mrs. Attridge a small strip near her bungalow.'

Possibly it is wrong, in these enlightened mid-twentieth century years that citizens should wish to retain their property, when it has been compulsorily acquired for totally inadequate consideration by a local authority, although curiously enough in earlier times this would have been regarded as oppression and extortion. Nevertheless, it remains true that a substantial number of citizens have not yet been educated to the point where they can view their own dispossession as a highly praiseworthy incident in the onward march of progress. Certainly Mr. Claud Attridge did not, for on the day following the events recorded in the newspaper extract given above, he was charged at the Stratford police court, and was remanded on bail for fourteen days on a charge of obstructing a police sergeant.

It is unfortunately true that no clear line of distinction can be drawn between judicial, quasi-judicial, and administrative functions in the wide powers conferred on government departments. As Dr. C. K. Allen points out,[6] there are few administrative actions, except the most mechanical and trivial, in which a judicious balancing of considerations is not necessary. On the other hand, there are judicial processes, judicial in form, which are in substance administrative, e.g. directions to trustees for the administration of a trust. Acts such as these, as we have seen, are survivals from the days when the Court of Chancery was very widely concerned with administration. Furthermore, as Dr. Allen also points out, even if it were possible to classify the powers exercised by Ministers, it will be found in practice that Statutes have classified as administrative, powers which are predominantly judicial or quasi-judicial, and conversely, they have sometimes treated as judicial, powers which equally clearly are administrative. Nevertheless, the Committee on Ministers' Powers heroically sought to establish such distinctions, and the courts have sometimes attempted to follow the classification put forward by the Committee. The judicial process, says the Committee has four characteristics: (1) There must be a presentation, either orally or in writing, of the case of each party; (2) the facts must be ascertained by means of evidence, adduced by each party, and cross-examined by the other; (3) there must be argument by the parties on any points of law which may arise; (4) there must be a decision upon the matter, based on stated conclusions concerning the facts, and the application of the relevant rules of law, by which the judge is bound. It is that last characteristic which is often decisive in respect of the judicial process. Once the judge has determined what the relevant law is, he is bound to apply it. He has no discretion to dispense with it.

[6] *Laws and Orders*, p. 69.

A quasi-judicial process, says the Committee, exhibits the first and second characteristics, sometimes the third, but never the fourth. The quasi-judge must know the two cases, and the facts supporting them, but he need not consider arguments about them, and his final decision is not conditioned by relevant rules of law. The formal difficulty, it will be seen, coincides with the difficulty which judges experience in distinguishing quasi-judicial from purely administrative acts. Nevertheless, one may be subject to judicial control, whilst the other is not.

The difficulties and uncertainties to which this attempted classification may lead are plainly apparent in the decision of the Court of Appeal in *Cooper* v. *Wilson*.[7] The facts of this case were extremely simple. The chief constable of Liverpool had provisionally dismissed a police sergeant, and the watch committee confirmed the dismissal. Under various Police Acts, the power to dismiss a constable in a borough police force is vested solely in the watch committee, and the question to be decided was whether the fact that the chief constable, who had issued a provisional dismissal, sat with the watch committee through the hearing invalidated the proceedings. Both Greer and Scott L. JJ. thought that this hearing was a quasi-judicial proceeding, and both learned Lords Justices were avowedly making an effort to apply the definitions contained in the Report of the Committee on Ministers' Powers. Scott L. J. indeed observed that the police regulations issued by the Home Secretary made the watch committee a domestic tribunal.

'to try and decide very important issues of fact, of guilt or innocence it may be on grave criminal charges, and anyhow in all cases, where the chief constable has proposed dismissal, on charges of great seriousness to the accused constable. On a criminal charge, presumably the watch committee would not act, but leave the matter to the ordinary criminal administration of justice; and in any case the decision of the watch committee would, in my view, be no bar to a trial of an issue "between the King and the prisoner" on the same charge in a criminal court. But as between the constable and the police authority—the watch committee itself—which employs him, is the decision of the watch committee on a trial under regulation 20 that the accused is guilty of the offences charged an

[7] [1937] 2 K.B. 309.

estoppel against an action for either damages for wrongful dismissal or for declarations that he did not commit the offences charged? That question does not arise here as the form of the action brought seems to me tacitly to have assumed that the watch committee was, by the regulations, given exclusive jurisdiction over the question of guily or innocence of the three charges of offences against the discipline code of the police regulations. But if this view be right—and I repeat that I express no opinion—it makes the function of the watch committee in point of degree approximate to the judicial rather than the quasi-judicial.'

Applying this view, the Lords Justices had no difficulty in holding that the requirements of natural justice had not been satisfied, so that the decision of the watch committee could not stand. The third member of the Court of Appeal, Macnaghten J., on the other hand, whilst accepting the fact that the proceedings of the watch committee were either judicial or quasi-judicial, could not find that they were unfair or biased.

The decision has provoked strong, and justified criticism from Professor Robson.[8] He points out that the watch committee is certainly not a domestic tribunal.

'If we regard the watch committee, in respect of part of its work, as an administrative authority exercising judicial functions, and thus acting as an administrative tribunal, we shall be nearer the truth and we shall have cleared the air of much ambiguous and nebulous phraseology. The functions which it exercises in that capacity are those in which it is called upon to hear and determine a controversy between parties, either in the first instance or on appeal or by way of an application to confirm the chief constable's decision.

'This is surely simpler, more lucid and nearer the truth than the picture conjured up of a quasi-judicial court presided over by a quasi-judge administering quasi-law in quasi-disputes. The quasi-parties give their quasi-evidence; the tribunal finds the quasi-facts and considers the quasi-precedents and the quasi-principles. It then applies the quasi-law in a quasi-judicial decision which is promulgated in a quasi-official document and given quasi-enforcement. The members of the tribunal, having concluded their quasi-judicial business, then go out and drink quasi-beer before taking lunch consisting of quasi-chicken croquettes. They then go home to their quasi-wives.'

[8] *Justice and Administrative Law.* 3rd Ed., pp.494-6.

The great problem presented by the proliferation of administrative tribunals of all kinds, their wide variations in composition and judicial technique, their miscellaneous provision for appeals and their relation to the ordinary courts is the subject of Professor Robson's stimulating criticisms in *Justice and Administrative Law*, which has profoundly influenced all study of the question. Professor Robson's approach is an exceedingly balanced one. He recognises the advantages which a system of administrative tribunals can give in so closely integrated a society as that of the West now is. He has a number of important reforms, both procedural and substantive to suggest, but also, from the date of the appearance of the first edition of his book (and before), he has argued in favour of the creation of an administrative court of appeal, with mixed administrative and judicial personnel, and sitting in a number of divisions. This would replace the existing lack of system in the organisation of appeal tribunals.

Although Professor Robson put forward this view with his usual lucidity to the Committee on Ministers' Powers, it was frigidly received. The lawyers thought it would weaken the already slender control exercised by the courts. The administrators, no doubt, preferred the present formlessness and lack of system as leaving more autonomy to each of the Departments. There were no grounds for the complacency of the lawyers, however, for in the next two decades, the administrators increasingly outwitted them, and today they become even more insistent that the remaining checks upon their absolutism should be relaxed. Accordingly, Professor Robson's proposal which, twenty years ago, was brushed aside as an 'unnecessary Continental innovation' would today be accepted as a safeguard; but, as Professor Robson is plainly conscious in his third edition, it is today the administrators who are highly suspicious of the purity of his intentions.

Chapter 8

The Courts and the Executive

THE last two chapters have been primarily concerned with the extent of the judicial and legislative powers which have been progressively secured by the Departments, and in the course of the discussion, it has been necessary to refer incidentally to the degree of control exercised by the Courts over the executive. In order to make the picture plainer, however, it will now be necessary to consider the functions of the Courts in somewhat greater detail.

The superior Courts in England, it has been noticed, have no great constitutional power entrusted to them to invalidate Parliamentary legislation, as the American Supreme Court has, and it is perhaps fortunate that they have not, for the exercise of this power by the American Supreme Court has more than once made it the storm-centre of controversy. At the time of the New Deal legislation, indeed, it appeared for a time as if the executive would be satisfied with nothing less than the curtailment or abolition of this great power. Even though it is regularly exercised, however, it is interesting to notice that it has not prevented the growth to major proportions of a situation similar to that which exists in Great Britain. Something will be said about the American problem in a later chapter. In England, the Courts can exercise a somewhat similar power in respect of delegated legislation by the invocation of the doctrine of *ultra vires*. Something has already been said on this point, and upon the efforts of the Departments to escape from the restrictions imposed by it through the insertion into statutes granting legislative power to the Departments of a power to amend the Act itself, or even of a power to amend the Act and any other Act as they may think fit. It will be profitable at this point to examine more closely one or two cases in which the existence of such clauses has prevented the Courts from effectively intervening on behalf of a subject. Of necessity, such cases are somewhat technical, for having regard to the wide powers conceded to Departments, the only obvious line of attack open to the subject is to claim, either that the action of the Ministry is beyond the purposes for which the Act was passed (necessarily a somewhat vague and often inconclusive enquiry) or that the Minister has failed to comply with the requirements of the Act, usually by omitting some step in the procedure prescribed by Parliament. Successive Housing Acts have provided a battleground for Department and subject, for the powers conceded have been increasingly extensive, their exercise has often involved the compulsory acquisition of the citizen's property, usually for an inadequate sum. Thus, Section 40 (2) of the Housing Act, 1936 (repealing the provisions of earlier Acts) directed that

'the compensation to be paid for land, including any buildings thereon, purchased as being land comprised in a clearance area shall be the value at the time the valuation is made of the land as a site cleared of buildings and available for development in accordance with the requirements of the building byelaws for the time being in force in the district.'

This is the infamous 'site value' clause under which widespread injustice and spoliation has been done to a thrifty and numerous section of the community. It meant, for example, that if a shop was built on a quarter of an acre site, and was included in a clearance order, the shopkeeper got nothing at all for the destruction of his business, and nothing at all for the shop premises which were demolished. He got the estimated price of quarter of an acre of land; and if he held his shop on a lease, he got nothing at all, as he was not the owner of the site. Since, therefore, ruin and destruction of livelihood could follow upon a clearance order, it is scarcely surprising that those affected by them sometimes scrutinised the circumstances of their promulgation closely. Even so, and even if they could show that the local authority was not proposing to proceed with clearance for some years, it did not follow that they had any remedy. As *Robins* v.

Minister of Health[1] showed, a local authority might confiscate a man's property, and then relet it to him for a high rent!

This case also illustrates a further point, viz. that the Ministry is prepared to take a wide view of its functions, and will confirm schemes prepared by local authorities, even when there is no prospect at all that they can be carried out at an early date. In this way, local authorities, actively encouraged by the Ministry of Health (and now by the Ministry of Town and Country Planning) have carried out large-scale expropriation of property-owners. One such scheme, under the Housing Act of 1925 was tested in Court in *R.* v. *Minister of Health; Ex parte Davies.*[2] The Act of 1925 was drafted in narrower terms than the Housing Act of 1936, on which *Robins* v. *Minister of Health*[1] was fought, and accordingly the Courts were able to intervene effectively on behalf of the subject. The points in issue in this case are very concisely set out in the opening paragraphs of Lord Justice Greene's judgment, which read as follows:

'This appeal raises a question of great importance and difficulty with regard to the true interpretation of several sections of the Housing Act of 1925. It is worthy of note in passing that that Act takes the place of four statutes which it repeals in whole or in part, and which were known as the Housing of the Working Classes Acts of 1890, 1894, 1900, and 1903. The title of the Act affords some ground for expecting that it is wider in its scope than the provision of houses for the working classes, the demolition and rebuilding, and the regulation of such demolition and rebuilding, and the letting and occupation of such houses.

'After receipt of an official representation by the medical officer made under Section 35 of the Act, the corporation of Derby took it into their consideration and made what purported to be an improvement scheme for an unhealthy area in their city, which for convenience be referred to as Area No. 2. William Davies, an owner of one of the houses affected by the scheme, after a public inquiry by an inspector, applied to the Court of King's Bench for a writ of prohibition directed to the Minister of Health prohibiting him from proceeding further in the matter of an Order confirming the scheme. The Court, on December 18, 1928, made an Order Absolute for such prohibition. This is an appeal by the Minister of Health against such Order Absolute. It is unnecessary to read

[1] [1939] 1 K.B. 537, Ante chapter II.
[2] [1929] 1 K.B. 619.

the whole of the scheme. In order to consider this question, it appears to me to be desirable to read, not only the clause, but to read also the clauses immediately preceding and following. (The three clauses were then read). The respondents contended in the Court below that the penultimate clause invalidated the scheme, because (1) it did not comply with the provisions of Section 35 of the Act, which requires that an improvement scheme must be a scheme "for the reconstruction and rearrangement of the streets and houses within the area or some of such streets and houses"; (2) it was in any event too indefinite—it left undecided what was to be done with the area. The Act contemplates a definite scheme, under which it will be shown what is to be done with the area after demolition, and the authority cannot reserve to themselves a power to dispose of it at a future time for any purpose they think fit.'

The Divisional court of the King's Bench Division held that the scheme did not comply with the requirements of the Act. It provided that the area when cleared 'should be sold, leased, or otherwise disposed of as the local authority may think fit', whilst the Act required that the local authority, in the scheme, should specify the use to which the land was to be put. The Court of Appeal unanimously took the same view as the Divisional Court. Apparently, therefore, a victory for the subject had been recorded, but the success was fleeting. In the Housing Act of 1936 the Department inserted a clause providing that the local authority should have complete discretion from the standpoint of user. The result was the decision in *Robins* v. *Minister of Health*.[3] Once again the Ministry had outmanoeuvred the Courts.

It is important to notice that in *Davis's Case*, the aggrieved subject had moved swiftly, and had invoked the assistance of the Courts after the local authority's scheme had been published, but before it had been confirmed. The result of the case was that the subject was granted a prohibition (on which something will be said later) restraining the Minister from confirming the scheme. What could the subject have done if the Minister *had* confirmed the scheme, having regard to the fact that the Act of 1925, like the later Acts, provided that the order, when confirmed by the Minister, should have effect 'as if enacted in the Act'? In the Divisional

[3] [1939] 1 K.B. 537.

Court, in *Davis's Case*, Lord Chief Justice Hewart had expressed the view that if the scheme had been confirmed by the Minister, the Courts would then have been powerless. This exact point came before the Divisional Court in *R.* v. *Ministry of Health; Ex parte Yaffé* two years later,[4] when Lord Hewart and Talbot J. followed the view expressed by Lord Hewart in Davis's Case. Swift J., however, thought that even at that stage, the Courts could effectively intervene, and the Court of Appeal reversed the decision of the Divisional Court, and substantially accepted the opinion of Swift J. This time, however, the Ministry pursued the question as far as the House of Lords, which held, by a majority of four to one, that when the scheme, as modified by the Minister, was confirmed by him, it took effect as if enacted in the Act, notwithstanding its earlier defects. The Court of Appeal, on the other hand, had taken the view that if a scheme failed to satisfy the requirements of the Act, it was *ultra vires*, and therefore there was no effective scheme for the Minister to confirm. The House of Lords, it will be seen, took the view that there was a scheme, albeit a defective one, which the Minister modified, and effectively confirmed. Thus, the protection given by the Courts in *Davis's Case* was applicable only when no valid scheme at all was prepared by the local authority, and in any event, even this possible redress was swept away in the wider terms of the Act of 1936.

With the substantial failure of the onslaught on schemes themselves, as reflected in the judgment of the House of Lords in *Yaffé's Case*, the point of attack changed, as might have been anticipated, to the conduct of public enquiries. Assuming that in holding a public enquiry, the Minister was discharging a judicial or 'quasi-judicial' function, then the Court might enquire into the proceedings to discover whether the requirements of 'natural justice' had been satisfied. This was done with some success in *Errington* v. *Minister of Health*.[5] The appellant in this case, had lodged objections against a clearance scheme relating to land in the centre of Jarrow. A Public Local Inquiry was held,

[4] [1931] A.C. 494.
[5] [1935] 1 K.B. 249.

with the result that the Ministry did not automatically confirm the scheme, but made suggestions that many of the desired improvements could be achieved by repairs and reconditioning. The Jarrow Corporation, however, pressed for the entire scheme to be confirmed, and eventually, a representative of the Ministry, together with the Inspector who held the inqury, met representatives of the Corporation in Jarrow, where they inspected the area, in the absence of the objectors, or any representatives of them. The result of this inspection was that the Minister confirmed the scheme. The Court of Appeal were able to hold that the Minister's action in confirming the scheme after public inquiry was quasi-judicial, and that since in this case the requirements of natural justice had not been fulfilled, the Order must be quashed.

It is not often that a Ministry trips up so obviously, however. Moreover, *Errington's Case* opened up a number of baffling problems upon the question when a Minister may be said to be acting quasi-judicially, and when administratively. Almost immediately after *Errington's Case* had been decided, *Frost* v. *Minister of Health*[6] was argued before Swift J. This arose out of a clearance order relating to Birkenhead. After the Corporation had made its draft order, and before any objections had been lodged, the Ministry of Health advised the Corporation to omit a number of houses from the scheme, without any fresh resolution being passed by the local authority. This was done, and the draft order when published omitted the houses mentioned by the Minister. Later, objections were lodged, and after they had been heard at a public inquiry, the Minister confirmed the scheme. Thereupon, some of the objectors sought to have the order confirming the scheme quashed. Swift J. held that he had no power to do this. The amendment of the scheme did not make it invalid under the Act, and when the Minister tendered his advice, before objections were lodged, he was acting administratively, not judicially or quasi-judicially. Twelve months later, a variation of this mode of attack again proved ineffective. In *Offer* v. *Ministry of Health*,[7] the facts

[6] [1935] 1 K.B. 286.
[7] [1936] 1 K.B. 40.

were similar, except that before the public inquiry was held, the Minister had sent an official to make a preliminary inspection of the area, the result of which was to encourage the Corporation to declare it a clearance area. The Court of Appeal held that this did not invalidate the order. In their view the Ministry was acting administratively before the dispute between citizens and local authority had arisen.

These decisions, however, by no means covered the difficulties which can arise from the merging of administrative and judicial functions in an executive Department. In *Horn* v. *Minister of Health*[8] the Court of Appeal was called upon to make the attempt to sort out a number of episodes into their respective spheres—administrative and quasi-judicial—and opinions have differed widely upon the results of their efforts. In this case, the Sunderland Corporation made a compulsory purchase order in respect of farmland owned by Horn. This was under the Housing Act of 1925. Horn objected, and a public local inquiry was held, at which Horn developed his objections. After the inquiry closed, but before the Minister had confirmed the compulsory purchase order, a deputation from the Sunderland Corporation had an interview with the Minister, not to discuss the inquiry, but to discuss the plans of the local authority to abate overcrowding under Section 1 of the Housing Act of 1935. Nothing appears to have been said at the interview about the confirmation of the compulsory purchase order then pending, but Horn asked for the order to be quashed on the ground that the Minister had failed to observe the principles of natural justice in receiving representatives of the corporation in his absence. The question to be resolved was whether this case came within the principle of *Errington's Case* or within that of *Frost's* and *Offer's Cases*. In *Errington's Case*, it will be remembered, the Minister had been in contact with the local authority in the absence of objectors between the time of the inquiry and the time when the order was confirmed—as was the case here. In *Frost's* and *Offer's Cases* the contact had occurred before the dispute between citizens and council had arisen, when it was clear that the Minister was acting administratively. In *Horn's Case*, however, the

[8] [1937] 1 K.B. 164.

Council deputation had interviewed the Minister on a different Act, and generally on a subject-matter of which the compulsory purchase order was a specific instance. The Court of Appeal held that here, too, the Minister was acting administratively and not quasi-judicially, so that the subject was without redress, and common sense would appear to coincide with the Court of Appeal's decision. As Scott L. J. said in his judgment,

> 'the administrative duties have to be carried out as part of the policy of Parliament imposed upon the Minister by the statute which he is administering, and Parliament must be taken quite deliberately to have decided that the exercise of the quasi-judicial functions of the Minister is compatible with the performance of his administrative duties under the Act.'

That may not be an ideal solution, but there it is, and once it has been settled that the Department is acting administratively, the subject is beyond the protection of the Courts. This was also the conclusion reached in *Franklin* v. *Minister of Town and Country Planning*,[9] a case which has already been discussed earlier in this volume. In that case, it will be remembered, the original decision of Henn Collins J. was not supported by higher Courts, which took a narrower view of their powers to control the Departments than the judge of first instance, who had expressed the same view in other decisions. Thus in *Re Plymouth (City Centre) Declaratory Order, 1946*[10] an application was made to quash an order made under the Town and Country Planning Act, 1944, by the Minister of Town and Country Planning, and relating to property in the centre of Plymouth. Section 1(1) of the Act provides:

> 'Where the Minister . . . *is satisfied* that is requisite, for the purpose of dealing satisfactorily with extensive war damage in the area of a local planning authority, that a part or parts of their area, consisting of land shown to his satisfaction to have sustained war damage, or of such land together with other land contiguous or adjacent thereto, should be laid out afresh and redeveloped as a whole, an order declaring all or any of the land in such a part of their area to be land subject to compulsory purchase for dealing with war damage may be made by the Minister.'

[9] [1937] 1 K.B. 164.
[10] [1947] L.J.R. 527.

The Plymouth order related not only to war-damaged property, but also to sound property contiguous to it. Henn Collins J. held that the Minister had no jurisdiction to make the order, since there was no evidence that he had satisfied himself on reasonable grounds that it was necessary for the redevelopment scheme. The order was therefore quashed to the extent that it related to the sound property. In effect, Henn Collins J. was maintaining that phrases such as 'is satisfied' and 'has reasonable cause to believe' are phrases which entitled the Courts to enquire into the propriety of administrative action.

This view of the matter did not commend itself to the Court of Appeal in *Robinson* v. *Minister of Town and Country Planning*,[11] an appeal from another judgment of Henn Collins J. in another Plymouth case, later in the same year. In that case the Minister had made a declaratory order under the Act of 1944 providing for the compulsory purchase of nine houses, three of which had been destroyed by enemy action, one damaged, and the other five were undamaged. Once again, Henn Collins J. quashed the order, but the Court of Appeal reversed this decision, and Lord Greene M. R. conceded the freedom of the executive in these matters in very wide terms.

'The words "requisite" and "satisfactorily" (he said) clearly indicate that the question is one of opinion and policy, matters which are peculiarly for the Minister himself to decide. No objective test is possible. If confirmation of this view is sought, it is to be found, for example, in the provisions of the First Schedule, under which the Minister, although bound to consider objections, is entitled to make his decision without any private hearing or public inquiry. In making his decision he may obviously be guided by his own views as to what is "expedient" for the purpose of dealing "satisfactorily" with extensive war damage, assisted, of course, by any advice which he may obtain from his own staff or from outside advisers. But the decision and the principles and policy which lead him to it are such as to commend themselves to him. This cannot be affected by the fact that he decides to order a public inquiry. The object of such an inquiry under the First Schedule can only be to elucidate matters upon which he desires to be better informed. Nothing that is said or done at it can bind his

[11] [1947] L.J.R. 1285.

discretion although it may have some bearing on the question of bona fides. In exercising his discretion he cannot be confined to the evidence given at the inquiry. Such matters form only part of the considerations which he is entitled to take into account. He may have and is entitled to have present to his mind his own views as to general policy as well as material acquired in a purely executive capacity, such as reports and opinions obtained from sources within or outside the Ministry.'

Here, therefore, we have the doctrine of departmental irresponsibility expressed in very broad terms, and it is instructive to compare the language of the case with that used by the courts in *Davis's Case* and *Yaffé's Case* in order to assess the extent of judicial abdication which has occurred in the course of fifteen or sixteen years. Its effects in relation to industry may be studied in the decision of Sellers J. in *Thorneloe and Clarkson* v. *Board of Trade*.[12] In that case, the effect of s.1(4) of the Industrial Organisation and Development Act, 1947, was under consideration. This subsection provides that a development council order

'shall not be made unless the Board of Trade is satisfied that the establishment of a development council for the industry is desired by a substantial number of the persons engaged in the industry.'

The Board of Trade, by the Clothing Industry Development Council Order 1949 made an order establishing a development council for the clothing industry, and clothing companies brought an action alleging that the order was *ultra vires*. It was shown that the order was desired by 1,000 firms out of a total of 24,000, and that it was opposed by 5,000 firms. Out of 474,000 employees in the industry 150,000 had expressed their desire for a development council. Sellers J. held that, in the absence of bad faith, the courts had no power to control the Board of Trade in the exercise of its discretion, or to test whether the desire was substantial or not. In the light of the decision of the Court of Appeal in the Plymouth case, no other decision could have been reached; but the case throws an interesting light on the 'new industrial democracy' in action.

With these decisions in mind, it will be valuable now to discuss briefly the mechanism by which the subject tests the

---

[12] (1950) 66 T.L.R. (Pt. 7) 1117.

action of a department in the courts. The most common mode of procedure is by seeking an order in the nature of one of the prerogative writs.

Until the Administration of Justice (Miscellaneous Provisions) Act, 1938, it was in fact the prerogative writs of *certiorari*, prohibition, and *mandamus* themselves which were used. That Act substituted an order in the nature of the appropriate writ, and simplified the procedure to some extent, but this did not affect more widely the actual working of the writs themselves, and accordingly, it will be convenient to discuss them, as if the writs themselves were still in operation.

Whether or not these writs are correctly described as 'prerogative' writs we need not inquire, although it may be noticed that Mr. de Smith has lately examined their history, and has reached the conclusion that this general description can be ascribed to Lord Mansfield, thus linking them with *habeas corpus*, which had been regarded as a prerogative writ from the time of James I.[13] Each of them, however, has a separate history, and its own distinctive procedural characteristics. *Certiorari* was in origin a royal demand for further information on some governmental matter. At an early date, it was used for the purpose of removing to the King's Courts at Westminster for trial cases which had been initiated before inferior courts of record. This function was progressively extended until, as Mr. de Smith observes, the Court of King's Bench, which monopolised the issue of the prerogative writs became

'a supreme court of administration, supervising much of the business of local government by keeping subordinate bodies within their legal limitations by writs of *certiorari* and prohibition, and ordering them to perform their duties by writs of *mandamus*. The modern High Court had succeeded to much of this jurisdiction, and there can be no doubt that the absence in the common-law systems of a distinct body of public law, whereby proceedings against public authorities are instituted only before special administrative courts and are governed by a special body of rules, is directly traceable to the extensive use of prerogative writs by the Court of King's Bench.'[14]

[13] *The Prerogative Writs* in (1951) *Cambridge Law Journal*, pp. 55-56.
[14] *Ibid.*, p. 48.

Having regard to the wide scope of this writ in early times, it might have been expected that the courts would frequently have availed themselves of it to test the decisions of government departments. This, however, is not the case, and *certiorari* has played a smaller part in the struggle between the courts and the executive than might have been expected. In effect, the courts have remained content with the restriction of the writ to judicial proceedings, although they have given a wide interpretation to the phrase 'judicial proceedings.' Thus, it is now clear that the granting of licences is a judicial proceeding for this purpose,[15] and in *R. v. London County Council, ex parte The Entertainments Protection Association*,[16] Scrutton, L. J. said:

'It is not necessary that it should be a court in the sense that this court is a court; it is enough if it is exercising, after hearing evidence, judicial functions in the sense that it has to decide on evidence between a proposal and an opposition; and it is not necessary to be strictly a court; if it is a tribunal which has to decide rights after hearing evidence and opposition, it is amenable to the writ of *certiorari*.'

In the same case, Fletcher Moulton L. J. defined the scope of *certiorari* possibly even more clearly. He says:

'The procedure of *certiorari* applied in many cases in which the body whose acts are criticised would not ordinarily be called a court, nor would its acts be ordinarily termed "judicial acts". The true view of the limitation would seem to be that the term "judicial act" is used in contrast with purely ministerial acts. To these latter the process of *certiorari* does not apply, as for instance to the issue of a warrant to enforce a rate, even though the rate is one which could itself be questioned by *certiorari*. In short, there must be the exercise of some right or duty to decide in order to provide scope for a writ of *certiorari* at common law.'

Certiorari and prohibition are often claimed together. In Short and Mellor's *Practice of the Crown Office*,[17] prohibition is described as

'a judicial writ, issuing out of a court of superior jurisdiction and directed to an inferior court for the purpose of preventing the inferior from usurping a jurisdiction with which it was not

---

[15] *R. v. Woodhouse* [1906] 2 K.B. 501.
[16] [1931] 2 K.B. 215.
[17] 2nd Ed., p.252.

legally vested, or, in other words, to compel courts entrusted with judicial duties to keep within the limits of their jurisdiction.'

Historically, prohibition played a great part in the struggle between the Common Law courts and the prerogative courts in the early part of the seventeenth century, and prohibitions granted by Coke whilst Chief Justice confined the activities of the ecclesiastical courts and the Court of Admiralty within narrow limits. Of its later history, Bankes L. J. says in *R. v. Electricity Commissioners: Ex parte London Electricity Joint Committee:*

'Originally, no doubt, the writ was issued only to inferior courts, using that expression in the ordinary meaning of the word "court". As statutory bodies were brought into existence exercising legal jurisdiction, so the issue of the writ came to be extended to such bodies. There are numerous instances of this in the books, commencing in quite early times. In the case of *R. v. Glamorganshire (Inhabitants)*, decided in Trinity Term, 12 Will. 3,[18] the court expressed the general opinion that it would examine the proceedings of all jurisdictions created by Act of Parliament, and if, under pretence of such Act, they proceeded to usurp jurisdiction greater than the Act warrants, the court could send a *certiorari* to them to have their proceedings returned to the court; to the end that the court might see that they keep themselves within their jurisdiction, and, if they exceed it, restrain them. It would appear from the judgments in *Re Ystradgynlais Tithe Commutation*[19] and *Re Appledore Tithe Commutation*[20] that in both these cases the court was willing to assume that a writ of prohibition could lie against the Tithe Commissioners. In *Chabot v. Lord Morpeth*,[21] the court certainly proceeded upon the assumption that a writ of prohibition might be issued to the Commissioners of Woods and Forests.'

R. v. Electricity Commissioners: Ex parte London Electricity Joint and Others[22] shows the furthest limits of the application of *certiorari* and also the application of the *ultra vires* doctrine to the activities of a statutory body functioning under the Board of Trade. Under the Electricity (Supply) Act, 1919, two statutory bodies were set up, the Electricity Commis-

[18] (1700) 1 Ld. Raym. 580.
[19] (1844) 13 L.J.Q.B. 287.
[20] (1845) 17 L.J.Q.B. 59.
[21] (1850) 19 L.J.Q.B. 377.
[22] [1924] 1 K.B. 171.

sioners and the Joint Electricity Authority. By the Act, the Electricity Commissioners were empowered to formulate a scheme enabling the Joint Electricity Authority to delegate their powers to committees. The Commissioners had powers to make an order giving effect to the scheme, such order being subject to confirmation by the Board of Trade. For the purpose of creating a single electricity authority for London and the Home Counties, the Commissioners, pro-pounded a scheme, which created the London and Home Counties Joint Electricity Committee. The scheme also provided that this committee should appoint two committees to which it should delegate its powers and duties under the scheme. Each of these committees had assigned to it a portion of the entire district. The Court of Appeal eventually held this scheme *ultra vires* the Act of 1919. In this case, both prohibition and *certiorari* had been asked for, and the Court of Appeal granted prohibition.

Lord Justice Atkin, in a notable judgment, continued the discussion of the two prerogative writs which had been initiated by Bankes L. J. He said:

'The matter comes before us upon rules for writs of pro-hibition and *certiorari* which have been discharged by the Divisional Court. Both writs are of great antiquity, forming part of the process by which the King's Courts restrained Courts of inferior jurisdiction from exceeding their powers. Prohibition restrains the tribunal from proceeding further in excess of jurisdiction; *certiorari* requires the record or the order of the Court to be sent up to the King's Bench Division, to have its legality enquired into and, if necessary, to have the order quashed. It is to be noted that both writs deal with questions of excessive jurisdiction; and doubtless in their origin dealt almost exclusively with the jurisdiction of what is understood in ordinary parlance as a Court of Justice. But the operation of the writs has extended to control the proceedings of bodies which do not claim to be, and would not be recognised as, Court of Justice. Whenever any body of persons having large authority to determine questions affecting the rights of subjects, and having the duty to act judicially, act in excess of their legal authority, they are subject to the controlling jurisdiction of the King's Bench Division, exercised in these writs.'

He then cites decisions to show how *certiorari* and prohi-bition have been used in respect of decisions of Justices of the Peace, Poor Law Commissioners, Boards of Guardians, the Board of Education, Licencing justices, Tithe Commissioners, Inclosure Commissioners, and Light Railway Commissioners, and he reaches the conclusion that both *certiorari* and prohibition would be applicable to the determinations of the Electricity Commissioners under the Electricity Acts.

Neither *certiorari* nor prohibition, however, can be used to inquire into the *bona fides* of a purely administrative act. For this, the appropriate remedy is *mandamus*. This is a direction from the High Court to a public body or an official, who is under an absolute, as distinct from a discretionary, duty to perform an act, to do it. Where, however, the duty is discretionary, the High Court cannot exercise control. The act need not necessarily be administrative. Thus, by means of mandamus, a lower court can be compelled to exercise jurisdiction which it is prepared wrongfully to renounce. In *R. v. Barker*[23] Lord Mansfield said:

'A *mandamus* is a prerogative writ; to the aid of which the subject is entitled, upon a proper case previously shown, to the satisfaction of the court. The original nature of the writ, and the end for which it was framed, direct upon what occasions it should be used. It was introduced, to prevent disorder from a failure of justice, and defect of police. Therefore it ought to be used upon all occasions where the law has established no specific remedy, and where in justice and good government there *ought* to be one. Within the last century, it has been liberally interposed for the benefit of the subject and advancement of justice.'

Nevertheless, as Lord Wright pointed out in *Stepney Borough Council* v. *J. Walker & Sons Ltd.*,[24] mandamus will not be granted where there already exists a sufficient and convenient remedy.

Besides these three prerogative writs, other legal redress may be available to the subject. The legality of a rule promulgated by a Department may be tested in advance by an action for a *declaration*. This procedure is limited in scope, and cannot be initiated without the Attorney-General's

[23] (1762) 3 Burr. 1265, 1267.
[24] [1934] A.C. 365.

fiat.[25] In some circumstances also, a subject might obtain an injunction to prevent a public authority acting illegally in respect of him. Somewhat surprisingly, this species of equitable relief seems to have been asked for only rarely, and then not always successfully, although Professor Hanbury, in a stimulating essay,[26] has suggested that the limits of equitable assistance to the harassed subject have perhaps not yet been reached. In substance, however, the subject is confined to the three prerogative writs and an action for a declaration, and the effectiveness of his remedy will depend upon two things: (1) the extent to which the Departments, in framing the legislation by virtue of which powers are transferred to them, can so frame those powers as to make recourse to these remedies ineffective, and (2) the vigour with which the courts are prepared to scrutinise the conduct of the executive.

In a recent essay in *The Canadian Bar Review*,[27] Mr. Clive Schmitthoff has suggested that in recent years, the province of the Common Law has expanded, through the precedents established by the use of the prerogative writs in respect of administrative law. He goes so far as to suggest[28] that

'the most significant legal development of the past fifty years is the almost complete absorption of administrative law in the fold of the common law. This development is an event of the first magnitude, which is comparable to the incorporation of the law merchant into the common law in the eighteenth century.'

This, he suggests, has been accomplished by extensions in the use of the three prerogative writs discussed in this chapter.

One could only wish so general and so optimistic a statement were true. Unfortunately, it is the precise converse of the truth. Lord Hewart, as has been pointed out, was profoundly concerned by the steady expansion of the areas in which administrators operated entirely free from legal restraint. Professor Robson and Dr. C. K. Allen, widely

[25] For some examples of its use, see *Dyson* v. *A.G.* [1911] 1 K.B. 410; *China Mutual S.N. Co. Ltd.* v. *Machay* [1918] 1 K.B. 33; *Bombay and Persia S.N. Co. Ltd.* v. *Machay*, [1920] 3 K.B. 402; *Nixon* v. *A.G.* [1931] A.C. 184; *Thomas* v. *A.G.* [1937] Ch. 72.

[26] *Equity in Public Law*, in *Essays in Equity*.

[27] (1951) 29 C.B.R. p. 469.

[28] P. 470.

divergent though their viewpoints are, concur on this point. Still more recently Lord Justice Denning, in *Freedom Under the Law*, the first series of Hamlyn lectures, devoted an entire lecture to a discussion of the limits of the power of the ordinary courts to intervene between the subject and the State. After noting the frequency with which appeals to the courts from decisions of administrative tribunals are prohibited, Lord Justice Denning continues:

'If any proof were needed that there should be an appeal to a superior court it is provided by cases which have been recently reported. One of them will undoubtedly rank as a leading case.[29] It arose in connexion with the new tribunals which have power to fix the rent of furnished lettings. The underlying principle of this legislation is that the landlord has in his control an essential supply, and it is his duty only to charge a reasonable rent. Not only the tenant, but the local authority, can compel him to perform this duty. They can apply on their own initiative to the tribunal to fix a reasonable rent, and, thereafter, the landlord is tied down to this amount. There is no appeal to the courts from the decision of the tribunal, nor even to the Minister. But the courts, as you will hear, have some degree of control so as to prevent them exceeding or abusing their jurisdiction.

'Let me, however, go on with the story. There is, as you know, a large block of flats in Paddington called Park West. In 1947 two of the tenants referred their tenancy agreements to the tribunal and got their rents reduced. Thereupon the Paddington Borough Council referred 302 of the other flats straightway to the tribunal. In eight of them the tribunal reduced the rents. Several points arose in the case, but the only one for present purposes is this: when the tribunal reduced the rents, they did not give the landlords any credit for the fact that the landlords were providing a lift, a swimming pool and many other amenities for the tenants, which were obviously of considerable value. The tenancy agreements contained nothing to bind the landlords to supply these amenities, and so the tribunals thought that, in consequence of recent decisions, they could not take them into account. Now that is a typical point of law upon which the High Court could have ruled, if there was a right of appeal to the Court. It was obviously desirable that there should be an authoritative ruling upon it. So the Solicitor-General did invite the Court to express an opinion on it for the guidance of tribunals; and the Court did so. But if that had not been done, the tribunals might have

[29] *R. v. Paddington and St. Marylebone Rent Tribunal: Ex parte Bull* [1949] 1 K.B. 666.

gone on indefinitely acting on a wrong view of the law—all because the Statute did not provide for any appeal to the courts.

'It should be clearly understood that, although the High Court has some degree of control over the tribunals it is not such as to enable it to correct many of the faults or injustices which may arise, unless the Statute gives an appeal. The High Court proceeds on the footing that if Parliament had thought fit to entrust jurisdiction on all these new matters to new tribunals without any appeal from them, then, so long as the tribunals do not exceed or abuse their jurisdiction, the High Court should not interfere with them. If a tribunal should come to a wrong conclusion on the fact, or, indeed, if there is no evidence on which it could come to its conclusion, the High Court cannot interfere; nor, if the tribunal comes to a wrong conclusion in point of law, can the High Court interfere. So long as the tribunal keeps within its jurisdiction, and is not guilty of any flagrantly unjust procedure, its decision is final both on facts and the law.'[30]

Nothing could more clearly demonstrate the untenability of Mr. Schmitthoff's hypothesis. It is historically unsound for two reasons: (1) the machinery of control by the prerogative writs has been part of English law for centuries, and in the time of Lord Mansfield was used over a wider area than it is today, as Lord Mansfield's own language shows; (2) the procedure whereby the law merchant was incorporated into English law was one whereby the Common Law courts took over a jurisdiction previously exercised by non-Common Law courts, extending English law to include mercantile law in the process. There is no sign at all that the courts today are incorporating the 'jurisprudence' of administrative tribunals, if that be the term, into the Common Law. If judicial pronouncements are any guide most of them would recoil in dismay at the prospect. Instead, the courts are seeking with difficulty to set limits beyond which administrative usurpation shall not pass. Very far from the Common Law replacing administrative tribunals, more and more are being created outside the Common Law year by year, and some of the cases discussed earlier in this book will show how, in spite of obvious willingness, the courts have failed to hold back the onward rush of administrative lawlessness.

[30] *Freedom Under the Law*, pp. 92-4.

Chapter 9

Taxation and Freedom

IN an age which has become accustomed to the presentation of an annual budget exceeding four thousand million pounds sterling, and in which the screw is turned ever more tightly upon the taxpayer, it is well to recall the original conceptions underlying our modern system of taxation. In theory, even today, the King asks Parliament for the means to carry on his government. This procedure is now no more than a historic relic, but it recalls the initial theory of our constitution, in the first centuries after the Norman Conquest, that the King should 'live of his own'. For generations, the King was the greatest landowner in the realm, at a period when land was the principal source of wealth. It followed, therefore, since the King's ministers were in fact, as well as in form, his servants, that the revenues of his estates should go far towards payment for the services which they gave him. This, however, was by no means the full extent of his revenues. By the feudal law, the King was entitled, independently of any grant, to certain customary 'aids', or payments from his feudal tenants. These aids were leviable for the knighting of his eldest son, for the marriage of his eldest daughter, and for the ransom of the King's person. An 'aid' of the third kind, it will be remembered, was levied to rescue Richard I from captivity sustained on his return from the Crusades. Beyond this, the feudal law granted the king certain other valuable rights. He could, for example, exercise the rights of wardship and marriage in respect of infant tenants-in-chief; he could forfeit the lands of those convicted of treason, and he could exercise the right of 'primer seisin' (i.e. to the revenues for the first year) on the succession of a tenant-in-chief. Over and above these rights, the King was entitled to the fees exacted by the Crown in litigation; he could sell rights of jurisdiction to towns or other local authorities, and he exacted heavy fees from those appointed to offices and dignities. Even today, some of these rights still survive. Fees are still exacted from litigants, and there exists a half-forgotten theory that the Courts of Justice, as far as possible should be self-supporting; and although the Crown has long since ceased to rely upon them, fees are still exacted in some cases from those who are granted dignities.

Nor was this all. At some period subsequent to the Norman Conquest, it had become accepted doctrine that the Crown could levy certain customs duties. It was by no means clear how far this prerogative right extended, and its existence was the cause of much controversy in early Stuart times, but the right certainly existed, since Magna Carta attempted to draw a distinction between those customs duties which could lawfully be imposed, which it termed *antiquae et rectae consuetudines*, and unjust customs dues (maletolts), which it would be lawful to resist.

Not unnaturally, strong Kings attempted to press their rights of revenue to the furthest possible limits, and there were frequent irregularities. The great significance of Magna Carta in its fiscal aspect is that it defines what dues can be levied by the King under the medieval feudal law of the land. Unfortunately, the conduct of government became ever more costly, and increasingly, the King was unable 'to live of his own'. More particularly, foreign wars were expensive, and the Kings (even Kings such as Edward III) were often hard pressed to raise sufficient revenue for the execution of their policies. Loans were an obvious expedient, and several of our medieval Kings were compelled to have recourse to Jewish or Lombard moneylenders. But the records of monarchs in the matter of repayment were not impressive, and security was frequently demanded. Thus, the Crown jewels were upon occasion pawned. When security was insufficient, a strong King was sometimes compelled to exact 'forced loans' and 'benevolences' (i.e. enforced gifts). These were resented and, where possible, resisted. There was a long controversy whether these were to be regarded as taxation (in which case they failed to conform with the terms of Magna Carta) or whether they were some special type of exaction. Even as late as the reign of Henry VII, the question was still unsettled.

The existence of this type of exaction, however, emphasises one important characteristic of medieval taxation. Insofar as the Kings required revenue beyond what was permitted by ancient custom under feudal law, it was regarded as a gift from the subject. If a subject did not consent to the imposition, he was not technically bound by it, and occasionally, as Maitland notices,[1] a powerful prelate or baron might successfully resist payment. Gradually, however, in the reigns of Henry III and Edward I, it became customary to secure the consent of representatives of each order of the realm. The greater barons and prelates assembled in Parliament agreed on behalf of their order to an additional tax. In the Commons, representatives of the lesser landowners, and of the towns and boroughs did the same on behalf of their orders. Until the Restoration in 1660 the lesser clergy voted their taxes separately in Convocation. So, progressively, the idea that representatives could bind their constituents in matters of taxation gained ground, and in this way Parliament was born. If the King will redress his subjects' grievances, his loyal subjects in return will grant him extra revenue to carry out his policy. Nevertheless, down to the Restoration in 1660, when the Crown surrendered many hereditary sources of revenue, two ideas remained implicit in all taxation: (1) that Parliamentary grants were exceptional; and (2) that the King's hereditary revenues should be made to go as far as possible. Unfortunately, the growing complexity of government, the decline in the value of money, and the passing of feudalism all served to make the hereditary royal revenues less adequate than they had been at first. Hence there arose frequent and increasing friction between Crown and Parliament over the extent and adequacy of the royal powers of taxation. All this would in any event have come to a head at the close of the Middle Ages, but the struggle between Crown and Parliament was delayed for a time by the sagacity of the Tudors. Henry VII administered his realm with extreme frugality. In

[1]*Constitutional History*, p. 95.

addition, he had the benefit of an unusually large number of escheats and forfeitures from the baronage, due to the Wars of the Roses, and to sporadic revolts during his reign. Yet another source of revenue was the heavy fines exacted from the nobles for breaches of the Statutes of Livery and Maintenance. Finally Henry, like his Yorkist predecessors, was compelled to resort increasingly to benevolences, first from the nobility, and later from the mercantile classes, whose wealth and power were growing rapidly as a result of his diplomacy.

Thus, Henry VII was one of the few sovereigns who was able to bequeath a full treasury to his successor. This accumulated wealth was rapidly dissipated, however, and Henry VIII in turn was compelled to look for additional sources of revenue. An effort was made to increase the revenue derived from the feudal dues, one aspect of this being the passing of the Statute of Uses in 1535. The preamble to this statute expressly recites that the practice of putting lands to use has, in the past, deprived the King of revenue. Much additional wealth fell in to the Crown on the dissolution of the monasteries. This, however, was also squandered, as his father's treasure had also been, and Henry VIII was compelled to resort to the debasement of the coinage (the contemporary equivalent to inflation) and to repudiation of debt for temporary relief. Both these expedients produced depression in commerce and in agriculture. Yet it is interesting that even so powerful, and so feared a monarch as Henry VIII was prepared to adopt these expedients, rather than lay the full extent of his financial embarrassment before Parliament.

In many respects, Elizabeth restored and extended the financial policy of her grandfather. She, too, encountered great resistance in Parliament to any general extension of taxation. She, therefore, resorted cautiously to benevolences, she sold monopolies, and she extended customs duties by proclamation. At every imposition of such extraordinary taxation, there was resentment, but no general resistance. For the greater part of the reign the menace of a Spanish invasion was very real, and responsible men hesitated to thwart measures upon which the safety of the realm might depend. Moreover, all the Tudors showed commercial acumen in their imposition of customs duties. These heredi- tary duties were automatically granted to each sovereign for life on his accession, but each of the Tudors sought to extend them. In so doing, they gained additional revenue, but the nominal reason for their action was to protect the English merchant and craftsman. So long as these customs dues hit the foreign merchant importing into the realm, and protected the English merchant, such a protective policy was distinctly popular. It was frequently reinforced, throughout the Tudor period, by legislation in a similar sense.

However, the entire question of levying customs duties by prerogative (other than the traditional hereditary duties permitted by Common Law) was raised in *Bates's Case* in 1606,[2] early in the reign of James I. Bates had refused to pay an additional duty of 5s. per cwt. on currants, over and above the statutory poundage of 2/6 per cwt. The four Barons of the Court of Exchequer, who tried the case, were unanimous that the impost was lawfully levied, since the customs were an incident of foreign commerce, which were in the absolute power of the King. Although the decision, and the judges who delivered it, were frequently denounced by Parliamentary apologists, Mr. Hubert Hall, in his *History of the Customs Revenue in England* has shown that it correctly represented the constitutional position at the time. Nevertheless, the movement of the age was against the exercise of prerogative powers of taxation, and in 1610 the Commons staged a four-day debate upon the question, from which there emerged the Petition of Grievances, which advanced the broad thesis that

'all impositions got without consent of Parliament may be quite abolished and taken away.'

A Bill in this sense passed the Commons, but was lost in the Lords. Both James I and Charles I therefore continued to exact, as opportunity offered, both customs duties and ben- evolences by prerogative, and accordingly, the Petition of Right in 1628 enacted that

[2] (1606) 2 St. Tri. 371.

'no man hereafter be compelled to make or yield any gift, loan, benevolence, tax, or such like charge, without common consent by Act of Parliament'.

The struggle was as yet by no means at an end. In the great *Ship-money Case* in 1637[3] the Crown sought to enforce the payment of a direct tax, in the form of ship-money, on all subjects, by virtue of the prerogative. Once again the issue was by no means so clear as is sometimes supposed, for ship-money had been frequently imposed by virtue of the prerogative on seaports in times past, and once again the tax could be said to arise out of the King's overriding duty to secure the safety of the realm. By a majority of seven to five, the Court of Exchequer decided in favour of the Crown. Accordingly, writs for the levy of ship-money continued to be issued annually until the assembly of the Long Parliament in 1640. That Parliament specifically declared all levies of taxation without Parliamentary authority to be illegal, and that verdict was repeated in the Bill of Rights in 1689.

Thus, the Crown's claim to independent taxing power was finally abolished, but with the acceptance of Parliamentary omnipotence in this, as in other fields of government, came the coincident responsibility of Parliament for the public revenue. Even Charles II was expected to conduct the national business from his hereditary revenues, with only occasional assistance from Parliament. It is therefore not surprising that neither revenue nor expenditure was accurately known, nor that Charles was compelled to resort to such discreditable expedients as gifts from Louis XIV to meet his expenditure. In the period between the flight of James II and the accession of George III many important changes took place. The King's personal income and expenditure were separated from the public finances of the realm, the King's annual revenue was stabilised and made payable out of the hereditary revenues, whilst the King's Ministers became responsible to Parliament for the raising and spending of public money. Until late in the nineteenth century, however, the aim of all Chancellors of the Exchequer was to keep the public expenditure within the narrowest possible limits, and to repay part of the National Debt as often as

[3] *R.* v. *Hampden* (1637) 3 St. Tr. 825.

opportunity offered. Even so late as 1874, at the conclusion of Gladstone's great Ministry, income-tax had been reduced to 3d. in the pound, and Gladstone, who regarded it as an exceptional tax, imposed originally in time of war, was looking forward to its final abolition.

Two factors made this aspiration impossible to realise. In the first place, Germany was about to undertake that process of industrialisation and preparation for world-power, which made her feared throughout the world, and which was directly responsible for the division of Europe into two armed camps. Into this struggle Great Britain was very reluctantly drawn, with the result, as has been pointed out in an earlier chapter, one section of the electorate demanded insistently that our armaments should be improved. The second factor was the progressive extensions of the franchise, which resulted in the transfer of political power at the polls to a class which was without a substantial stake in the country. The aspirations of this class required to be satisfied by successive developments of the social services, and by financial measures which became ever-increasing transfers of wealth from one section of the community to another. Although the struggle between the adherents of the two policies was continuous, it had the consequence that whatever government was in power, expenditure soared. When, as occurred in the Liberal Government of 1906, both views were strongly represented in the same Cabinet, expenditure mounted faster than before. The search was unceasingly for new sources of taxable wealth. No matter how many of these were discovered, expenditure constantly outran revenue, and indebtedness has continued to mount. It is worth while remembering, however, that the national budget only passed the £100,000,000 mark at the beginning of the present century, and that the first £1,000 million budget dates from the late thirties, when rearmament for the Second World War was already embarked upon. The year 1951 saw the first four thousand million budget. Even when full allowance has been made for inflation and a depreciated currency, the figure is still staggering. It is plain that a budget of these proportions, with a peace-time standard rate of income-tax of 10/- in the pound has deprived the

E

individual of virtually all possibility of achieving financial independence, by the thrifty accumulation of annual surpluses. He has been reduced to the status of a State-dependant, and even his hope of enjoying such a pension as the State may choose to allot him when his capacity to work has gone depends upon the continued workability of State insurance schemes, and ultimately upon the capacity of future governments to raise taxation of these staggering proportions. It is too often overlooked, in considering State insurance schemes, that sums raised by way of contributions are not appropriated to any fund. They are swept away into the general expendible funds of government, and the security that the commitment will eventually be honoured is exactly the same as that which supports the Post-War Credits of war-time finance.

It is quite clear that today, we are passing through an era of financial chaos, in which all standards are progressively swept away. We have seen that, in origin, a tax was an exceptional impost, levied to supplement a royal revenue that should normally have been adequate. After the Revolution of 1688, it became the means of carrying on the public administration, to be used with every possible economy. At the end of the nineteenth century, it became a means of transferring an increasing share of the national wealth from one section of the community to another. Today, it has become a means of achieving a planned economy in which the individual is no more than a cog in the machine, whose precarious existence depends no longer on his own efforts, but on the success of the master-plan. It follows therefore that the State takes ever-more extensive powers to enforce this preconceived plan upon the community as a whole. Progressively, therefore, personal liberty is curtailed, and controls become a normal instrument of government. The ordinary citizen will no doubt have noticed that Government spokesmen have described the abandonment of these controls as 'concessions', and a short time ago Dr. Dalton described his removal of various irritating restrictions on domestic comfort as an 'experiment in freedom'. This attitude of mind is extremely significant. Freedom, it would seem, today exists on sufferance. If citizens are too exuberant, their fetters will be re-imposed. Mr. Harold Wilson, it will be remembered, suspended negotiations with the Argentine to restore meat to the Englishman's diet as a penalty for the independence of a section of the trading community. Clearly, dictatorship is in the air. This, however, should provoke no great surprise, for it is an inescapable consequence of a rigidly-planned economy. 'The Plan' is a Procrustean bed, and if the individual fails to fit it, then he must be pruned to shape. From this standpoint, therefore, the difference between the planned State of East and West is a difference in degree only. In the West the State has so far stopped short of physical compulsions (other than that which follows failure to comply with any one of innumerable regulations) to enforce conformity with the plan. Moreover, the Western State still admits that the authors of the plan may be replaced by others, professing different ideals, by constitutional means. Nevertheless, both for employer and employed, the plan substitutes a remote and imperfectly conceived objective for individual effort, with the consequence that the sense of frustration develops, and responsibility and initiative decay. Consequently, the attention of the planners has been turned increasingly towards a search for 'incentives'. Should that enquiry prove insufficiently rewarding, there remains only the question of compulsion. So long, however, as political opinion remains as evenly balanced as it is today, compulsion remains outside the range of political activity. Even though physical compulsion as yet remains unused as an instrument to enforce conformity with a plan which seeks to control, not only the individual's property and livelihood, but the incidents of his daily life, the weapons at its disposal are already numerous and formidable. Prominent amongst them is retrospective legislation in the field of taxation. In the Finance Act of 1950 there appeared such a provision, retrospectively making liable to tax certain capital payments which admittedly were not subject to tax at the time when they were made. It may be conceded at once that precedents for the course taken by the Chancellor of the Exchequer in 1950 can be found in Finance Acts of inter-war years. This, however, proves only that the criticisms now made apply, not to some particular government, but to government generally, for oppressive use of power. A suggestion was made in contemporary newspaper discussion that because similar clauses could be found in earlier Finance Acts, then the practice was sanctified by 'precedent' —an argument which, if conceded, would legalise successful burglary. Further, it was suggested that the rule against retrospective legislation applies in reality only to criminal law, and finally, that capital payments of the kind made taxable in the Budget of 1950 were 'anti-social', and should therefore be suppressed, whether or not in fact they were technically legal when made. This last argument merits careful attention. It bears all the hall-marks of totalitarian doctrine, and it implies that anything of which the ruling clique disapprove can be suppressed without going to the trouble of passing special legislation to condemn it.

There can be no doubt that taxation statutes have in the past always been regarded as governed by the rule restraining retrospective legislation, even though that principle was occasionally infringed in the inter-war years. Indeed, the claim now made by the Executive to catch for purposes of taxation sums of money which under the existing law are not taxable is precisely the same as that made by the first two Stuarts, and which was then decisively rejected by Parliament. Today, however, the Executive possesses a docile Parliamentary majority which exists to give legislative force to ministerial exhortations. Hence the present controversy. No one questions the legal right of Parliament (i.e. the Cabinet) to legislate on any topic it likes so long as it retains sufficient discipline over its followers. The question is simply one of constitutional ethics; and lest this aspect of the matter should be lightly dismissed, it must be added that today constitutional ethics have become more important than constitutional law. With the destruction of the House of Lords as an important political force, any Government can pass any legislation whatever, which it considers to be necessary. What legislation it will enact depends upon the opinions it holds upon the rights of citizens, and whether it proposes to continue in office by the normal processes of elective government. If its opinions are absolutist, then the life and livelihood of every citizen are at its mercy.

The aspect of the provisions in the Finance Act of 1950 which received the most attention was that the practices aimed at were a serious example of tax-avoidance which it was the duty of the Chancellor of the Exchequer to stop. To this, the reply was promptly made: By all means stop it by a clause suppressing the practice *in the future*, but do not make taxable retrospectively something which was untaxable at the time when it was done. This limitation, in turn, was described as a technicality, unworthy of serious consideration. One point must be made at the outset. The attack is not, or at least should not be, concentrated upon the then Chancellor of the Exchequer, Sir Stafford Cripps, or even upon the Labour Government. Mr. Neville Chamberlain, as Chancellor of the Exchequer, in his speech on the Finance Bill of 1936 (in times less difficult than those following the Second World War) expressed himself in stronger terms than Sir Stafford Cripps, and in fact made a clause in the Act of 1936 retrospective in operation for the previous year—thereby giving just one more illustration of his quite remarkable lack of political instinct. During the same debate, no less eminent a lawyer than Sir John Simon (as he then was) expressed himself as being in full agreement with what was done.

The question therefore cannot be regarded as a party question. Both parties have sinned, and this can scarcely be regarded as surprising. Whilst in office, they possess a weapon —taxation—of virtually unlimited power. Since the need of modern governments is always for more money, it is not remarkable that the weapon is relied on ever more extensively. For this reason, it is regrettable that the instrument by which taxes are levied is precisely the same as our instrument for legislative change. It has become progressively easier to manipulate during the past century. Undoubtedly this has encouraged governments to become increasingly extravagant and wasteful. The last Chancellor of the Exchequer to make any stand against this tendency was Sir Michael Hicks Beach, at the end of the nineteenth century, and his failure to evoke any response from his colleagues has already been noticed.

The present relationship between taxpayer and Treasury has often been compared with a game of hide and seek.

Each successive Finance Act puts an end to various schemes of tax-avoidance, and a new crop promptly emerges. Chancellors of the Exchequer, in curbing them, can sometimes secure a little fleeting popularity by describing them as 'anti-social', and by suggesting that such methods of tax-avoidance, if successful, make it more expensive for the rest of us. From a financial point of view, this is a gross exaggeration, and from the standpoint of political ethics, it overlooks the fact that it is solely the extent of the Government's exactions from those possessing rather more wealth than the rest of us that has made this game of hide and seek necessary. No more need be said on this point than that the schemes of tax-avoidance now practised were completely unknown until taxation became so penal in incidence that Prime Ministers were paid a portion of their salaries tax-free in order that they, at least, might be able to meet their obligations. Even this, however, does not go to the root of the matter. The rule against retrospective legislation in the sphere of taxation strikes at the foundations of our legal and political existence. It is one of the most important manifestations of the basic principles of our Common Law. Magna Carta laid down the broad principle that no taxes could be imposed without Parliamentary consent, and although, as has been shown ealier in this chapter, a limited power to impose customs duties remained vested in the Crown, the extent of this power was one of the main causes of contention between King and Parliament in Stuart times, and the Bill of Rights in 1689 finally settled the question against any imposition of taxes, of whatever kind, without Parliamentary authority. Taxation, therefore, must be levied in statutory form, and a statute which imposes a tax is a statute which removes from the subject property to which Government would otherwise have no title. Accordingly, therefore, the *onus* is always on the revenue to show that what is claimed is within the words of the statute. The Courts have again and again affirmed this principle. As Lord Hanworth put it in *Dewar* v. *Inland Revenue Commissioners:*[4]

'Either in the clear words of a taxing statute the subject is liable or, if he is not within the words, he is not liable.'

[4] [1935] 2 K.B. 351, 360.

From this it follows that if the subject so arranges his proprietary and contractual obligations that tax is not assessable where otherwise it would be, then provided he contravenes no other rule of law (e.g. penalising fraud) he is beyond the reach of the Revenue. This, too, has been repeatedly affirmed in a succession of judicial pronouncements of the very highest authority. For example, in *Levene* v. *Inland Revenue Commissioners*[5] Lord Sumner said:

> 'It is trite law that His Majesty's subjects are free if they can to make their own arrangements so that their cases may fall outside the scope of the taxing Acts. They incur no legal penalties and, strictly speaking, no moral censure if, having considered the lines drawn by the Legislature for the imposition of taxes, they make it their business to walk outside them.'

Again, in *Inland Revenue Commissioners* v. *Duke of Westminster*,[6] the Revenue made a determined effort to establish the proposition that, although the transaction under consideration did not fall formally within the provisions of any taxing legislation, nevertheless, in substance it was taxable. The House of Lords, however, would have nothing to do with this doctrine, and Lord Tomlin commented:

> 'Every man is entitled if he can to order his affairs so as that the tax attaching under the appropriate Acts is less than it otherwise would be. If he succeeds in ordering them so as to secure this result, then, however unappreciative the Commissioners of Inland Revenue or his fellow-taxpayers may be of his ingenuity, he cannot be compelled to pay an increased tax. This so-called doctrine of "the substance" seems to me to be nothing more than an attempt to make a man pay notwithstanding that he has so ordered his affairs that the amount of tax sought from him is not legally claimable. . . . There may, of course, be cases where documents are not *bona fide*, nor intended to be acted upon, but are only used as a cloak to conceal a different transaction. No such case is made or even suggested here. The deeds of covenant are admittedly *bona fide*, and have been given their proper legal operation. They cannot be ignored or treated as operating in some different way because as a result less duty is payable than would have been the case if some other arrangement—called for the purpose of the appellants' argument "the substance"—has been made'.

[5] [1928] A.C. 217, 227.
[6] [1936] A.C. 1.

The doctrine of 'the substance' is a pernicious doctrine, which, if conceded, would threaten all financial security. It could be used to attack any transaction which the officials, or Government of the day, chose to call 'anti-social'. Notwithstanding some hesitation by some judges in recent years, it remains the case that the courts have unanimously pronounced against it. Hence the eagerness of the Treasury to attack specific transactions retrospectively.

It is, of course, common knowledge that a high degree of ingenuity is now exercised to place transactions in such a form that they attract as little taxation as possible. The draftsman is not always successful, however. Indeed, his failures are probably more important than his successes, and of one recent example of failure, Lord Greene said in *Lord Howard de Walden* v. *Inland Revenue Commissioners:*[7]

> 'For years a battle of manoeuvre has been waged between the legislature and those who are minded to throw the burden of taxation off their own shoulders on to those of their fellow-subjects. In that battle the legislature has often been worsted by the skill, determination and resourcefulness of its opponents of whom the present appellant has not been the least successful. It would not shock us in the least to find that the legislature has determined to put an end to the struggle by imposing the severest of penalties. It scarcely lies in the mouth of the taxpayer who plays with fire to complain of burnt fingers.'

It is, however, worth while enquiring why tax-avoidance occupies such an important place in the legal and commercial life, not only of this, but of every other important trading nation outside the Soviet Union, and also why it is simply a twentieth-century phenomenon. Is not the reason that taxation, as a method of State-intervention in the lives and commercial activities of its manufacturing and commercial classes, has now reached the point where it is considered to be a form of oppression? If it is said that industrialists, merchants and others ought not to feel that way, that is no answer to the fact that they do. Indeed, the merchant or industrialist feels about taxation precisely what the employee feels about a controlled economy, in which inflation is a condition of daily existence, and in which high paper wages fail to produce him the things he wants, but which the

[7] [1942] 1 K.B. 389, 397.

Government thinks either that he ought not to want, or alternatively, that he ought to want only in strictly limited and rationed amounts. The employee reacts in one way to excessive control, the employer in another. It is quite idle to denounce both as 'anti-social'. Abuse does not alter facts.

Further, each successive Budget makes additional and grave inroads, not only upon personal liberty, but upon principles which lawyers for centuries have regarded as essential features of English political life. It has been shown how the Finance Act of 1950 violated the principle forbidding retrospective legislation. In his first Budget, Mr. Gaitskell ventured further along the road to totalitarianism than his predecessor, Sir Stafford Cripps, ever chose to do. Three separate clauses were completely at variance with previous constitutional practice. Thus, Clause 23 gave a surveyor of taxes power to require anyone, including a banker, to make a return of all interest paid by him to his clients or customers, provided that the interest paid exceeds £15. This provision strikes at the root of the relation of banker and customer. At one blow, one's banker becomes the agent of the tax-gatherer, as usual unpaid. Again, Clause 28 triumphantly overrides the repeatedly-expressed views of the Courts, and gaily concedes to the Treasury the doctrine of 'the sub-stance' for which it has in the past unsuccessfully agitated, and in addition gives them this power retrospectively. Clause 28 gives the Commissioners of Income Tax power to disallow any transaction effected *before or after* the passing of the Finance Act, 1951, if they think that one of the main purposes of this transaction was the avoidance or *reduction* of liability to profits tax. Thus, the subject may no longer take any active steps to avert the rapacity of the taxgatherer. He can merely stand mesmerised awaiting his doom. It is perhaps, a trifle in the middle of the twentieth century that this single clause destroys the security which the subject has laboriously won from arbitrary power in the seven centuries which have elapsed since Magna Carta was wrested from a corrupt tyrant. It would seem that so long as these things are done in the name, not of a tyrannical King, but of an omnivorous State, the public conscience is not outraged, or perhaps it is drugged into apathy by the relentlessness

E*

of the present-day exactions. Nor is this by any means all, in an instrument of extortion which transcends 'Morton's Fork' for ingenuity. Clause 32 attempts to deal with those who, aghast at the pace with which the spoliation of England is proceeding, seek to move their businesses overseas. Since 1939, it has been the position that such transfers need Treasury authority, if they are within the regulations governing foreign exchange. This, however, did not affect transfers within the sterling area. By Clause 32, however, a new test is introduced—the avoidance, real or supposed (and it should be remembered that Clause 28 applies to this, too) of United Kingdom taxation. Such a provision, it need scarcely be added, goes as far as any restriction ever attempted in Nazi Germany. That it was economically unsound can scarcely be questioned, for as the City Editor of the *Sunday Times* pointed out,

'it is to the public interest that new businesses should come to this country, bringing with them new money and work. Unless they are free to go, they will not come. Again, it is to the public interest that businesses in London should be encouraged to operate overseas. That is one of the ways in which we both earn income and foreign exchange and ensure our supplies of raw materials.'

How far Clause 32 can be pressed is shown by an example given by a correspondent to *The Times* of May 12, 1951. He points out that if a man and wife who possess a controlling interest in a United Kingdom company should chose to live in Jersey and conduct their business from there, they might expose themselves to a penalty of £10,000 and or two years' imprisonment. It is true that such penalties might not normally be claimed, but the fact that they exist indicates how far, simply by means of financial control, the Treasury has now destroyed personal freedom of movement. Commenting on Clause 32, *The Times*, in an important leading article on May 14 said:

'The control and the taxable capacity of overseas enterprises can no doubt be imprisoned in this country if they are already here; but control of new enterprises will certainly not be brought here so long as this constraint prevails. This can mean only that this country, as time goes on, will control a wasting and ageing body of oversea resources, whilst the new, vigorous, and virgin resources will pass into other hands—at a time when, with the supply and control of raw materials so important to the nation, the advantages of close and continuing association with oversea resources are clearer than ever before.'

In other words, this clause is another step, and an extremely important one, on the road to national bankruptcy. On Clause 28, *The Times* commented:

'Where a person has carried out any transactions, one of the main purposes of which (in many cases it might not be a "purpose" but only a result "to be expected") is to reduce liability to profits tax, this clause empowers the Revenue to rearrange the person's affairs in retrospect so as to ignore anything which he has done which would diminish his tax liability. Hitherto it has been only retroactive legislation that has seriously impaired the citizen's right to arrange his affairs within the law so as to attract the least amount of tax. To give retroactive executive power to the Revenue to arrange the citizen's affairs by selecting out of the past that particular arrangement of his affairs which would best suit the taxgatherer is a strange and important innovation. This and some other parts of the Finance Bill will be critically examined by those who still believe that tax law should not hamper or frustrate the ordinary actions of business life and should even conform to Adam Smith's first principle that "the tax which each individual is bound to pay ought to be certain and not arbitrary" '.

To say that this clause is an example of financial tyranny is to make a serious understatement. At long last the Revenue have broken down the citizen's last line of resistance, and they can now plunder him almost at leisure. In facing the omnipotence of the State in its exactions the citizen no longer has the security of the law. He must make what terms he can with the taxgatherers who alone will decide the extent of their demands on him. Even Charles I did not venture so far. These clauses in the Finance Act of 1951 simply emphasise once more that we are suffering today from the disease of over-government. Just as the capitalist world has seen the great combine drive out the small enterprise, so that great monopolist trusts have developed, culminating in the gigantic State-monopolies of this country and the Soviet Union, and as in the industrial world the big unions have eaten up the lesser unions, so in the political world the great party machine has steadily grown in power and destroyed its lesser competitors. In some States the process has already reached the point where one party alone is tolerated. In Great Britain, the British Dominions, some parts of Western Europe and the United States, however, we have the two-party State which can survive only so long as the underlying assumptions of our political association are accepted generally by both parties. But the maintenance of that agreement in Great Britain and the British Dominions is becoming increasingly difficult because of the increasing range of official intervention in every aspect of human life, and because the rigidity of party discipline gives the Government in power (in reality, a small group of its leaders) quasi-dictatorial powers. Such powers tend to become ever more extensive. In their financial aspect, because of the increasing elaborateness of the machinery of control, the powers tend to be used more comprehensively to appropriate an ever-larger amount of the individual's income, and to fetter the spending of the fraction that remains. It is only necessary to think of the use in Great Britain during the past thirty years of such (originally temporary) taxes as entertainment tax, purchase tax, and betting tax, and the enormous increases in income-tax and surtax, and in the duties on alcoholic drinks, tobacco and petrol to appreciate what has been happening. One needs to be no prophet of doom to realise where this may eventually end. The financial history of France in the two decades which preceded the French Revolution is a valuable pointer. Unfortunately it is the case that the appetite for control and taxation grows with what it feeds upon. That appetite is perhaps at its most voracious in the Soviet Union, but the appetite of Government in the Western world grows apace. It is also true that the efficiency of control descends sharply with each increase in its complexity. In Imperial China the machinery developed to such a point that, in theory, the magistrates controlled every aspect of the citizen's life from the cradle to the grave in accord with the principles of Confucian philosophy. The result was that large numbers of officials were busily engaged in writing to one another either about nothing at all, or about totally fictitious episodes, such as wars against frontier tribes in which the writer scored imaginary victories, or domestic perils successfully averted by the exercise of great resource. The citizen, for his part, had perfected his own technique for the purpose of circumventing authority. The result was a destruction of all sense of public responsibility, and a cult of family preservation which, though understandable, has been one of China's main weaknesses in modern times. It would be an odd conclusion to so much Western planning if we were to achieve a similar result. To preserve a balance between freedom and control in the mid-twentieth century conditions of economic and political insecurity is a task of immense difficulty; but it must be attempted, if the modern State is to remain a satisfactory— or even an endurable—setting for the social activities of the individual.

Chapter 10

Land in Chains

I

NO claim for originality can be made for the title of this chapter, for it was used by more than one legal writer in the nineteenth century, when advocating reform of the land law. This circumstance may serve as a reminder of the services rendered to the community by a succession of eminent conveyancers who alone were in a position to tell the public what the defects of the existing land law were, and how they could be most effectively removed.

The condition of the land law at the end of the nineteenth century was remarkable. From the time of the first Reform Bill until the end of the century there had been a succession of important and carefully-drafted Real Property Statutes. In spite of them, however, the fundamentals of the land law remained unaltered. In the words of Professor Dicey, in a notable contribution to the *Law Quarterly Review* in 1905:[1]

> 'The paradox of the modern English land law may thus be summed up: the constitution of England has, whilst preserving monarchical forms, become a democracy, but the land law of England remains the law appropriate to an aristocratic State.'

Maitland, in his lectures on Constitutional History which were delivered at Cambridge during the session 1887-8, has explained some of the main reasons for this remarkable paradox. Although in the Middle Ages, the land law was the basis of all public law at first, the vigour of the English people, coupled with the power of a centralised royal administration, succeeded in separating the land law from the business of government at an earlier date than was generally possible on the Continent, with the result that our constitutional development was continuous, whilst the land law tended to remain a repository for outworn forms. As Maitland observes

---

[1] Vol. 21, *Law Quarterly Review*, p. 221.

in his review of the place of feudalism in English constitutional development, feudalism was probably at its zenith in the land law during the eighteenth century. In the political sphere at this date, the consequences of the great constitutional settlement of 1688 were already profound, and the essentials of the modern constitution had been established.

At the time when Professor Dicey pointed out the unsatisfactory state of the land law, in 1905, it was still feudal in form, even though it had been slowly and painfully adjusted to the needs of an industrial society; and all critics started from the proposition that more fundamental changes than any which had hitherto been attempted must speedily be brought about. Even at the dawn of the present century, the two basic doctrines upon which the land law was built were those of Tenure and of Estates. In the first centuries after the Conquest, Tenure had been a reality. Indeed, it was the chief characteristic of land-holding. Land was enjoyed in return for services to be overlord; and one of the main causes of the decline of feudalism was the decline in value of the feudal services. In 1660 an Act had been passed formally abolishing feudal services which had long been of little economic significance; yet the intricacies of tenure remained, and by the art of conveyancers, they had been gradually developed to a condition of almost intolerable complexity. Nor was this all. Our law knew two entirely different kinds of tenure—the free and the unfree. Originally, the distinction had a far-reaching social and economic significance. In the nineteenth century, the existence of two kinds of tenure was an unnecessary complication, which legislation sought to minimise, but declined to abolish. Superimposed on both was the conception of leasehold tenure and the abstruse complexities of equitable and legal estates. In these circumstances, it was not surprising that the establishment of title—a necessary condition precedent to the transfer of land—was a cumbrous and expensive business. One method of simplification would have been the establishment of a national register of titles to land. This had been contemplated from the time of Edward I onwards, as Professor Holdsworth shows,[2] but legislation to this end had

---

[2] 'The Reform of the Land Law,' *Essays in Law and History*, p. 100.

always been frustrated by the attachment of landowners to a system of private conveyancing. In this field, even the strictures of Bentham proved to be ineffective to achieve a major change, even though the conscience of Parliament was sufficiently stirred, just before the passing of the first Reform Bill, to appoint a Real Property Commission to study the whole question. The conclusions reached in their first report, which appeared in 1829, governed the reform which was undertaken during the next seventy years. The complacency with which the Commissioners surveyed even the unreformed fabric is strikingly reflected in their opening remarks. They observed:

'We have the satisfaction to report that the Law of Real Property seems to us to require very few essential alterations; and that those which we shall feel it our duty to suggest are chiefly modal. When the object of transactions respecting land is accomplished, and the estates and interests in it which are recognised are actually created and secured, the Law of England, except in a few comparatively unimportant particulars, appears to become almost as near to perfection as can be expected in any human institution. The owner of the soil is, we think, vested with exactly the dominion and power of disposition over it required for the public good, and landed property in England is admirably made to answer all the purposes to which it is applicable. Settlements bestow upon the present possessor of an estate the benefits of ownership, and secure the property to his posterity. . . . In England families are preserved, and purchasers always find a supply of land in the market. A testamentary power is given, which stimulates industry and encourages accumulation; and while capricious limitations are restrained, property is allowed to be moulded to the circumstances and wants of every family. When no disposition is made by will, the whole landed estate descends to the son or other heir male. This, which is called the Law of Primogeniture, appears far better adapted to the constitution and habits of this kingdom than the opposite Law of Equal Partibility, which, in a few generations, would break down the aristocracy of the country, and, by the endless subdivision of the soil, must ultimately be unfavourable to agriculture, and injurious to the best interests of the State.'

This extract from the Report really goes to the root of the whole question. The general law of descent was reinforced by a widespread use of the family settlement to secure the undivided descent of the great estates of the landowning aristocracy; and this preserved, at one and the same time, the privileges and power of an aristocracy and also a remarkably efficient system of agriculture.

Unfortunately for the order of landowners, however, their hour had already struck when the real Property Commissioners reported. The first Reform Act transferred their political ascendancy to the manufacturing middle classes, who demanded an increasing supply of cheap and well fed labour. This demand denuded the countryside of its reservoir of agricultural labour, and at the same time made inevitable the repeal of the Corn Laws, the growth of Free Trade, and the importation of agricultural produce. Thus, as the nineteenth century progressed, land ceased to be the chief source of wealth, power, and privilege, and with the introduction of the limited liability company, it became possible for the aristocracy to participate extensively in industry and commerce.

With this change in the national economy which was due to the growth of industry and commerce came a changed outlook upon the ownership of land. It was no longer a foundation of privilege and a symbol of political power; nor was it an inheritance to be transmitted in almost the identical condition in which it had been received. It was increasingly a commodity to be developed. Some parts of it might be needed for housing development; some might be the subject of compulsory purchase for the construction of railways; other parts again might be leased for the opening of collieries or factories. When any of these developments had taken place, the character of the neighbourhood might have changed to such an extent that the sale of the remainder of the land might be desirable. Even where the character of large estates remained substantially unaltered, it might still be a matter for consideration whether it might be wise to sell land and invest the proceeds in industry. In all these cases the family settlement, hitherto regarded as the guarantee and charter of family ascendancy, might sink to the level of an obstacle to development. It followed, therefore, that in the second half of the nineteenth century, a succession of statutes grappled with the problem of the family settlement, with the object of giving the limited owner (usually the 'tenant for life') powers wide enough to permit development or, with the consent of the trustees, the sale of the land, without at the same time prejudicing the rights of those entitled to interests following upon that of the tenant for life. Little by little, the functions of the tenant for life changed. He became a trustee of a complex of valuable rights and interests for all those who were granted interests in the settlement, and accordingly, the ownership of land became simply one aspect of this comprehensive function. The Settled Land Act of 1925 has given express recognition to this principle.

These changes, and many others, which were brought about by nineteenth century statutes, failed to touch the core of the problem. Land transfer became easier, and either the trustees of a settlement, with the concurrence of the tenant for life, or the tenant for life himself, could sell settled land; but land transfer was still cumbrous and costly. A register of title was instituted in the second half of the nineteenth century, but the registration of land titles remained almost a dead letter, since the initiative lay with the landowner himself; and he and his legal advisers still preferred a system of private conveyancing. The land law was still unnecessarily complicated by the co-existence of freehold, copyhold and leasehold tenure, and by the development of an intricate system of legal and equitable estates and interests in land at different periods of history. Moreover, new conceptions of the social responsibility of the landowner, embodied in the first Town Planning Acts, were gradually introducing a further complicating factor into a law which was already unduly complex. The powers given to local authorities by these Acts to control the use of land were factors which prospective buyers of land must take increasingly into account when considering purchase. Accordingly, the local land charge became yet another circumstance for which careful search must be made, thereby adding to the expense, difficulty, and uncertainty of transfer.

2

The conclusion of the first World War marked an important change in the national outlook upon the land law. Amongst other things, it had shown that land was still a national asset, upon the productivity of which, in an emergency, the survival of the nation might depend. Moreover, the sharply-ascending rates of taxation and death duties accelerated the pace at which the great estates were broken up; whilst large landowners themselves sought to transfer their wealth from land to commerce and industry. Accordingly, when the Scott Committee reported on land transfer in 1919, its main conclusion was that the land law itself needed far-reaching reforms and simplifications, in order that the process of transfer might be progressively assimilated to that governing the transfer of personal property. The result was the comprehensive property legislation which was enacted in 1925, and which owed much to the energy of Lord Birkenhead. The reforms which those acts brought about were far-reaching, and in many respects they were also overdue. For example, they reduced the number of estates and interests which could exist in land, and the Act of 1922 abolished copyhold tenure altogether. No more than the empty shell of freehold tenure remained, and at this late date, it became the practical equivalent of the absolute ownership of chattels. At long last, primogeniture was abolished, and common rules of descent for real and personal property were introduced. Moreover, compulsory registration of many *charges* on land (but not title to land itself) was widely extended. Even so, however, some reforms which might have been expected, were not undertaken. Yet another Land Registration Act was placed on the statute-book, but once again the opportunity to institute a national system of registered titles was missed. The Act simply continued the system of voluntary registration with the addition of machinery whereby local authorities could, if they wished, declare their areas compulsory registration areas. Comparatively little use has been made of this power, although London, Middlesex, and the County boroughs of Croydon, Eastbourne and Hastings are now compulsory registration areas. At the end of the recent war, during which numerous documents of title disappeared as a result of enemy bombing, a committee under the chairmanship of the late Lord Rushcliffe, again considered the question of a national system of registration of title, and once again, disappointingly, reported against it. Few people today, however, doubt that a national system must be introduced at an early date.

Again, the legislation of 1925 preserved two distinct methods of settlement—the 'strict' settlement, which is the traditional settlement of the great landowner, much modified to meet the changed conditions of the twentieth century, and the settlement by way of trust for sale. Many lawyers have doubted whether such duplication is necessary, and today, the survival of the strict settlement seems a little archaic. Discussions in Parliament upon the Bill to abolish restraints on anticipation has shown that modern rates of taxation may cause even the settlement of great funds of personal property to work out very differently from what the creator of the settlement anticipated. At the present time, the whole machinery of trusts and settlements is working under increased strain.

Surprisingly, one great branch of the land law was not widely affected by the legislation of 1925—the law of land-lord and tenant. One section of it, which governed the relations of house owners and short-term tenants—had been subjected to statutory control as a consequence of the cessation of building during the war, and the post-war shortage of houses. Control remained, with successive modifications, during the inter-war years, and was widely extended again in 1939. Throughout its existence, however, rent restriction has preserved a number of unsatisfactory features which are attributable to the fact that it was introduced as an emergency measure; and an investigation of the whole question, leading to a new and simpler body of legislation, is urgently needed.

Altogether apart from this special question, however, the law of landlord and tenant had many anomalies and obscurities in 1919, and it may be regretted that an opportunity to modernise and simplify the branch of the law was then missed. The result has been that piecemeal modification has from time to time been achieved in successive Agricultural Holdings Acts and, for urban business tenancies, in the Landlord and Tenant Act, 1927. Such acts, however, do not cover the whole of the ground, and where they do not, the law on such questions as compensation for fixtures, and for loss of goodwill, or for failure to renew a lease, preserves a number of features which reflect the social conditions of an era which has gone. Today, however, these questions are of rapidly diminishing importance in agricultural tenancies, in view of the provisions of the Agricultural Holdings Act, 1948.

3

It will be apparent from what has already been written that the seventy years of reform which followed the report of the Real Property Commissioners in 1829 removed a number of archaisms from the law of real property, and achieved a number of improvements in detail in the system of land transfer, although in this period none of the fundamental changes, which were widely advocated, were brought about. During the next three decades, rapidly changing conditions and the first World War were responsible for a new approach to the land law in the Property legislation of 1925. This legislation brought about many important and far-reaching reforms, although in some respects it probably did not go far enough. Notwithstanding this criticism, however, it is true to say that the 1925 legislation had at long last struck off most of the feudal fetters which had so seriously impeded the transfer of land. Today, however, land is once again in fetters, which are clogging its full utilisation to a degree which has not been experienced for over a century. How has this paradoxical and unexpected result been achieved?

If, as Professor Holdsworth has pointed out, the first World War produced a new social consciousness of the unsatisfactory state of the land law,[3] the second World War was responsible for a more widespread and far-reaching sense of dissatisfaction with its condition. Once again, the need for the fullest utilisation of our national resources had been demonstrated, and this time public opinion had reached the conclusion that no anti-social assertions of private right should be permitted to stand in the way of such utilisation. As a necessary condition precedent to such utilisation, however, it followed that there should be planning on the national

[3] 'The Reform of the Land Law', in *Essays in Law and History*, p. 121.

scale. Accordingly, the Town and Country Planning Act of 1947 gives powers of planning and control on a scale not hitherto contemplated. Moreover, in view of the importance of agriculture in the national economy, the Agriculture Act, 1947, and the Agricultural Holdings Act, 1948, have revolutionised the position of the entire farming community. Because public dissatisfaction with the Town and Country Planning Act has grown rapidly in intensity, the equally far-reaching provisions of the Agriculture Act and the Agricultural Holdings Act have not been so generally appreciated. Nevertheless, they cut right across the traditional development of agriculture in this country, and as the extent of the powers conferred upon the Ministry of Agriculture are more widely appreciated, there can be little doubt that criticisms of this Act, and dissatisfaction with the regime it creates will increase sharply. These two Acts, and the Town and Country Planning Act, 1947, leave little more to the owner of land than the empty shell of bare title. The text-books of legal practitioners have not, in the past, been conspicuous for their awareness of social trends. For that reason, the following observations from the *Preface* to the tenth edition of *Jackson's Agricultural Holdings*, which was published in 1949, is of considerable significance. Discussing the effect of the Act of 1948, the learned editor, Mr. Aggs, writes:

'From a perusal of the Act it will be realised that the age-long relationship of landlord and tenant under which the industry has in the past been carried on has largely disappeared, and that there has now been introduced into that relationship the overriding powers of the Minister of Agriculture and Fisheries acting through the county agricultural executive committees.

'Thus scarcely any freedom of contract remains for either landlord or tenant and even the terms of the tenancy are prescribed for them and, if not adopted, can be varied by arbitration so as to accord with the statutory requirement.

'Landlords will find themselves under severe restrictions regarding notices to quit, and though this may mean a greater measure of security for the tenant, yet instead of having to deal with the landlord and his agent whom he often regarded as a helpful partner in his undertaking, he will now have to comply with the orders and directions of the Minister and the officials of the agricultural executive committee and he will frequently have to take professional advice as to what are his rights and obligations.

'It is thought that the result of this trend in legislation may be that the "tenant farmer" will gradually cease to exist and instead a relationship of owner and manager will take the place of the former relationship of landlord and tenant. Some such new arrangement will probably be adopted on the larger estates as farms become vacant.'

As some indication of the change which has come over the face of agriculture since the war, it may be pointed out that before 1939, the staff employed by the Ministry of Agriculture was less than 2,000. Today it exceeds 15,000, i.e. there is one official for every twenty farmers. Nearly 7,000 of them serve on country agricultural committees, which were war-time creations which have become a permanent feature of British farming. Another 1674 run the National Agriculture Advisory Service. This unquestionably does a great deal of immensely important work, but at the other end of the scale, it has been responsible for pamphlets of which two are 'How to Build a Bonfire', and 'How to make Sandwiches'. The county committees, of which there are over 60, each with its staff of technicians, and office staffs, include within their province the task of telling farmers what crops are to be grown, the hiring out of machinery and casual labour, looking after the various subsidy schemes, and the allocation of feeding stuffs. Possibly their most important function of all, however, is the holding of enquiries at the direction of the Ministry to establish cases of bad management, leading to a supervision order or a dispossession order. Such enquiries are classic examples of administrative tribunals at their worst. They are staffed by neighbouring farmers, who therefore are necessarily interested parties. In addition, their terms of reference are ambiguous to the points of incomprehensibility. Thus Section 11 (1) of the Act states:

'For the purposes of this Act, the occupier of an agricultural unit(!) shall be deemed to fulfil his responsibilities to farm it in accordance with the rules of good husbandry insofar as the extent to which and the manner in which the unit is being farmed (as respects both the kind of operations carried out and the way in which they are carried out) is such that, having regard to the character and situation of the unit, the standard of management thereof by the owner and other relevant circumstances, the occupier is maintaining a reasonable standard of efficient production, as respects both the kind of produce and the quality thereof, while keeping the unit in a condition to enable such a standard to be maintained in the future.'

It will be seen that this clause, when translated into English, has the effect of putting a farmer into the hands of his neighbours, with whom he may be on the worst of terms. These very wide and ill-defined powers are being freely used. Down to the middle of 1951, no less than 2,750 farmers had come under the supervision of the county committees, and 130 had been dispossessed. Thus, 130 farmers had been deprived of land and livelihood by amateur tribunals from whom there is no possibility of appeal to the courts.

Inasmuch as freedom of contract has virtually disappeared, and as a farmer can now be evicted at the instance of the Ministry for failure to farm 'efficiently,' or in accordance with the plan, it is plain that, after a brief absence of a quarter of a century from our land law, feudalism has now returned in a new and ominous form. Moreover, some of the other trends indicated by the editor of *Jackson* are already appearing. Today, there is a steady change from individual ownership of agricultural land, to ownership by a company; and farming in compliance with the orders of the State, as feudal overlord, is being carried out by skilled and highly-paid managers. It is not difficult to see in these land companies, owning substantial areas, the successors of the *majores barones* of an earlier feudal age. The ensuing struggle between them and their feudal overlord will be interesting to watch. At present, under the Acts of 1947, and 1948, the last word appears to be with the State, through the Ministry of Agriculture, but the history of our land law shows such a situation to have existed on several previous occasions. Yet major barons, whether individual or corporate, are a stubborn race, and farming, like the medieval profession of arms, is not learned in a day. Throughout the history of the land law the pendulum has swung between public control and private interest. There was a considerable element of public control after the Norman Conquest, and the Domesday Survey might not inaptly be regarded as a medieval counterpart to a Royal Commission on the use and taxable value of the land. Today, once again the element of public control is dominant; but the pendulum is still swinging.

If the two Acts mentioned above have placed agricultural land again in fetters, the Town and Country Planning Act has done even more for land capable of non-agricultural development. Indeed, it represents a very formidable obstacle to the development of land at the present time. Broadly, it rests on two general principles: (1) that the development of all land in the country should conform to an overriding plan, and should not be spasmodic; (2) that the increment in value arising from development should accrue to the State and not to the individual owner. On the other hand, since the vesting of this development value in the State will remove from the landowner wealth previously vested in him, the Act fixed a global figure of £300,000,000 from which all existing owners of land capable of development could draw compensation. How this round figure has been reached does not appear. At this stage of the national development, there are probably few who would question the wisdom of the first principle. Almost every modern town, and many adjacent areas, could furnish illustrations of the evils of absence of planning in the past. As far as this aspect of planning is concerned, therefore, the issue is not one of planning or non-planning, but of the reasonableness or unreasonableness of the planning which is being undertaken. It was said of Guy Fawkes, when arrested after the discovery of the Gunpowder Plot, that he was interrogated before being racked, during racking, and after racking. The plight of the unfortunate who wishes to undertake the development of land today is little better. He is interrogated before planning, during planning, and after planning. Indeed, Great Britain today illustrates in acute measure the misfortunes of a country which has surrendered unconditionally to the planners. Very soon, it will be impossible to place a dustbin in the backyard without planning permission. It has already been held that planning permission is necessary before a board can be exhibited announcing a sale of property. A house-owner has been directed to paint the tiles of his house another colour to conform with a local 'plan'. To place a heap of stones on land is a change of use, which requires planning permission. As yet, it is not necessary before opening or closing a hole in the ground to obtain planning permission, and therefore planning permission is not as yet necessary in order to be buried in land which has been designated a burial ground, although presumably, if at some future date, the planning authority decides upon a better site for the burial ground we shall all run the risk of being dug up again. This may, perhaps, seem a somewhat extreme case, but it is worth while remembering that today, local authorities, in pursuance of obligations laid upon them by the Ministry, are preparing 'over-all' (blessed word) plans of their areas, and in so doing, are not unnaturally viewing their responsibilities in the widest terms. In one plan with which I am acquainted, it is suggested that the gas-works should be transferred to the other side of the city! No doubt there are good reasons for such a suggestion. There may also be good reasons for moving the city bodily to some healthier neighbourhood. It is, as was suggested above, entirely a question of reasonableness, and reasonableness in planning is a question of degree.

Unfortunately, such an idealistic view of the future as is involved in this 'over-all' plan has a deterrent effect on industry today. As many plans are as yet incomplete, and if complete, are not yet presented to the Minister, many planning permissions are today given with a time-limit, so that the developer is told his buildings may have to be demolished at the expiration of that period. That may not deter the boldest, but many valuable developments are being abandoned in face of such a risk, coupled with liability to development charge.

When the Act was under discussion, there was little public appreciation of what was involved. It is only since the impact of this imposition upon members of all classes has been experienced that public opinion has shown a resentment, which is rising daily. Where the nature of the impost was understood at all, it was widely assumed at this time when the Act was before Parliament that a small percentage tax alone was involved. It is certainly true that the framers of the Act made the nature of the charge plain, but public opinion was not conscious of the comprehensive nature of the legislation. It was not contemplated, for example, that a cobbler who erected a small lean-to shed behind his house to carry on his trade more efficiently would have to pay £400 development charge. Nor was it appreciated that the conversion of two flats back to the single house from which they had been made by the removal of inner partitions was a change of use attracting development charge. As the Act stands at present, much property in this country is probably sterilised to its present use for an indefinite period. Where it is not, the existence of the tax is a substantial measure of inflation. Suppose, for example, a limited company wishes to erect a new factory, costing £25,000, to manufacture an article which would have been sold at five shillings before the Act. Development charge amounting to many thousands of pounds will have to be paid. There will be only one way in which the company can recover this outlay. It will be added to the sales price of the article it manufactures. If the company does not do this, it will be unable to continue in business. This tax on development, it must be remembered, represents the full amount of the development, and it is levied without the possibility of appeal to any Court. In this respect, in fact, it directly resembles the fines levied by the Star Chamber, and it is as arbitrary in incidence, as the account given by Lord Halifax in the House of Lords of his own negotiations to settle development charge on a converted garage sufficiently showed. It has been suggested that the burden imposed by development charge upon land has been much exaggerated, inasmuch as land values have fallen, or should have fallen. Practical experience shows, however, that development charges are today frequently far in excess of the total price charged for land before the Act—so that even if the land were given away, the recipient who wishes to develop it would still be the loser. It is only the purchaser who preserves the existing use who may gain —which surely was not the object of the Act. Indeed, the whole impost rests upon the fallacy that development value may be calculated. Moreover, each time the use of land is changed, liability for a fresh payment exists. Few Acts have so quickly frustrated the purpose for which they were passed as this part of the Town and Country Planning Act, 1947.

Nor is this all. The recent decision in *Earl Fitzwilliam's Wentworth Estates* v. *Minister of Town and Country Planning*,[4] to which reference has already been made in an earlier chapter shows that, in effect, the possibility of land nationalisation has been conceded to the Ministry, without this fundamental question ever having been discussed by Parliament. Section 43(1) of the Act provides:

> 'that the Minister may authorize the Central Land Board to acquire land compulsorily if he is satisfied that it is expedient in the public interest that the board should acquire land for any such purpose as aforesaid, and that the board are unable to acquire the land by agreement on reasonable terms'.

In the case under consideration, the Board exercised compulsory powers of purchase when the Estates Company failed to sell land for building at existing use value, as indicated by the Board in a circular. As Denning L. J. said in a dissenting judgment in the Court of Appeal, this had the effect of giving to the Board, or the Ministry, or both, a power to legislate independently of Parliamentary control, for which there was no warrant in the Act. The majority of the Court of Appeal, however, thought that the Act gave the Board the general power of compulsory purchase which they claimed to have exercised in this case, and the House of Lords agreed with them. Few people, however, could have appreciated the full significance of this, when the Act was being placed on the Statute Book in 1947.

Today, therefore, new fetters have been forged for the land; the fetters of a new feudalism, and of crippling new imposts, frustrating development. The whole question of land law urgently needs fresh investigation, in the course of which the economic consequences of the existing legislation should be fully examined.

[4] [1951] 2 K.B. 284.

Chapter 11

The Problem of State Monopolies

IT was pointed out in Chapter 2 that this country since the end of the fighting in 1945 has gone a considerable way upon the Moscow road through the setting up of gigantic State monopolies in which the ownership of most of our essential services and heavy industries—transport, fuel and power, coal, iron and steel—is vested. Moreover, it is gradually becoming apparent that neither Parliament nor public is either satisfied or fully informed about these gigantic and unprofitable enterprises. It is also a matter upon which the curious may reflect that so far the lawyers, whether academic or practising, have been extremely hesitant to analyse the legal implications of successive nationalisation Acts.[1]

Looked at from one point of view, the setting up of State monopolies in activities in which the amalgamation of competing enterprises has already proceeded very far is simply the final stage in the history of commercial and industrial enterprise in the West in the last two centuries. In the earliest phase, when it is national policy for industrialisation to proceed as rapidly as possible, conditions are established in which highly competitive enterprises can be set up with moderate capital. Later there follows the state of consolidation, in which redundancy is to a considerable degree eliminated, and in which uneconomic units are either merged or dissolved. For example, the railway boom in the middle of the nineteenth century produced a large number of railway enterprises, most of them highly competitive and some of them weak and ineffective. Rationalisation by way

[1] Two notable exceptions are contributions by Professor W. Friedmann and C. Winter, LL.M., to *Law and Contemporary Problems* (Duke University, 1951).

of amalgamation had already proceeded very far when, after the 1914-18 war had demonstrated the importance of unified control in time of war, the merger of 1921 reduced the ordinary railway companies of this country to four, each with a fairly clearly-defined area of operation. From that point to nationalisation after a second war in which our transport system had functioned under even greater strain than during the war of 1914-18 could therefore be regarded, and was widely regarded, as no more than the last step in a process which had been going on for over half a century.

Such a view does not take all relevant factors into account, however. An alternative route by which this movement could have reached its conclusion would have been by a merger of the four railway companies, either of their own initiative, or at government prompting, into a single company, comprising the shareholders of the pre-existing companies. The fact that this apparently simpler method was not adopted indicates that the recent changes have occurred in response to the operation of some social or political theory. They are, in fact, the product of that brand of Socialism to which organised labour was converted thirty or forty years ago by the Fabians, acting under the leadership of the Webbs. This is an aspect of the matter to which we will return later in this chapter. For the present, however, we will examine the mechanism by which nationalisation has been carried out. This has sometimes been described as the establishment of public corporations. Such a term is very misleading. The proceedings of these State monopolies are a good deal more private than the proceedings of public companies. Further the outstanding characteristic of a corporation, whether public in the true sense (e.g. a local authority) or commercial, is that it is an aggregate of persons, united in membership for the achievement of some purpose. The modern State monopolies, however, have no members to whom they can be made responsible. It is true that English law also knows the corporation sole, which is the result of the incorporation of a succession of persons occupying the same office. Such a type of corporation is somewhat anomalous, and in any event, the State monopoly bears no more resemblance to the corporation sole that it does to the corporation aggregate.

It will be valuable to examine what is constituted by a nationalisation Act by examining the Iron and Steel Act, 1949, by virtue of which, after bitter conflict, the iron and steel industries were nationalised. Part I of the Act established the Iron and Steel Corporation of Great Britain, a monster compared with which the greatest steel combine which existed before the Act was an infant. The Corporation, says Section 1(2), consists, not as one would expect from such a name, of persons having some financial stake in the industry but of a chairman and not less than six nor more than ten other members,

> 'and the chairman and all other members shall be appointed by the Minister from amongst persons appearing to him to be persons who have had wide experience of, and shown capacity in, the production of iron ore or iron or steel, industrial, commercial or financial matters, administration or the organisation of workers.'

The so-called corporation, therefore, is not a corporation at all, except that it has legal personality so that it can sue or be sued as a unit. It is, in fact, an emanation of the Ministry which, by a pleasant trick of nomenclature well known to government departments, has been called something else to make it more palatable to the public at large.

This point is made plain beyond the possibility of ambiguity by the terms of Section 4, which reads as follows :

> '(1) The Minister may, after consultation with the Corporation, give to the Corporation directions of a general character as to the exercise and performance by the Corporation of the functions (including the exercise of rights conferred by the holding of interests in companies) in relation to matters which appear to him to affect the national interest, and the Corporation shall give effect to any such directions.
>
> '(2) In carrying out any such measure of reorganisation or any such work of development as involves substantial outlay on capital account, and in securing the carrying out by publicly-owned companies of any such measure or work, the Corporation shall act in accordance with a general programme settled from time to time with the approval of the Minister.

'(3) In making or securing provision for the training and education of persons employed by the Corporation or any publicly-owned company, and for research, the Corporation shall act in accordance with a general programme as aforesaid.

'(4) Without prejudice to the preceding provisions of this section, the Minister may, after consultation with the Corporation, direct the Corporation—

'(a) to discontinue or restrict any of their activities or to dispose of any part of their assets; or

'(b) to secure the discontinuance or restriction of any of the activities of a publicly-owned company, or the disposal of the whole or any part of the assets of any such company, or the winding-up of any such company;

'and the Corporation shall give effect to any such direction.'

All this is very clear. The Departments, having to an important and increasing degree emancipated themselves from the control of Parliament and the Courts, now enjoy a stranglehold upon the economic life of the country, operating through dummy monopolies, whose officials are appointed by them and are responsible to them, and whose activities are subject to control and supervision by the Departments on all questions of broad policy. The Iron and Steel Act, 1949, reflecting as it does the fierce struggle which preceded it, has been completely clear in its statement of both the legal position, and the situation in terms of power. It is perhaps, unnecessary to add that Section 7 of the Act gives the Corporation power to purchase compulsorily

'any land required for the exercise and performance of their function or the carrying on of any activity by a publicly-owned company.'

May it not be, however, that somewhere in this gigantic power complex, the interests of the ordinary public have been remembered? Section 6 is instructive on this point. It provides for the establishment of an Iron and Steel Consumers Council, to comprise an independent (*sic*) chairman appointed by the Minister, two members of the Corporation (i.e. the Board of Control appointed by the Department) nominated by the Corporation, and finally

'not less than fifteen nor more than thirty other persons appointed by the Minister, after consultation with such bodies (which may include organisations representing workers) as he thinks fit, to represent the interests of persons (hereinafter in this section referred to as "the consumers") who are consumers of the products of any of the principal activities of the Corporation and the public-owned companies.'

If it were suggested that a legislative body should be selected (the word elected cannot be used) in the manner in which this shadowy Consumers' Council is, the adjective 'dictatorial' would be rightly applied to the process. Even so, however, the Act takes every possible precaution to prevent the Council from doing anything effective. By Section 4, the Council may 'consider', 'consider and report', 'consider and make recommendations', and finally 'make representations' concerning various matters. The reader will observe the fine shades of distinction introduced by the department in respect of these nebulous functions. It is hardly surprising that Consumers' Councils have been still-born. Few people have heard of them, none but Departmental officials know how they are selected, and their representations and considerations remain in the files of the appropriate State monopoly whilst prices continue to rise, and deficits to increase. The unchallengeable fact is that the ordinary citizen has very considerably less share in the operation of nationalised enterprise than he had in the operation of the enterprise before nationalisation. The last element of freedom of choice as a consumer has been removed from him; it is no longer possible for him to buy any shareholding in the enterprise. Officials are appointed without any reference whatever to him, even indirectly; the consumers' councils are selected by, and responsible only to the nationalised industry and its parent Ministry, and in any event, they do not possess anything beyond the most shadowy of advisory powers. The nationalised industry has the appearance of some Frankenstein monster, groping in a world in which, from the standpoint of intelligence, it is scarcely safe to be let at large, insensitive to opinion, and seeking to escape from departmental fetters which, in the last resort, will bring it to ruin.

It is very important indeed to appreciate that the corporate structure of the State monopoly is merely a façade behind which nominees of a State department operate. In an ordinary public company, the shareholders have certain rights

F

guaranteed by law. They appoint and remove directors, and they can proceed against the directors in the Courts for negligence and misfeasance. It may be that even today the rights of the shareholder against a director are not so extensive as some would wish. Nevertheless, their existence may operate as a check upon the activities of directors. There is nothing to correspond with this in the structure of State monopolies. Members of their Boards can only be responsible to the Departments which appoint them. Remembering that in the view of many, the standard of diligence required from the directors of public companies is still surprisingly low, and that presumably no higher legal standard of duty is required from the members of boards of nationalised industries, the position in law appears extremely unsatisfactory.

It may, perhaps, be suggested that although there is no possibility of control by shareholders, and although consumers councils have proved completely ineffective to influence the policy of the giant State monopolies, an adequate protection of the interests of the general public is provided by the control exercised by Departments of State. Unfortunately this is not the case. The failure of the groundnuts scheme threw into sharp relief the complacency and incompetence of a public department when faced with novel problems, whilst the prosecution and conviction of the chairman and deputy-chairman of the Yorkshire Electricity Board, as well as the Board itself, for violation of building regulations by building in excess of the limits imposed by licences to the extent of over £30,000 showed in striking fashion the extent to which members of these Boards now regard themselves as a privileged caste, above the rules of law which govern ordinary citizens. Unfortunately also the case demonstrated how utterly ineffective the alleged control exercised by a government department can be. Even apart from the deliberate law-breaking proved in this case, the trial had two other disturbing features. The Lord Chief Justice not only punished the persons principally responsible for law-breaking by the Electricity Board. He also imposed a fine of £20,000 upon the Board itself. Inasmuch as this was not to be paid by the members of the Board personally, this meant either that the consumers supplied by the York-shire Electricity Board will have to pay the fine, or that the taxpayers as a whole will have to pay it by way of a subsidy for a deficit. It would seem, therefore, that a very desirable alteration in the law would be a statutory provision giving power to surcharge the members of the Board personally where penalties imposed upon the Board can be traced either to the personal and wilful misfeasance or to the culpable negligence of its members. A further unsatisfactory feature of the case was the tacit assumption of all parties that the lavish scale even of *lawful* expenditure at Scarcroft was justified. It was assumed that large-scale additions to buildings, and lavish equipment were appropriate for these mighty potentates of State monopolies. Their estimates of expenditure are apparently not subjected to the scrutiny to which the estimates of such essential services as the Army, the Navy and the Air Force must submit. There appears to be no justification whatever for such an irresponsible procedure. Reviewing the Scarcroft case in a leading article, the *Evening Standard* of November 20th, 1950, after pointing out the double check of democratic control and strict and impartial financial scrutiny which exists in respect of central and local government, draws attention to the privileged position enjoyed by the State monopolies, and after discussing the laxity which was responsible for the Scarcroft case, added:

'Presumably it was hoped that control from Whitehall would prevent such a situation ever arising. But the futility of setting one bureaucracy to watch over another appears from the part played by the Ministry of Fuel in the affairs of the Yorkshire Board. The details have yet to be exposed, but on the best possible interpretation the Ministry knew little of what was happening in Yorkshire and cared less.

'The Scarcroft scandal throws light on reforms which should be brought into immediate effect.

'1. The finances of all Boards should be made subject to the full inquisitorial powers of the Select Committee on Public Accounts or of a similar committee of Parliament set up for this particular purpose.

'2. Ministers should be made responsible to the House of Commons personally, and not as agents passing on information supplied, for answering questions on the operations of Boards under their jurisdiction.'

This is sound criticism. Further reference will be made to it in the final chapter.

If we seek the origin of the mania for nationalisation which continues to impair the judgment of left-wing publicists, it will be found ultimately in the writings of the Webbs, and particularly in *A Constitution for the Socialist Commonwealth of Great Britain*, published in 1920. By no stretch of the imagination can this be regarded as an inspired work. It is crude in technique, and it shows regrettable ignorance of the principles either of constitutional history or political science. For example, the authors put forward the naïve suggestion that the 'essentially political functions of government', whatever that may mean, should be concentrated in a Political Parliament, with an executive responsible to it, while 'all the other functions of the House of Commons' should be transferred to a second national assembly, with a second executive responsible to it. The primary function of the second assembly would be to exercise control over the nation's economies and social activities, including taxation, the social services and property. One can well imagine the constitutional conflicts which would arise from the establishment of such a quaint mixture. Their upshot can be predicted with some confidence, for the whole of English constitutional history confirms the hypothesis that he who controls the purse controls the State—more especially as the setting up of such a constitution was to be an incident in the nationalisation of industry. It is no novelty to suggest that the Webbs had the outlook of industrious civil servants. Their writings afford abundant proof of it; yet it is remarkable that they nowhere stop to consider the extent to which, even at the date when they wrote, the departments were encroaching upon Parliamentary sovereignty and personal freedom. Elsewhere in the same volume, they purport to analyse, in terms borrowed from Marx, the economic inequalities that exist in a capitalist society. They somewhat plaintively observe:

> 'The continued existence of the functionless rich—of persons who deliberately live by owning instead of by working, and whose futile occupations, often licentious pleasures and inherently insolent manners undermine the intellectual and moral standards of the community—adds insult to injury.'

One is surprised to find that these sentiments appear, not in the works of the well-known novelist, Mr. Hall Caine, but in those of persons who had undertaken a good deal of social research, and who were intended to be taken seriously. By some astonishing abeyance of the critical faculty, they have been taken seriously by many persons who are considerably their intellectual superiors, and who are not usually lacking in the critical faculty. For example, some of the arguments used by Sir Stafford Cripps in the debates on the Steel Bill in 1949 appear to have been drawn directly from this treasure-house of inaccurate generalities. However, as the climax of this emotional approach, the Webbs observe:

> 'What the Socialist aims at is the substitution, for this Dictatorship of the Capitalist, of Government of the people and for the people, in all the industries and services by which the people live. Only in this way can either the genuine participation of the whole body of the people in the administration of its own affairs, and the people's effective consciousness of consent to what is done in its names, ever be realised.'

What the Socialist has got, as distinct from what he aimed at, is the exact opposite of those noble aspirations. He has got a rigid mechanism, remote from and indifferent to public opinion, operated at a handsome loss by departmentally appointed officials with salaries as large as those ever paid to capitalist directors, with the added advantage that their losses and official expenses can be underwritten by a beneficent State. On these points, the reports so far published by the Public Accounts Committee of the House of Commons on the finance of nationalised industries make illuminating reading.

It will be evident that the Webbs, and following them left-wing publicists, have advocated the nationalisation of industry on three main grounds: (1) that private ownership has resulted in a great waste of productive power; (2) that it was necessary to reduce great inequalities of wealth, and (3) that public ownership of the means of production has removed from a small minority a complex of power which threatened personal freedom. Not one of these arguments bears prolonged examination. For example, as Lord Brand has pointed out,[2] if the first were true, it would follow that the Soviet Union would be industrially considerably more efficient than the United States, which few believe. Public ownership of industry and transport may have an important part to play in backward economies, where investment surpluses are very small, but that does not prove it to be a remedy of universal application. The second argument has ceased to have relevance in a community in which taxation has reached the heights which exists in England today. Moreover, nationalisation has not abolished wide disparities between the wages and salaries of the rank and file, and the salaries of the heads of the bureaucracy and industry; and it is interesting to notice that there has been no visible reluctance amongst trade union leaders and others in Britain to accept the high salaries paid to members of the Boards of nationalised industries. Finally, insofar as the third argument is concerned, the effect of nationalisation has been to remove power from one group to another, which operates in response to the promptings of the government of the day operating through the departments. Whether this is a change for the better or not still remains to be seen. As is plainly apparent from the language of the nationalisation Acts themselves, the departments have no intention whatever of allowing public interest the power to make effective intervention in the liaison between State monopoly and the parent department. The reason for this is also clear. Industry must operate subject to an over-all plan, whether in war or peace. In a period of rearmament, it is armaments which will secure priority. At other times, the entire country will be repeatedly spurred on to greater efforts in the field of exports. The acceptance of the principle of 'the plan' for the country's economic life of necessity excludes the element of personal choice. It takes us a long way on the Moscow road, and brings us within sight of the day when the individual will be a 'unit of production' and no more. If it should be that the planners, after all, have made a gigantic mistake, it will not be difficult to know where to place the responsibility for it. Unless the urge to power can be controlled within reasonable limits, the security and freedom

[2] 'Nationalisation' in *Lloyd's Bank Review*, April, 1949.

of the ordinary citizen become increasingly precarious, for as the enjoyment of power by those in possession fails to bring to the rank and file the benefits which have been so widely promised, there remains only the possibility of taking still more power, either to make a last effort to procure the elusive benefits for which change was instituted or else to control their disappointed rank and file when the futility of the proceedings at last becomes manifest. The history of the French and Russian Revolutions is very instructive on this point. The conception of the great pool of wealth which is available for universal distribution is a recurrent one in the mind of the revolutionary, but as Lord Brand has pointed out, nationalisation of industry has, in fact, no bearing even on the great problem of the central control of the nation's money structure. Post-war governments in England have forgotten Lord Keynes' conclusion that

> 'it is not the ownership of the instruments of production which it is important for the State to assume. If the State is able to determine the aggregate amount of resources devoted to augmenting the instruments and the basic reward of those who own them it will have accomplished all that is necessary.'[3]

The establishment of the State monopolies, therefore, is intended to represent the practical realisation of Socialist theories, as formulated by the Webbs and by the Fabians round about the time of the war of 1914-18.

The source of their inspiration is not open to argument, for Professor Friedmann notices:

> 'The Soviet Union proceeded, only a few years after the Revolution, to develop the institutions of the State Trusts for the running of major industrial State enterprises. These trusts are constituted as autonomous legal units; they received their charter from the Supreme Council of National Economy, which also appoints the members of the board, they have two types of capital assets which roughly correspond to the distinction between fixed and floating assets of British company law. The fixed assets belong to the State, the floating assets belong to the trusts. That is to say, they are State property at one remove and can be freely disposed of. The trusts enter into contractual and other legal transactions and legal disputes between them are settled by State arbitration which appears

[3] Lord Brand loc. cit.

to have developed principles of mixed contract and administrative law.'[4]

There, in fact, are to be found all the essential characteristics of the British State monopolies, which now control the nationalised industries. Professor Friedmann opens his interesting analysis by remarking that

'the Public Corporation is emerging as the chosen legal instrument of the Labour Government for the public control of basic industries in an economy still based on private enterprise.'

Exactly. Professor Friedmann makes the point even clearer when, at a later stage in his study, he points out that it is not easy to classify public corporations. They may be regarded as parts of, or extensions of, the executive; as a new type of public company; or as analogous to statutory public corporations, e.g. local authorities. Discussing the possibility that they can be regarded as a new species of public company, he remarks:

'Although there is a certain similarity in form, the public corporations are essentially instruments of public policy under the direction of the Government, which is responsible to Parliament. The public function overshadows the private form but even the formal similarity is limited, because of the absence of private shareholders and the appointment of the managing board by the Minister.'[5]

A word may perhaps be added upon the legal status oi public corporations. It was decided by the Court of Appeal in *Tamlin* v. *Hannaford*[6] that they do not rank as government departments, with the immunities, derived from the Crown, that such executive departments enjoy. Lord Justice Dening, delivering the judgment of the Court described the status of the Transport Commission as follows:

'The Transport Act, 1947, brings into being the British Transport Commission, which is a statutory corporation of a kind comparatively new to English law. It has many of the qualities which belong to corporations of other kinds to which we have been accustomed. It has, for instance, defined powers which it cannot exceed; and it is directed by a group of men

---

[4] 'The New Public Corporations', in *The Modern Law Review*, 1947, pp. 233-4.
[5] *Ibid*, p. 379.
[6] [1950] 1 K.B. 18.

whose duty it is to see that those powers are properly used. It may own property, carry on business, borrow and lend money, just as any other corporation may do, so long as it keeps within the bounds which Parliament has set. But the significant difference in this corporation is that there are no shareholders to subscribe the capital or to have any voice in its affairs. The money which the corporation needs is not raised by the issue of shares but by borrowing; and its borrowing is not secured by debentures, but is guaranteed by the Treasury. If it cannot repay, the loss falls on the Consolidated Fund of the United Kingdom; that is to say, on the taxpayers. There are no shareholders to check the directors or to fix their remuneration. There are no profits to be made or distributed. The duty of the corporation is to make revenue and expenditure balance one another, taking, of course, one year with another, but not to make profits. If it should make losses and be unable to pay its debts, its property is liable to execution, but it is not liable to be wound up at the suit of any creditors. The taxpayer would no doubt, be expected to come to its rescue before the creditors stepped in. Indeed, the taxpayer is the universal guarantor of the corporation. But for him it could not have acquired its business at all, nor could it now continue it for a single day. It is his guarantee that has rendered shares, debentures, and such like all unnecessary. He is clearly entitled to have his interest protected against extravagance or mismanagement.

'But there are other persons who have also a vital interest in its affairs. All those who use the services which it provides—and who does not?—and all whose supplies depend on it, in short everyone in the land, is concerned in seeing that it is properly run. The protection of the interests of all these—taxpayer, user and beneficiary—is entrusted by Parliament to the Minister of Transport. He is given powers over this corporation which are as great as those possessed by a man who holds all the shares in a private company, subject, however, as such a man is not, to a duty to account to Parliament for his stewardship. It is the Minister who appoints the directors—the members of the Commission—and fixes their remuneration. They must give him any information he wants; and, lest they should not prove amenable to his suggestions as to the policy they should adopt, he is given power to give them directions of a general nature, in matters which appear to him to affect the national interest, as to which he is the sole judge, and they are then bound to obey. These are great powers but still we cannot regard the corporation as being his agent, any more than a company is the agent of the shareholders, or even of a sole shareholder. In the eye of the law, the corporation is its own master and is answerable as fully as any other person or corporation. It is not the Crown and has none of the immunities or privileges of the Crown. Its servants are not civil servants, and its property is not Crown property. It is as much bound by Acts of Parliament as any other subject of the King. It is, of course, a public authority, and its purposes, no doubt, are public purposes, but it is not a government department nor do its powers fall within the province of government.'

The public corporation, in fact, is not a sub-department of an Executive department; it is its creature. One further point may be added. Being the creation of statute, a public corporation is subject to the doctrine of *ultra vires*, and it can therefore be restrained if it seeks to go beyond the terms laid down to limit its activities.[7]

By the terms of their creation, however, it has been shown that the State monopolies are, in effect, subject to the control and direction of parent departments, and they are therefore no more democratic, in the sense of being responsible to popular opinion, than the departments themselves are. May it not be argued, however, that in spite of this structure they are responsible to Parliament, as the 'Grand Inquest of the Nation'? This is a question concerning which Parliament, Press and public have all been increasingly concerned in recent years. It has become, since the programme of nationalisation took effect, a major constitutional question.

It will be profitable, therefore, in discussing this question to consider what constitutional machinery already exists, whereby control or influence in the working of these vast monopolies can be exerted. Each of them prepares an annual report on the year's working, and following its approval by the Minister, and its subsequent publication, a date is specified for a debate in Parliament on the report. Of necessity, this involves a considerable time-lag. Thus, the first report of the British Transport Commission, covering the year 1948, was published on September 7th, 1949, and the debate on it in the House of Commons took place on December 1st, 1949. Thus, a whole year elapsed before the opportunity arose for an informed discussion, even on the general principles in accordance with which the Transport Commission was working. Manifestly, the evils of this system are greater

---

[7] *Smith* v. *London Transport Executive* [1949] 2 All E.R. 295; *National Coal Board* v. *Hornby* [1949] 2 All E.R. 615.

when the monopoly is working uneconomically or ineffici-
ently, and the weaknesses of this procedure were fully exposed
in the catastrophic muddle produced by the Overseas Food
Corporation in its notorious ground-nuts scheme. Even so,
however, when after adverse criticisms on the accounts of
the enterprise from the Public Accounts Committee of the
House of Commons, this unfortunate episode was debated in
the House of Lords on December 14th, 1949, Lord Hall took
the disturbing view that in spite of the gross waste of public
money, there was no point in having an inquiry. What was
past was past, and the financial situation would be clearer
when the Public Accounts Committee made its report to the
House of Commons. The extent to which this complacency
was justified may be discovered by those who care to do so
by perusal of the illuminating volume on the Ground Nuts
adventure which was published shortly afterwards.

At the present time, the position of the members of State
boards and of the Minister in charge of the parent department may be summed up as follows: The Minister answers
in Parliament on the general running of the Board. It is no
part of his duty to answer questions relating to day to day
administration.

It will be generally agreed that any other principle would
make the Minister's position almost untenable. Nevertheless,
there is a real and growing danger than in these circumstances Parliamentary control will be completely illusory.
Even Mr. Morrison appeared to contemplate that situation
without undue concern in opening a debate on the control of
nationalised industries in the House of Commons on October
25th, 1950, for he said:

> 'It was often argued that when it came to sheer business of
> commercial matters the machinery of the State necessarily
> worked slower than that of ordinary commercial concerns.
> There was truth in that, not because of any inherent incom-
> petence in the Civil Service or in State administration but
> because Ministers were absolutely responsible to Parliament for
> everything that happened in their departments. It was right
> that that should be so. The Civil Service machine must there-
> fore be cautious and careful because of the possibility of Parlia-
> mentary trouble, or trouble with the public, or criticism in the
> Press.

'There was a series of economic, industrial, or commercial concerns regarding which it was appropriate that they should be managed by public corporations rather than by State departments. When Parliament set up public corporations it was trying to get the best of both worlds; and sometimes got it. It was trying, on the one hand, to have a public concern or public authority, and on the other to graft on to it a commercial or business management capable of acting with speed and in a situation whereby it could make mistakes without causing an immediate Parliamentary crisis or embarrassment for a Minister.

'It followed that if a public corporation was set up in order to get the advantages of commercial management and it was freed from meticulous Parliamentary control, then details of Parliamentary question and ministerial management and supervision and control would have to be given up.'

A few months later on July 4, 1951, the House of Lords debated the same question, this time with particular reference to the position of peers who served on the Boards of nationalised industries. This raised the question whether such peers should be called upon to answer in the House of Lords for the work of their monopolies. Speaking on behalf of the Government on this point, Viscount Alexander said:

'Nothing should be done which might impair the responsibility of Ministers to Parliament or prejudice the freedom of the Boards from meticulous political supervision of their day-to-day management. Ministers alone were responsible to Parliament for the way in which the Boards were conducted. The chairman and members of any Board were responsible to the Minister by whom they were removed. Anything which weakened the position of Ministers *ipso facto* weakened Parliament, and no Board member should be expected to assume a role of accountability to Parliament which was proper to the responsible Minister."

This makes somewhat clearer than Mr. Morrison's statement did that the official view is that the Boards are the creatures of the Ministries. This adds point to the comment of Mr. Bird upon the course of debates on reports of nationalised industries:

"The Minister opens the debate with a formal statement which need do no more than recapitulate some of the main points in the Public Relations Officer's summary of the report. He then turns to more current topics—coal prices or transport charges—and by the time the first Opposition speaker has made his much interrupted reply, the stage is set, not for a sober review, but rather for a display of backbench backbiting. It becomes a rambling and incoherent debate, to which even the sheepish silence of the average shareholders' meeting might be preferred.'[8]

It requires a more lively imagination than the ordinary citizen possesses to see in this an effective Parliamentary control. Indeed, scepticism with regard to the operation of nationalised industries is now widespread amongst those who have the best opportunities for observing them at close quarters. The various nationalisation Acts contain provisions for consultation between Boards and workpeople. Thus, Section 95 of the Transport Act, 1947, makes it the duty of the Transport Commission to consult with workers' organisations concerning the safety, health and welfare of persons employed by it. There is, unhappily, little evidence that this duty has been widely exercised. Thus, during 1950 and 1951, railwaymen of the Western Region of the Transport Commission's railways were seeking to discuss with the Commission the abandonment of safety-signalling devices in operation before nationalisation. Failing in their purpose, they asked the Minister of Transport to receive a delegation to discuss the matter—a request which was refused. Again, the National Union of Mineworkers has been so disturbed by the working of the National Coal Board that it has set up an investigation into the expenditure of public money by the Board. These things are scarcely indicative of 'that participation of the whole body of the people in the administration of its own affairs', so naïvely predicted by the Webbs.

A further point of constitutional importance has emerged during the debates on nationalisation. It is that the Minister may refuse to disclose to Parliament directions given by him to a public corporation, where he considers that it is contrary to the national interest to make such a disclosure. Professor Friedmann rightly attacks this privilege as a violation of British constitutional practice. As he observes:

'The cases where the disclosure of the directors to a public corporation would be against the national interest should be

8 'Public Boards and Public Accountability', in *Lloyd's Bank Review*, January, 1950, p. 15.

rare indeed. Where they do exist, it should not be beyond the
ingenuity of Parliamentary procedure to provide for secrecy.'[9]

Actually, however, it would seem that in practice, Ministers
have preferred to avoid giving formal directions on policy
wherever possible, but have preferred to exercise their un-
doubted power to influence the working of the monopoly
by means of a consultation or a conference with members
of Boards.[10] In this way, of course, the possibility of Parliamentary scrutiny of what is decided is avoided altogether.
This situation is the more unsatisfactory inasmuch as the
effect of such discussions is frequently to modify policy which
may be commercially sound in the light of the political or
social economic theories favoured by the Minister. If the
result of such persuasion is a heavy financial loss, then the
Board of the monopoly is not unreasonable in expecting
the Ministry to underwrite it, and to undertake the defence
of the policy in Parliament.

Two further points in the working of nationalised industries should be noticed. The first relates to the reference of
their affairs to the Public Accounts Committee of the House
of Commons. This only occurs when they get into financial
difficulties, and must therefore be rescued by fresh grants
of public money. Even the most confirmed enthusiast for
nationalisation can scarcely visualise this as a permanent
condition of their existence. Since they are monopolist,
they can ultimately fix the prices in exchange for which the
public can enjoy their services. Yet the fixing of rates to
obliterate deficits will be no guarantee of efficient management, nor any assurance that the public interest has been
safeguarded since the possibility of alternative service has
been destroyed. This involves therefore consideration of a
second point. In 1948, there was placed on the Statute
Book the Monopolies and Restrictive Practices (Inquiry and
Control) Act, which provides for the setting up of a Commission of Enquiry, to investigate particular trades and industries whose activities appear to fall within the terms of the
Act. For reasons which are by no means apparent, the State

---

[9] 'The New Public Corporations', in *The Modern Law Review*, 1947, p. 392.

[10] E. Davies, 'Ministerial Control and Parliamentary Responsibility of
Nationalised Industries', *Political Quarterly*, 1950, p. 150.

monopolies have been excluded from the purview of the Commission, whose activities in respect of them might possibly have embarrassed the parent Ministry in the manner indicated by Viscount Alexander in the debate in the House of Lords in July, 1951.

The remarkable immunity of State monopolies from the supervision of the Public Accounts Committee of the House of Commons is accompanied, as we have seen, by their exemption from the requirement to submit to audit by the Comptroller and Auditor-General. This second immunity applies only to the monopolies which control industrial undertakings. It does not extend to such bodies as the New Town Development Corporation to which the public authority analogy is applicable to a greater degree. The defence of this additional immunity, advanced by Labour Ministers, was based on the fallacious analogy between State monopolies and public companies, an analogy which, as we have seen, is utterly misleading. There is no responsibility to any body of shareholders, and insofar as responsibility exists at all, it is to a government department, and through that department, to Parliament. There can thus be no justification for the continuation of this immunity, which has rendered situations such as that revealed in the Scarcroft scandal possible.

The nationalised undertakings are bound by the Acts creating them to prepare annual reports at the end of each financial year for presentation to the Minister, who is under a statutory obligation to lay it before Parliament. Such reports will normally include any directions by the Minister unless, as has been mentioned above, he has informed the corporation that it is against the national interest or, in the cases of electricity, transport, gas, iron and steel, it is against the interests of national security to do so. Moreover, in the case of the Iron and Steel Corporation, the Minister can exclude a direction if he accepts the contention of the corporation that it is contrary to the commercial interests of the corporation to publish it. The reports so far published, have been voluminous, extending to several hundred pages. They have been widely commented on in the Press, although only a brief account of their contents could be given. The presentation of the reports to Parliament has been accompanied by a debate of one-day's duration, during which Government and Parliament have attempted to grapple with the problems that the establishment of these monopolistic leviathans has created. This procedure has proved far from satisfactory, however, since of necessity, the Minister has appeared before Parliament in the role of defender of the monopoly, and of his department's policy in respect of it. This has prevented the debate from doing more than raise a wide variety of points, to which no precise answers need be given. In the last resort, the Minister has been able to rely on the governmental majority to ward off scrutiny that has appeared to him to search too closely into the mechanism of monopoly-departmental relationship.

Although in the debates in the House of Commons and in the House of Lords, anxiety over the unsatisfactory working of nationalised industries has been general, the Labour Government repeatedly rejected proposals for a higher degree of Parliamentary or public control than exists at present. At bottom, the issue is again a constitutional one, for as Lord Salisbury put it, in the House of Lords,

> 'if an industry was privately owned the shareholders could at the annual meeting outvote and, if necessary, dismiss the directors or they could sell their shares. Once an industry was nationalized the shareholders could not get out of the concern and if they endeavoured to exercise some control through their elected representatives in Parliament it was unlikely, no matter how badly an industry was being administered, that the directors, who were ultimately the Government, would be defeated in the House of Commons.'

It is only necessary to express the problem in these terms to expose the fallacy of comparing the position of the public in respect of nationalised industries to that of shareholders. A shareholder has, in any circumstances, *some* minimum of rights conferred by law.

The only concession which the Labour Government made to rising public feeling was the suggestion that each nationalised industry might be the subject of a seven-yearly enquiry, although neither Mr. Morrison nor Mr. Noel-Baker, who both put forward this suggestion in the debate on October 25th, 1950, specified how the enquiry should be conducted, who should conduct it, or what their powers should be. This certainly falls very far short of what many want to see. Mr. Butler, speaking for the Opposition, advocated the reference to the activities of the State monopolies to the Monopolies Commission, and the laying of their accounts before the Public Accounts Committee. He also wanted to see the Consumers' Councils made effective. For that, they should be independent of the department, and representative of local associations. In the House of Lords, Lord Strabolgi pointed out that three methods of Parliamentary control had been widely advocated: (1) a permanent standing committee of members of both Houses, with power to examine Ministers and members of nationalised Boards; (2) the setting up of a select committee every three, four or five years to examine each nationalised industry. Such a committee should have the assistance of the Comptroller and Auditor-General; (3) the reference of the affairs of nationalised industries to the Monopolies Commission. He himself favoured the third course.

Whatever method of control be ultimately adopted, it will be apparent that State monopolies have so far been a further adventure in departmental irresponsibility. Behind the façade of public ownership, departments have pursued their respective policies in industry and trade, not always with conspicuous success, and very largely immune from constitutional check. This has been a strange consequence of the rather crude delineation of the control of industry by the people three or four decades ago.

Chapter 12

The Control of Administrative Power
Abroad

BEFORE the task of summing up the constitutional changes which have been described in the preceding chapters is attempted, it will be profitable to say something briefly of the treatment of similar problems abroad. Obviously the experience of no two countries is exactly the same, but some picture of differing modes of approach can be obtained from a rapid consideration of French and American practice.

1. The Administrative Problem in France

In many respects the French approach to this problem stands in sharp contrast to our own, and this difference can be traced ultimately to a different political and constitutional evolution. For example, one striking feature of French experience is the progressive and orderly development of a genuine administrative law in the past century and a half, precisely at the time when there have been numerous and widely-different experiments in government, most of them unsuccessful. Possibly it may be that political instability has brought home to the French people the necessity for a partially autonomous administration, with a fully developed theory of administrative responsibility for its acts. Again, the weakness and impermanence of French governments has made it all the more necessary that administration should proceed, largely unaffected by changes in the political arena.

The point of departure in the evolution of the modern French administrative system is to be found in the various constitutional experiments which followed the outbreak of the French Revolution in 1789. That revolution was necessary because, although French had faced similar constitutional problems to those which overshadowed English politics in the seventeenth century, they had been solved in a different way. In France, as in England, in the Middle Ages, representative institutions had gradually taken shape in the States-General, but this had failed to achieve the organic unity which Parliament had done in England by the close of the Middle Ages, and it therefore proved an ineffective barrier to royal despotism. Accordingly, in the eighteenth century, France was a centralised, and almost absolute monarchy. Whereas in England in 1688 the principle of Parliamentary sovereignty had finally triumphed, so that the legislative power of Parliament had superseded the rival claims of the Crown, in France legislative power had been concentrated in the King and therefore the distinction between law and ordinance had ceased to be of importance. Both emanated from the King, so that whereas in England the legislature had triumphed, in France it was the executive which had become all powerful, as it did again under Napoleon. This explains, to a considerable degree why the various constitutional experiments embarked upon before the advent of Napoleon, sought to establish as complete a separation of powers—legislative, judicial and executive—as was possible. It explains also why even today France tolerates the existence of a relatively weak executive with equanimity, and why, in addition, it is necessary for the departments to have the power to keep the administrative machine in motion, to a considerable extent independently of political change. Failure to understand the political background of the modern French administrative system is possibly the main reason for Dicey's profound misunderstanding of it.[1]

Throughout the various constitutional changes which France has experienced since the outbreak of the first revolution at the end of the eighteenth century, the practical application of the theory of the separation of powers has preserved the conception of an administration which is independent in its own sphere. In this respect the French

[1] The chief features of successive French constitutions are admirably summarised in Part II of *Government by Decree* by M. A. Sieghart.

system differs sharply from our own, in which, in theory, the administration enjoys simply those functions which are conceded to it by Parliament. Moreover, as a result of the reorganisation of French administration carried out during the First Empire, some of which had proved permanent, the central administration is admittedly supreme in respect of local administration, although in the past half-century there has been some tendency towards decentralisation. Thus, in the local administration (the *commune*), the Mayor is elected by the Municipal Council, which is also elected, but the Mayor's function is dual. 'As a representative of the *commune* he has autonomous powers, which include an ordaining power in matters of police; as an agent of the State he is the lowest link of the hierarchical order and is subject to hierarchical discipline and hierarchical control. The Municipal Council is mainly concerned with local finance and local expenditure, but is, as a rule, not responsible for public order and matters of police.'[2]

Above the *commune* is the department, whose administrative representatives are the *préfet*, who is the representative of the central government, and as such is subject to control from the centre, and a General Council elected by a direct adult suffrage. Both *commune* and department have, in addition, local administrations which, though not formally subject to the hierarchical control of the superior central administration, are nevertheless subject to its *tutelle administrative*, which expresses itself in the power to annul decisions of communal and departmental councils, where it would appear that they have trespassed upon the functions of the central administration.

Probably the most striking point of contrast between the English and French administrative systems, however, is to be found in the autonomous powers of the French Central Departments of State. We have seen that this is due to a mixture of causes—to the fact that the French Royal executive during the period of the monarchy was never brought under Parliamentary control as it was in England; it was also due to the practical application of the doctrine of the separation of powers at the time of the first revolution. Finally, it has

[2] Sieghart *op. cit.* p. 207.

been due to practical necessity, for France has undergone a long succession of constitutional experiments since 1789, and even during the Third and Fourth Republics, there has been the recurrent difficulty of establishing a stable ministry. Through all these changes, the permanent administration has continued to function, and in order that it might do this effectively, it has been necessary to concede to it autonomy within its own sphere. One important practical consequence of this is that in France the departments possess a power of law-making which is not the consequence of concession from the Assembly, as it is in England. It is autonomous, and it extends, not only to those spheres in which the departments can be regarded as implementing, by means of more detailed regulations, the commands of Parliament, as expressed in general laws, but also to spheres where the Assembly may not have legislated, but which are regarded as traditionally, by constitutional usage, within the sphere of activity of that department. Such regulations are described by Duguit, in his treatise on the French constitution as *règlements autonomes*, and they deal with either the organisation of the administrative service itself, or with police matters, in the Continental, as distinct from the English, sense of the word. These include not only public security and public order, but also many matters of public health. Two things must be noticed in connexion with this autonomous power of the administration, however. Where important extensions of it are contemplated (e.g. in connexion with modern extensions of the social services), these are embodied in statutes. Indeed, this must be the case where a new department is created. Secondly, the legislation of the departments is limited by existing Statute Law. Unless a statute otherwise provides, departmental ordinances have no power to alter it. Finally, the Courts are frequently called upon to determine whether a department has trespassed beyond its true limits. For the determination of these questions either a special tribunal of conflicts with equal numbers of ordinary and administrative judges or the *Conseil d'État* is the forum.

The logical division of governmental powers into legislative, judicial and administrative, and the achievement of the autonomy of each, has not necessarily worked in favour of personal freedom. As Mr. C. J. Hamson noted recently in his special articles in *The Times*,[3] the fact that in France the ordinary police are regarded as part of the judiciary, and not of the executive, has meant that their acts are frequently subject to no judicial scrutiny. In this respect, therefore, our system today works more effectively in protection of individual liberties than the French. On the other hand, what the French have done, and what we have so far failed to do, is to bring a wide range of administrative acts within the scrutiny of the Courts. This it has done through the creation of the *Conseil d'État*. Of this court (though it is in reality more than a court) Mr. Hamson says:

'The *Conseil d'État* has, in the critical particular, been spectacularly successful. Not only has it subjected to its control the whole of the administrative machine of a modern State but it has established itself as a Court in every sense of the word, with its judges holding office, in fact, during good behaviour until a retiring age and free from any subservience to the executive. Indeed, if they have any bias it is in favour of the subject and of what they term the equality of sacrifice. Having established its jurisdiction, the *Conseil* centralized and universalized it, as the King's Courts once did in England; it is *le juge de droit commun en matière administrative*; there is no administrative act which it may not examine and sanction, if needs be by *annulation* and the award of damages; full appeal (*appel*) lies to it as of right from any administrative tribunal, and even if that tribunal is specially empowered to render final judgment, a *recours en cassation* (which may roughly be translated as an appeal upon point of law or of form) is always open. So firmly established is its jurisdiction that it would seem barely credible to a Frenchman to attempt to withdraw from the administrative court cognizance of any administrative act.'

The *Conseil d'État* combines in itself a number of distinct judicial functions. It hears at first instance claims by a subject that a branch of the administration has acted *ultra vires*, and also all cases in which the subject seeks *annulation* of some administrative decision. Further it decides all those *contentieux de pleine juridiction* (which may be described as proceedings to secure redress against damage caused by an administrative decision, where *annulation* itself is not usually available), for which no special administrative tribunal

[3] February 20, 1951: February 21, 1951.

has been established. Again, the *Conseil d'État* has appellate jurisdiction in respect of those *contentieux de pleine jurisdiction* which are decided at first instance by the Councils of the Prefect and by some special and colonial administrative courts. Lastly, the *Conseil d'État* has jurisdiction *en cassation* in respect of every decision of an administrative tribunal for which there is no ordinary appeal to the *Conseil d'État*. The principal difference between an appeal and jurisdiction *en cassation* is that where the latter is invoked, the appellant is asking for *annulation* of the administrative decision on the ground of *ultra vires*. In form, however, it is not a complaint against the act of an administrator (as the *Conseil's* jurisdiction at first instance in respect of *annulation* is). It is an appeal against the *ultra vires* act of an administrative judge.

In view of this complete and powerful system of administrative courts in France, it is very nearly true to say that for every administrative wrong there is a remedy, which can be pursued, not in the ordinary Courts, but in the Administrative Courts. Much of the effectiveness of the system necessarily depends upon the vigour and vision of the administrative judges themselves, and in particular, those of the *Conseil d'État*. The testimony of recent writers is that they have shown no hesitation in maintaining and in extending their jurisdiction in respect of the activities of the departments. Thus, both Mr. Hamson and Mrs. Sieghart notice that the *Conseil d'État* exercises jurisdiction, not only where the claim is in respect of *excès* or *détournement de pouvoir* (which occurs when an authority, though acting within its competence, uses its powers for a different purpose from that for which they were conferred), but also in respect of administrative non-discretionary acts if they are deemed to be *insuffisamment motivé*, that is to say, if the administrative order does not set out upon the fact of it correctly and sufficiently the grounds for the order. In the case of discretionary powers, if an order based on such a power is attacked by a subject, the *Conseil d'État* requires the Department to set out its reasons for acting, and the Court then has power to enquire into their sufficiency. Should the Department persist in refusing to give reasons for its action, the *Conseil d'État* will now proceed to judgment on the basis that the allegations of the plaintiff attacking the Department are correct. Recently, the Court has gone even further. If the Department alleges for the exercise of a discretionary power a reason which on the fact of it is adequate, the Court may nevertheless annul the order, if it appears to be based on a *fait matériellement inexact*.

It will be evident even to the non-specialist that we are here in territory into which we in England have not as yet entered. In England, as we have seen, as soon as the character of an Act has been determined to be administrative and not quasi-judicial, the Courts are powerless to aid the subject. Moreover, the extent of the control exercised by the *Conseil d'État* can be perceived from examples drawn from the decisions of that Court. They show a detailed scrutiny of administrative motives from which the English Courts have, upon occasion, ostentatiously dissociated themselves. As Mr. Hamson has remarked:

'We seem to have fallen between two stools: anxious to maintain a theoretically universal rule of law, we preserve merely the fiction of a formal legalism and in fact abandon the executive to its own unattractive instincts.'

It hardly needs to be added that it is principally of the *Conseil d'État* that Professor Robson is thinking when he advocates the establishment of an administrative Court of Appeal in England.

2. *The Administrative Problem in the United States*

American experience in the control of administrative power has some striking lessons for the English reader. In the first place, he is conscious from the outset that he is dealing with social experience not too dissimilar from his own. Moreover, that experience has taken place in a legal setting which is derived from the same source as our own— the Common Law which was continuously developed by judicial wisdom and political tolerance in the period between the Norman Conquest and the American War of Independence, at the time, significantly, when Lord Mansfield was Lord Chief Justice, and when Blackstone's *Commentaries* had just been published. On the other hand, the English reader is conscious from the outset of the overriding importance

of the American Constitution, and of the doctrine of separation of powers which it embodied, in all legal and political
discussion. Finally, he is aware of the vigour of American
thought in its readiness to accept the existence of new
problems, calling for precise methods of investigation, to
be followed by remedial measures. It is fashionable today
to regard American society as less responsive to the need for
social change than our own. Such criticisms are superficial
and inaccurate. A distinguished young American lawyer
whose researches upon English and American administrative law have recently been published, concluded his survey
of *American Administrative Law* with the following observations:

'The role of the State has expanded as much in America
in the past century as it has in this country,[4] and has been
accompanied by as great an expansion of governmental power.
It is significant, however, that this new development—the
growth of administrative law—had proceeded along different
lines in America from those it has followed here. The tendency
in America has been towards the *judicialization* of these new
forces of social control—towards fitting them into the existing
constitutional framework, and, above all, towards their sub-
ordination to law. American administrative agencies thus bid
fair to repeat the history of the executive tribunals of the sixteenth century, which, in time, were fitted into their place in
the pre-existing legal order. The Executive in this country,[4]
on the other hand, has become by far the dominant agency of
social control, upsetting the historic balance between the
branches of government. The *real* power of the Executive has
been growing enormously at the expense of the theoretical
parliamentary hegemony. This shift in the "constitutional
centre of gravity" is not peculiar to this country.[4] It is a characteristic of the present century, and when carried to an extreme,
leads to the authoritarian state. It is surely of some significance
in the evaluation of supposedly inevitable developments here,
that this trend has been resisted in America to a much greater
extent than it has on this side of the Atlantic. It is in the problem of the canalization of executive power that the American
experience should prove of the greatest value as a guide in this
country."[5]

In facing the problem of administrative encroachment,
the United States has started with the very great advantage

[4] i.e. Great Britain.
[5] Schwarz, *American Administrative Law*, p. 128.

of a written Constitution, attributing specific functions to President, Congress, and the Courts, and with a division of power between federal and states governments. To the Supreme Court there has been attributed the function of preventing encroachments by one part of government against another through its interpretation of the constitution, Inevitably in its decisions it has not escaped criticism, and on more than one occasion, it has appeared to provoke a major constitutional crisis by adopting an interpretation which has failed to satisfy the desires of powerful interests or persons. Nevertheless, the fact that, over a long period, the balance has been fairly evenly preserved, and that on the whole, the desires of the American people have been correctly reflected is shown by the fact that these crisis have not issued either in abridgment of the function of the courts, or in an overthrow of the system established by the Constitution. Many of President Franklin Roosevelt's measures in the achievement of a 'New Deal' involved far-reaching extensions of the functions and powers of the administrative departments and agencies. It was no doubt as galling to the American Executive as it would be to their English counterparts to find that some of what they proposed was invalidated as too great an encroachment upon individual rights. Nevertheless, it should not be overlooked that the Courts had accepted an important part of the Executive's measures when, on a narrower interpretation of the Constitution, it would have been possible to hold that bad as well. The Courts, that is to say, were not hostile either to social change, or to an extension of the powers of the administration; but, under the American Constitution, they were charged with the duty of preventing the overthrow of the balance which the Constitution had sought to establish, and when they considered the point of danger had been reached, the Executive's measures were declared void.

The possession of such a power by the Courts may seem strange to English eyes, yet it has been constantly exercised in America. It is applicable alike to encroachments by the Executive and to encroachments by Congress, and finally, to encroachments by both, as was the case with much of that part of the New Deal legislation which was invalidated by the Courts during the first Presidency of Franklin Roosevelt.

In the United States there are two types of administrative organ which exercise general governmental powers giving rise to the problem of effective control. In the first place, some federal government departments themselves exercise wide powers. Professor Schwarz points out that there are nine of these, of which the most important is the Department of Agriculture, which exercises powers under about forty-four regulatory statutes.

> 'The most important of these are the Packers and Stockyards Act (fixing of rates and charges of stockyards, and commission men, and prevention of unfair practices by packers), the Commodities Exchange Act (supervision of exchanges on which grain, butter, eggs and potatoes are dealt in), the Agricultural Marketing Act (orders fixing the price of milk to be paid farmers and marketing quotas for fruits and vegetables), the Agricultural Adjustment Act of 1938 (marketing quotas for wheat, cotton, corn, and tobacco), the Sugar Act (marketing quotas for sugar), the Pure Food and Drugs Act, the Tobacco Inspection Act, the Poisonous Insecticides Act, and so on.'[6]

Where federal departments exercise functions such as these, there are fairly close resemblances between them and their British counterparts. It should be pointed out, however, that rule-making by the American department runs the risk of being invalidated on one of two distinct grounds. In the first place, the department in legislating may have gone outside the terms of the statute conferring power on it. This is an ordinary *ultra vires* question, such as constantly arises with regard to departmental legislation in England. Even if the rules are within the statute conferring rule-making power, however, the statute itself may be invalidated, as being beyond the competence of Congress to pass. In practice, departmental legislation is most frequently invalidated on the first ground, but the second is always there, and some of the New Deal legislation failed because it was held to be unconstitutional.

The second type of American administrative agency is the Commission, of which the first to be created was the Interstate Commerce Commission, which owes its origin to

---

[6] *op. cit.* pp. 9-10, citing Feller, *Administrative Justice* (1938) in 2 7 *Survey Graphic* 494.

the Interstate Commerce Act of 1887. Such commissions, like the departments, have the power to make rules binding on the community within the terms of their delegation, and they also possess the power to adjudicate in respect of breaches of those rules. On the other hand, the federal Commissions differ sharply from the British national monopoly corporations, in that their Boards enjoy security of tenure. Their members are appointed for a fixed term, are irremovable by the President, and unlike the heads of the administrative departments, they are not accountable to him. The result is that, within the sphere of activity committed to them by Congress, they tend to become independent specialists, independent of politics. This may, upon occasion, lead to difficulties in co-ordinating the policy of the executive with that of the commissions, but it is a further illustration of the American distrust of centralised omnipotence. Moreover, unlike the British nationalised monopolies, the Commissions do not own the industries which they regulate.

If we turn to the powers of adjudication possessed by the administrative agencies, we shall again find some striking differences from the English system, or rather lack of system. The American system of administrative adjudication is a good deal more formal, although it is recognised that the primary object of departmental activity is not an adjudication of private rights, but the promotion of a social policy. It is here that the American counterpart to the English concept of 'natural justice' has scope for operation. The federal and state constitutions provide that no person may be deprived of life, liberty or property otherwise than by 'due process of law'. Accordingly the federal courts are free to scrutinise the proceedings of administrative tribunals in order to ensure that this constitutional requirement has been satisfied. Hence, the administrative agencies, in order to protect themselves, have evolved a procedure for hearings which, though it avoids the technicality of the procedure in the ordinary courts, has nevertheless clearly defined stages and characteristics. In this way, some of the worst mistakes of some of our English administrative tribunals are avoided. Nevertheless, most American administrative agencies are open to the same fundamental criticism as their

English counterpart that they combine within themselves the functions of legislator, prosecutor and judge. This is a striking departure from the principle of the separation of powers, upon which the American Constitution is nominally based. Americans, however, have recognised that in a swiftly-changing society, it is impossible to apply this principle with rigidity. They have admitted the fact of successive and increasing delegation of legislative power to administrative agencies. Nevertheless, it is always possible for the Courts to hold any specific example delegation void as too wide. This is in fact what occurred in the celebrated case of *Schechter Poultry Corporation* v. *United States*,[7] when the Supreme Court invalidated a large part of the National Industrial Recovery Act of 1933. Section 3 of the Act authorized the President to approve 'codes of fair competition' for particular trades and industries. When the code was approved, its provisions constituted the 'standards of fair competition' for the trade or industry, and breach of such standards was punishable by penalties. In the majority of the Supreme Court invalidating this Act, judges so different in outlook as Chief Justice Hughes and Mr. Justice Cardozo concurred in the view that delegation in such terms could not occur under the constitution. Where in any particular case the line is to be drawn will remain a matter of judicial decision, but the *Schechter Case*, and similar decisions of the Supreme Court stress the fact that there exists in the American Constitution a power in the judiciary to prevent excessive delegations of power by the legislature to the executive—a provision which is conspicuously lacking from the English constitution.

One other important safeguard in respect of delegated legislation exists in the United States. No American administrative agency has power to amend a statute, either that which conferred power on it, or any other. Accordingly, nothing similar to the 'Henry VIII clause' can appear in American legislation. The result is that in the United States, discussion upon the question of preventing the abuse of rule-making power has concentrated upon the procedure to be followed, and not upon the question of abdication

[7] (1935) 295 U.S. 495.

of power by Congress. For example, the desirability of consultation and conferences with interests affected by the proposed sub-legislation has been stressed, and progressively that this has tended to become a characteristic of the rule-making process, as practised by the agencies. Again, the American Administrative Procedure Act of 1946 has laid down certain minimum conditions of publicity for proposed rule-making, where the proposed rules are substantive in nature. Following publication of such notice, the agency must give interested persons an opportunity to present their views, either orally or in writing. In many cases this occurs at a public hearing. Such hearings are most frequently informal, but where the hearings affect clearly-defined and competing interests, they may assume an 'adversary' character, in which case they will tend to assume a judicial character, with pleas for the exclusion of documents, cross-examination of persons giving evidence, and so forth. It may be that this type of procedure is not ideally suited for important questions, but it should be remembered that, since the independent administrative agency is not under the direct control of the department, and since neither an independent agency nor a rule-making department is directly responsible to Congress, Congress does not ordinarily possess the power to approve or annul administrative regulations, such as is possessed by Parliament here, although in the case of the Reorganisation Act of 1939, which gave the President wide powers to reorganise the executive by Presidential order, the procedure which is usual in Britain was followed, and Congress retained the power to nullify Presidential orders.

The American administrative agencies exercise a wide power of adjudication in matters comparable in variety and importance with those which come before administrative tribunals in England. In the United States, however, control over administrative tribunals by the ordinary Courts is wider and more effective. Indeed, as Professor Schwarz points out,[8] it has been assimilated to appeals from lower courts. In the first place, the statute conceding power to the agency often provides, directly or indirectly for judicial review. Thus, the agency may have to seek the assistance of

[8] *op. cit.* p. 109.

the Court to carry out its decision. Alternatively, the statute may provide that the administrative decision should be operative unless the person affected seeks to obtain judicial review of it in the ordinary Courts. This is now the most common method of dealing with administrative decisions.

Where, however, the statute is silent on the question, the subject may seek the assistance of the Courts by applying for some specific remedy, which is normally the injunction. This remedy has been very widely used to restrain administrative activities in the United States, and the almost complete absence of any similar development in England therefore stands in sharp contrast with American experience. Undoubtedly it is due to the fact that the American Courts, under the Constitution, occupy a more powerful position, *vis-à-vis* the executive, than their English counterparts. Since they have the power to declare either Congressional legislation or a Presidential act invalid as unconstitutional, their exercise of a general power of review over administrative decisions has been regarded as a matter of course, and the general principle of judicial review has been emphatically reaffirmed in the Administrative Procedure Act of 1946, and its function has been defined as 'a check on the administrative branch of government—a check against excess of power and abusive exercise of power in derogation of private right.'[9] Indeed, in the United States the problem has been rather to define the limits of the power of the Courts to overthrow the decisions of administrative agencies, and the Courts themselves have developed a 'substantial evidence' rule—i.e. that the ordinary Courts will not disturb a finding of fact of an administrative tribunal, if it is supported by substantial evidence. The question of deciding the weight of the evidence is one for the administrative agency itself. How far, under the limits of this rule a Court can, or should, re-examine the findings of fact of the administrative agency is a question which has been extensively discussed in the United States, but the position may be sharply contrasted with that which exists in Great Britain where, in the bulk of cases coming before administrative tribunals today there is no appeal to the ordinary Courts either on questions of law or

[9] *Report of the Attorney-General's Committee*, p. 76.

of fact. Both the American and English Courts, however, proceed upon the basis that where jurisdiction is conferred on an administrative agency in certain circumstances, it is for the ordinary Courts to determine whether those circumstances exist. This is, of course, a finding of fact, but collateral to the decision upon the facts in issue in the case.[10]

How important it is that an administrative agency should not be able finally to decide the limits of the power to adjudicate conferred upon it by statute may be seen from the determined efforts of the worst of English administrative tribunals, the Rent Courts, to escape from the limits prescribed by the Furnished Houses (Rent Control) Act, 1946.[11]

[10] Per. Coleridge J. in *Bunbury* v. *Fuller* (1853) 23 L.J.Ex. 29; and per Luxmore L.J. in *White and Collins* v. *Minister of Health* [1939] 2 K.B. 838.

[11] A recent example is *R.* v. *Fulham Rent Tribunal: Ex parte Marks* [1951] W.N. 405.

Chapter 13

The Constitutional Problem Today

THE purpose of the preceding chapters has been to draw attention to the existence in Great Britain of a major constitutional problem directly affecting the future welfare of every citizen. The problem may be shortly defined as the difficulty of maintaining either any constitutional system in the real sense of the word, or any security, either of person or property, in face of the continual and relentless encroachments of the executive. It may perhaps be suggested by way of minimising the gravity of the situation in which we now stand that as British people are habitually reasonable people, the formal dangers of our position do not accurately reflect the true situation. This, however, is no answer. No-one doubts that the vast bulk of the population of these islands are, not only reasonable, but politically mature. By that is meant primarily that they can endure opposition, even when it is based upon premises which they reject, and that they can act with restraint in the day of power. Unfortunately, however, we live in a century in which political maturity and political tolerance are qualities which are not necessarily so widespread as they were a century ago, and when the dangers arising from the accession to power of an intolerant body of extremists is greater. In the days of prosperity and stability, all political activity is confined within fairly narrow limits, since there is a natural reluctance to disturb a system which is obviously working well. It is in times of difficulty that the dangers from extremists are greatest, as the experience of Continental Europe since 1919 abundantly shows. It is then that desperate remedies have the best chance of being tried, and when there may be a general disposition to entrust a group, or even a single man, with uncontrolled powers to make far-reaching experiments. Under the conditions which now exist in Great Britain this can be quickly and *legally* achieved by continuing the present process of delegating governmental powers, legislative and judicial, to government departments, and by continuing either to exclude or to confine within narrow limits the right of recourse to the ordinary courts.

It is not sufficiently appreciated here that this is exactly how the majority of continental authoritarian regimes of the inter-war period came into existence. As contrasted with the stable conditions of the pre-war years, the experience of the inter-war years appeared to be so abnormal that it could only be faced with the assistance of special powers to meet emergency situations. But these situations lasted longer, and their inroads upon social life proved to be more far-reaching, than had been expected. Thus the use of emergency powers came to be regarded as normal. Nor was Great Britain entirely immune from this habit of thought. Reference has already been made to the writings of an influential group within the Labour Party during the inter-war years, who wished to transform English society by precisely the methods which were being widely employed upon the Continent, even though the objects in view may have differed.

Describing the rise of the Nazis to power in Germany during the inter-war period, a German legal writer of eminence describes exactly this revolution in governmental technique. He points out that even in a community where the Rule of Law has won general acceptance, there may be emergency situations (e.g. a general strike) in which the normal guarantees of personal liberty may have to yield to fuller grants of governmental power. Even so, however, the Rule of Law has been impaired if the grant goes further, or endures longer, than the necessities of the situation justify. He continues in his account of inter-war Germany:

'The Rule of Law was broken often and for some years continuously by the various German emergency measures. The decisive thing was not the invalidation of law by emergency powers during the critical days of 1923, but the getting used to it. In the most quiet times between 1924 and 1929 it would have been possible to draw some conclusions from the experience gathered and to bring the problems of emergency measures under legal control by defining conditions and limits, review and repeal, and by regulating the relations between the different authorities concerned. But neither the parliament nor the government and its professional legal advisers nor the lawyers energetically endeavoured to create such a legal order. There was no feeling for the necessity of law and rules in face of these doubtful and dangerous situations. When after 1930 Germany was continuously ruled by emergency legislation, when Chancellors changed, but the emergency powers remained, people did not know and became indifferent to whether the emergency measures were within the law, hard at its border or beyond its limits. Acknowledgment of half-legal government made illegal government possible.'[1]

At a later point in the same essay, the writer draws certain other conclusions from German experience, having a startling relevance to the position in Great Britain today:

'Delegation of power does not necessarily conflict with the Rule of Law, but the danger is always near. A certain separation of powers, both in local and higher administration, is the best way to avoid arbitrary decisions. The aim of achieving the highest efficiency was stronger in Germany than the conception of dangers connected with an almighty bureaucracy. So, by virtue of delegated authority, legislative, executive and judicial powers were often concentrated in one hand. In the struggle against scarcity of dwellings, for instance, the same magistrate might combine three functions which are normally under separate controls. He might have to issue the regulations governing conditions under which rooms had to be placed at his disposal, he could order a certain individual to give up a certain room in favour of another individual and pass judgment on a complaint connected with such an order. Delegations of this kind may often be necessary and sometimes harmless. The harmlessness depends on the working of controls, either bureaucratic or democratic. Parliamentary committees of enquiry and the activity of a vigilant opposition may control the administration as effectively as the Courts. But without controls delegation in the long run demoralizes the officials and embitters and injures the individuals. This was the German situation in 1918 when the arbitrary decisions were unavoidable in such a system, the general fear of arbitrary decisions and the distrust of all decisions whatsoever totally destroyed respect for law and government. In critical times the common man's ordinary experience of the public administration is of the same importance as matters of high politics.

[1] 'The Place of Law in Germany', (1943) 59 *Law Quarterly Review*, p. 134, 143-4.

'In connexion with these problems of control it has to be kept in mind that under German law there was not always and not even regularly an appeal to the Courts against infringements of law by government officials and public authorities.

'Delegations were often of such a wide compass that nearly all measures the government wanted to carry through could be covered by its wording. Consequently regulations could be issued which had nothing to do with the purpose of the delegation and which entered spheres which, for political reasons, were closed to ordinary legislation. The classic example is the reform of the law of procedure by order in council, issued under a law which contained an especially broad delegation (1924). The reform of civil and penal procedure, whether good or bad in itself, was not necessary in order to overcome the inflation or the difficulties brought about by it and it was for these purposes that the delegation was given. The reform was an old and deep desire of the high officials of the Ministry of Justice. For many reasons it was never possible to get the parliament actively interested in the reform bills. Then, in 1924, the delegated powers were a gift from heaven for the civil service. The government, which was governed by the bureaucracy in all matters without obvious political interest, issued the new statutes. This was, if not against the law, against its spirit and it was certainly not compatible with the Rule of Law in its political meaning.'[2]

These, and similar episodes will help to explain why the transformation of government in Germany from the Weimar Republic to the fully developed authoritarianism of the Nazis was carried out with complete legality. Indeed, the Social Democrats who were the backbone of the Weimar Republic, prepared their own downfall by the easy recourse to wide delegations of power to achieve social reform which an ambitious bureaucracy suggested to them. Hence it followed that although the judiciary of Republican Germany had a high sense of judicial independence (which was guaranteed by the Constitution) and although the German republic and civil service was as able and as incorruptible as our own, neither was in a position to offer prolonged resistance to the authoritarian onslaught.

It may perhaps be objected, however, that the Germans have a predisposition towards authoritarian rule (a highly debatable assertion) and that with them 'Might is Right'.

[2] *Ibid.*, p. 147.

Whatever may be the truth upon these topics, it cannot be questioned that the democratic tradition in France is as deep-rooted as it is with us, or that their attachment to personal freedom is as great. Yet after the collapse of French resistance in 1940, the National Assembly on July 10th was content to confer the widest powers upon the French executive, until a new constitution should be adopted. Thus, by a delegation of power in comprehensive terms, the French Assembly created an authoritarian regime by completely legal and constitutional means. Thereafter, Marshal Petain governed by decrees, which derived their formal validity from the law of July 10th, 1940. By this means, also, Marshal Petain would have enjoyed full powers to enact a new Constitution for France, had it not been for the saving clause that any new Constitution must be ratified by referendum. So long as two-thirds of French territory remained under German occupation, such a referendum was impossible. Accordingly, in his constitutional changes, and in them only, Marshal Petain broke the link of continuity and exceeded the terms of the delegation of power to him.[3] It is significant that in neither Germany nor France did any hint of resistance proceed from the bureaucracy which was able to hold itself free from responsibility by political neutrality.

Both Germany and France possessed written constitutions, making it necessary to comply with special provisions in order to secure constitutional change. In Great Britain, however, the process would be easier. A simple Act of Parliament would do all that is necessary. Indeed, in our own hour of peril, in 1940, we established something like a formal dictatorship of the Executive. Yet this dictatorship was superimposed upon our normal Parliamentary government, and was subject throughout to Parliamentary criticism. Much of the apparatus was abandoned at an early date after hostilities had ceased. It is not from such measures, taken to counter a ruthless foe in time of war, that democracy has reason to be afraid. In that respect the English people have qualities similar to those of the Romans, who did not hesitate to give a dictator unlimited powers so long as the enemy was at the gate, but who required the powers to be aban-

[3] M. A. Sieghart, *Government by Decree*, pp. 193-194.

G*

doned as soon as the emergency had passed. Such a reaction to extreme danger is a sign of vigour. It differs fundamentally from the steady and insidious curtailment of freedom which occurs under the plea of social necessity.

A survey of our political and social history during the past three-quarters of a century suggests two important general conclusions:

(1) That the increasing fondness for executive power is not the monopoly of any one political party. It is, or has been a characteristic of all, though with different degrees of emphasis.

(2) The usurpation of government by the departments is dangerous *per se*. It becomes very much more dangerous, however, when it is allied with a collectivist philosophy, for at that point the barriers which might otherwise prove in ordinary circumstances adequate are swept away.

These two conclusions will be elaborated in turn. Maitland, it will be remembered, writing in the second half of the nineteenth century, remarked that we had become a much-governed people. This was at a time when the newly-aroused social conscience was giving effect to its aspirations in legislation designed to improve the common lot. This resulted in the creation of boards of many kinds—for example, school boards and boards of guardians, charged with the duty of executing social policy under special statutes. This expression of democratic freedom in local activity was in harmony with our long tradition of local government. Since then, however, the scene has been transformed. In the first place, these local boards have progressively been merged in all-purpose units of local government. This has been accompanied by the development of efficient municipal civil services, whose functions have steadily expanded at the expense of effective control by local councils. Today, the elected councillor is to a substantial degree in the hands of his permanent officials. This is partly because the nature of their work has increased enormously in bulk and complexity with the steady extension of social legislation, and because the local officials themselves must work in close association with Whitehall, which not only exercises constant supervision over what they do, but also supplies much of the finance, on the fulfilment of specific conditions. The result is that the local councillor feels an increasing sense of frustration, and there has been in consequence, a progressive decline of interest in local government, which directly corresponds with the increase in central control. It is difficult to see what alternative could exist, however, so long as social services are planned on a national basis. Yet a glance at a modern statute, such as the Housing Act, or the Education Act, will show how little initiative today remains either to the local official or the local councillor. As the patterns of conduct traced by Whitehall become ever more clearly defined, it remains only for the local authority to ensure that these patterns are being adhered to in the area over which they exercise powers of local government.

It is possible to regard the present emergence of the executive as the dominant factor in our political life from two distinct points of view: (1) as a phase in the struggle between Parliament and the Executive which is the main theme of our constitutional history, or (2) in its wider context, as a phase in modern political evolution, for, as we have seen, this problem recurs in the recent political history of the United States, France, Germany, and indeed, of every considerable State.

Ever since the Norman Conquest it is possible to trace in our political life the desire of representatives of the community at large to set limits to the power of the Executive. This has found expression in several ways. The medieval Common Lawyers elaborated the theory of a common law which bound the sovereign as much as it bound the subject. The King ruled, but in accordance with laws which could only be changed with the consent of all. Such changes could only be expressed in formal compacts between King and nation, of which Magna Carta is the supreme example. But once the principle of representation was established, it was possible for a deliberative body, which ultimately became Parliament, to speak on behalf of the nation. So for a time during the Middle Ages, the King actually did legislate with the advice of the representatives of the people, assembled in Parliament, the balance between them, though fluctuating with the personality of the sovereign, not being too violently disturbed. With the Tudors, the Executive showed plain signs of emancipating itself from medieval limits. Parliament could be used as a convenient instrument to ratify any change, no matter how far-reaching. Thus Parliament could separate the nation from Rome, suppress the monasteries, change the national religion, and modify the order of succession. Behind its apparently unlimited legislative competence, however, was the force of royal power which, by means of an active council and prerogative courts with jurisdiction which increasingly encroached upon that of the Common Law Courts, constantly checked undue assertions of Parliamentary independence. The seventeenth century struggle ended the royal assertions of executive power independently of Parliamentary control, and from 1688 until the second half of the nineteenth century, Parliament not only exercised an unlimited legislative power, but to a considerable degree controlled the Executive as well. When, during the reign of George III, and in response to royal prompting, the Executive again showed signs of challenging this control, both Parliament (and especially the House of Commons) and the Courts were strong enough to defeat it.

Since the middle of the nineteenth century, however, the Executive has again shown the plainest signs, not only of emancipating itself from Parliamentary control, but of dominating Parliament to an extent that neither the Stuarts nor George III were able to do. Some reasons for this have already been noticed. The progressive extensions of the franchise have made the individual member far more dependent upon his party organisation than was formerly the case, and have enabled political leaders to appeal directly to the electorate at large, over the heads of their representatives. This has been facilitated by the spread of popular education, the increasing mobility of all classes of the community, and the development of such inventions as the telegraph and telephone, the radio, and now television.

Side by side with these changes, there have been others. A transfer of power from one class of the community inevitably involves also a change in social outlook. Although we have travelled a long way from the days when the electors of closed corporations put up their votes for public auction, a dominating class still requires tangible rewards from its representatives. If the class is a wide one, the organisation needed to satisfy its desires will be elaborate. Thus, education, national health insurance, housing and the other social services have prompted the creation of large and highly-skilled public services operating under the control of a State department, and each possessing a strong sense of corporate loyalty. It is idle to assume that the political chiefs of the departments concerned effectively control this vast machine. Today, it is indeed much if they even understand how it works; but to a considerable degree, it continues of its own momentum. It possesses a capacity to make and modify the rules governing its activities which makes it, to a substantial degree, independent not only of Parliamentary control, but also of effective Ministerial supervision. In any event, the steady growth of departmental tradition, and the folklore of departmental outlook upon administrative problems within its sphere, quells all but the boldest. A century ago, when the departmental staffs were still in their infancy, and when there still existed a sharp cleavage between a ruling class and the instruments of government, departmental employees were in a very real sense the Minister's servants. Now he is lucky if he is not theirs.

Accordingly, no real picture of the government of Great Britain can be obtained until it is realised that outside the hurly-burly of popular elections, unchanged by fluctuations in the political climate, well over a million civil servants now industriously carry on the work of government, looking to their permanent departmental heads for guidance, approval and ultimate promotion. To them, the political head is a remote, and sometimes troublesome, phenomenon, whom the permanent heads will do their best to bring under proper control. At all costs, and in spite of all complications, the machine must continue to work smoothly, and since the interventions of the uninitiated are apt to show a lamentable lack of comprehension of the objectives to be attained, the more they are left in the dark the better—especially if they are Members of Parliament. Thus, as the independent sphere of activity of this vast and ever-growing machine widens, Parliamentary control becomes increasingly formal and ineffective. Parliament, in fact, is predestined, if present tendencies continue, to become merely a ratifying body and a suitable forum for the ventilation of grievances. The process of evolution is interesting and significant. In Parliament, the House of Commons has swallowed the House of Peers, insofar as effective governmental power is concerned. Now the Departments are swallowing Parliament.

Continental, and especially German, experience has shown, however, that this is not the whole story. Every modern department cultivates neutralism in politics, not only because that way safety lies, but because many of the day-to-day questions of government are questions which can be, and often are, decided independently of party views upon them. The relation of the political heads to the permanent officials thus becomes clear. The political heads set the course, and the permanent officials navigate. Their services are equally at the disposal of any government, whatever its complexion. They are, that is to say, an additional instrument of almost unlimited potentiality, at the disposal of a party in power. In Germany and in France, and indeed in other European countries, they have provided a secure bridge upon which parties either of the Left or the Right have been able to cross legally from Parliamentarianism to authoritarian rule.

At this point it should be emphasised that the extra-Parliamentary powers possessed by the Departments cannot be attributed to the activities of any single political party. All three have helped to disturb the balance of the constitution, and the blame can be fairly accurately apportioned. Putting the matter another way, it can be said that all three have responded to the dominating social forces of the age. When the Liberals, in response to the insistent promptings of the newly-enfranchised working class, especially as expressed by the trade unions whose growth they had fostered, turned from social reform to social reorganisation, they swept away progressively the barriers which impeded the achievement of their aims. The strongest was the House of Lords, and this was under constant attack from 1880 onwards. It capitulated in the great constitutional struggle of 1909-10, and with the passing of the Parliament Act of

1911 the era of one-chamber government was inaugurated. In this respect the Labour Government, in its Parliament Act of 1949, merely carried the policy of its Liberal predecessor one stage further. The Act of 1911, however, must be considered in association with other items of Liberal legislation. The Finance Act of 1894 laid the foundations of modern confiscatory legislation in its graduated scale of death duties. In the following half-century the great accumulations of wealth have been remorselessly destroyed. The Lloyd George budget of 1909 traced the outlines of the modern 'social service' State; whilst the statute book for the period 1880-1914 shows how readily the departments availed themselves of the changed social outlook to enlarge their spheres of freedom from Parliamentary control.

Not all these advances took place under Liberal Governments however. The period of Conservative rule from 1885 until 1905 shows no perceptible change in governmental outlook. Equally in the inter-war period of Conservative dominance, successive governments availed themselves with the same freedom as their Liberal predecessors of the powers of departmental legislation and adjudication which docile majorities in the House of Commons were so ready to concede. Similarly Conservative leaders as we have seen,[4] were as ready to press the claims of the Executive in respect of taxation to their furthest limits as their Liberal predecessors had been. But the most serious criticism of Conservative policy which can be made in this respect is that during the whole inter-war period, they made no effort whatever to solve the constitutional problem which had been avowedly left unsolved in 1911. The preamble to the Parliament Act of 1911 says:

'Whereas it is intended to substitute for the House of Lords as it at present exists a second chamber constituted on a popular instead of a hereditary basis, but such substitution cannot be immediately brought into operation.

'And whereas provision will require hereafter to be made by Parliament in a measure effecting such substitution for limiting and defining the powers of the new Second Chamber, but it is expedient to make such provision as in this Act appears for restricting the existing powers of the House of Lords——'

[4] ante. pp. 18–19, 125.

Nothing could be clearer, therefore than that the Liberal Party at this date contemplated the establishment of an effective Second Chamber on a popular basis. Such a body would no doubt have possessed powers comparable with those possessed by the American Senate, or the second chambers of the British Dominions. To have solved this problem during the inter-war years would have been to have shown political foresight, and to introduce a badly-needed element of stability into our constitutional structure. The Conservatives, however, appeared to be ignorant that a problem of any importance existed. Today, it is almost certain that the opportunity no longer exists.

It will be evident, therefore, that when the Labour Party came to power in 1945, they found an instrument ready forged to their hands. The by-passing of Parliament by the departments was already advanced. So was the domination of Parliament by the Executive. What the Labour Party since 1945 did was to make abundantly plain, even to the non-expert, the almost unlimited possibilities for social revolution within the formal framework of our constitution. It was not necessary for them to put Parliament in commission, as the Nazis did after 1933, and as Sir Stafford Cripps and his colleagues suggested might be necessary here. For one thing, the powers of the vested interests which might have been expected to offer stubborn resistance were already crumbling as a result of the inroads of the past half-century, and of the upheavals of two world wars. In particular, although the House of Lords in 1911 had still been left with a by no means negligible power to delay unwelcome legislation, even this power had atrophied during the long period of Conservative rule in the inter-war years and after the second war, the Lords were too weak to attempt to revive it. The second Parliament Act of 1948 was therefore no more than a measure of insurance on the part of the Labour Party. Although the House of Lords discharges many useful governmental functions of a minor character, it is powerless to impede the achievement of major governmental policy. No-one at this date would suggest that it should be otherwise, for today the only effective brake which can be placed upon the policy of an all-powerful Executive is one which must proceed from the consciousness of wide-spread support, and this the Lords, as a body, demonstrably, do not possess.

It is only the natural order of things that the Labour Government should have exploited the technique of departmental aggrandisement to an extent not attempted by their predecessors. A social service State, owning vast State monopolies in the field of industry and trade, requires powerful departments, responsive to official promptings to control them. Simply through the achievement of this policy, the power of the Government of the day has increased enormously since 1939. It controls the lives and welfare of every one of us. As successive crises in nationalised industries have shown, we are now dependent for our very existence as a community upon the capacity of the departments to keep them running at any rate with some semblance of success. If there are signs that the powers already possessed are not adequate, it cannot be doubted that a Parliamentary majority will be prepared to concede still more. As *The Times* well expressed it in a leading article upon the future of the Labour Party on May 15th, 1951:

'At its annual conference in 1919 the Labour Party took a fateful step when, following the lead of Sidney Webb, it committed itself not only to Socialism, but to one particular definition of Socialism which happened at the time to have found acceptance with the Fabian Society. By this definition Socialism is identified with the increase (almost unlimited in the economic field) of the State's power and activity. It is a direct consequence of this decision that an important element among those in the Labour Party who doubt the direction which the party has taken consists of those who looked for more power for the workers and for ordinary people and have been given instead the huge, impersonal and management-controlled public corporation. Mr. Bevan, in his indictment of the "economists", partly voices their vague but real resentment against the State managers who, as they see it, have annexed Socialism. There is nothing in the history of Socialist thought to suggest that the State is the natural and inevitable instrument by which Socialism is to be attained. From Proudhon to William Morris to the Guild Socialists, distrust of the State has been a constant element in the development of Socialist ideas. It is the tragedy of the Labour movement that it has been so intent on extending the authority of the State that it has overlooked the purpose of its existence.'

The leader-writer argues strongly for a redefinition of Socialist policy in the light of post-war experience, and he concludes:

'Two lessons stand out clearly. The first is that the unquestioning faith in the power and activity of the State, inherited from the Webbs, has proved illusory. The second is that the redistribution of income cannot solve the problem of poverty or bring equality of opportunity appreciably nearer. Like their opponents, the Labour Party must seek an economic policy which will release the potential productive energy of the country. The State must be envisaged as stimulating enterprise for the social good, instead of confining and controlling it. The pursuit of equality must be redefined—not as a depressing, levelling process, but as the creation of a genuine equality of opportunity which will encourage and reward effort, instead of cramping it. There is no reason why such a policy should not be conceived in Socialist terms. It will require a clear-headed and unemotional approach to contemporary problems; and a start could best be made by abandoning the great fallacy of modern Socialist thought—that the State and the community are synonymous.'

Very far from being synonymous, State and community in Britain are now in open conflict, for the State is manifestly strangling the community. Nor is this surprising. The Webbs had as their ideal for Britain a paradise for the routine-bound administrator, an ideal which is repugnant at once to the British character and tradition. Limited by nature to a restricted territorial area, the British in the past three centuries have extended their energies and their commercial and industrial talents to every corner of the globe by their resource, adaptability and initiative. It is manifestly ludicrous to imagine that they will maintain their position by the development of opposite qualities. In this respect the groundnuts scheme is a suggestive pointer to our future overseas. Even this, however, is by no means the full story. The concentration of industry and commerce in State-monopolies implies the existence of a master-plan, into which the activities of these unwieldy enterprises can be fitted. No doubt the construction of such a plan calls for the exercise of initiative and inventiveness on the part of the planners. For the rest of the community, it implies a routine-bound existence which is made bearable by the offer of State benefits at every stage in exchange for the capacity to shape one's own destinies. It is, in fact, the policy of 'Mother knows best', carried by logical deduction, to the point of absurdity.

Unfortunately, there are even graver implications. When the process of constructing State-monopolies has been carried to its furthest point, we shall have an electorate which is predominantly composed of their employees. These will have a vested interest in the maintenance of the system for their own benefit. To change will not only be hazardous, but politically impossible. In fact, therefore, the continuation of the policy which is now being brought into force to its logical conclusion inevitably involves the establishment, by progressive stages, of the one-party State. This may be easier than is sometimes supposed, for with the decline in the importance of Parliament, and by the steady recruitment of the more highly trained members of the community to the departments and State-monopolies, the standard of party organisation may also be expected to decline. In any event, with the progressive curtailment of individual initiative by official planning, much of the purpose of party conflict passes. Already the revolt against *étatism* has made its appearance in all parties. The struggle to curb it, and to maintain what remains of our personal freedom, is being progressively recognised as more fundamental than mere differences in party programmes.

The problem which therefore faces all peoples which are still attached to the democratic way of life is to find some means of curbing the power of the executive, and preventing it from usurping the entire functions of government. The nineteenth century assumption that this would be achieved by successive extensions of the franchise has proved completely fallacious. The executive, as it has ventured to interfere increasingly with the lives of its subjects, has at the same time taken care to ensure that its servants and dependents (including the State-monopolies) are removed from the sphere of popular control. Its techniques grow ever more audacious. Today, in Britain, it is not only that wide powers of legislation, in fact if not in theory immune from Parliamentary control, have been granted to the departments. In addition, these powers in turn are habitually delegated by the departments to its own agents. Instances of sub-delegation to the fourth and fifth degree are not uncommon. In addition, the case of *Earl Fitzwilliam's Wentworth Estates Co.* v. *Minister of Town and Country Planning* illustrates how what has been called departmental *quasi-legislation* by circulars and explanatory memoranda, can acquire compulsive force. To what extent this was developing was shown by Mr. R. E. Megarry in a note in *The Law Quarterly Review* as long ago as 1944,[5] where he remarks:

> 'No lawyer will view with pleasure a process whereby statutes may acquire an administrative gloss both between State and subject and between subject and subject (the State intervening), and the unrepealed words of the statute book may be emasculated, not by the Legislature or the judiciary but by mere administrative process.'

This process has been pushed a good deal further since Mr. Megarry wrote. A particularly audacious recent example was discussed by the City Editor of the *Sunday Times* on September 9, 1951. In the preceding week, Sir Wilfrid Eady, Joint Second Secretary to the Treasury, wrote to Lord Kennet, the Chairman of the Capital Issues Committee on the Chancellor of the Exchequer's dividend limitation proposals in relation to the terms of new capital issues. Sir Wilfrid pointed out that companies which raised money through an issue with a substantial bonus element might get an advantage over permitted dividend distributions as compared with companies raising money through an issue to the market. He therefore suggested that this point should be borne in mind by the Committee when considering the terms of a new issue. As the City Editor pointed out, this comes dangerously near to a usurpation of legislative functions by the Treasury. No Bill to limit dividends at this date had even been drafted, much less introduced into Parliament or passed. Nevertheless, the Capital Issues Committee was being invited to act as if the Bill had already been passed, and a leading Civil Servant sees nothing incongruous, to put it no more strongly, in acting as an instrument whereby Parliament is by-passed. This, it will be remembered was precisely the process whereby Parliamentary government

[5] 60 *Law Quarterly Review*, pp. 125-8.

was overthrown in Germany in the inter-war period. Even in Great Britain such semi-dictatorial techniques already pass almost without comment.

It is plain, therefore, that we are already approaching the dangerous half-light in which the boundaries of what is legal and what is not are barely perceptible. Nor should we take comfort in the fact that most modern States are facing similar problems. That is undoubtedly true, but most of them are facing these problems within a stronger constitutional framework than our own. We have no written constitution, and no special constitutional machinery. Any change, no matter how far-reaching, can be achieved by ordinary legislation. For all practical purposes, that change depends upon votes of a single Chamber, in which the majority party is closely-controlled by the Government of the day. The United States, for example, has a written constitution, changed only by special constitutional machinery. It has an effective Senate, as well as States Governments with spheres of activity upon which the Central Government cannot trespass, and finally, Congress has greater independence of the Executive, headed by the President, than our own House of Commons enjoys. It should also be added that the legal accountability of Ministers for their public conduct has ended with the passing of impeachment. Political accountability, in theory to the House of Commons, is in practice to the Government of which they are members. Thus, Great Britain today is a country in which an all-powerful Executive, acting through a subservient Parliamentary majority in one sphere, and subservient Departments, interfering with the life of the citizen at all points, and operating gigantic State-monopolies, exercises despotic power. It is therefore not to be wondered at that Communists and other political extremists assure us that they are prepared to work constitutionally. If they had fashioned the constitutional machinery themselves, it could scarcely have been apter for their purpose.

It is for this reason that no attempt has been made in this book to discuss at length the safeguards, actual or possible, which could check the relentless advance of administrative tyranny in Great Britain. Within the existing framework, such safeguards could not be effective. Everyone of them could be swept away by a Parliamentary majority. It is, in fact, the very existence of a formally unfettered Parliamentary sovereignty that is the main source of weakness in our existing institutions, when the legal sovereign has shown itself so willing to delegate its powers as Parliament has done during the past half century. If the temper of the times remains favourable to increasing interference with the lives of citizens, towards the destruction of individual initiative, and towards the concentration of economic wealth in the State, then any safeguards which legal and political ingenuity may devise will remain as ineffective as consumers' Councils within State-monopolies are today. Behind the high sounding generalities of present-day politics, the issue is really a very simple one. It is whether we should accustom ourselves to the ant-like existence of the fully-integrated and planned State, or whether we believe that individual initiative and increased opportunity are more likely to produce more tolerable conditions of life for the bulk of our citizens. In the long run, it is impossible to preserve freedom of the mind when the power to choose has been removed from the citizen in more and more areas of his daily life. In the end, there will have been produced something approximating to the planned stagnation of the Chinese Empire. That would be an odd fate for a people who built the Common Law and who were responsible for Magna Carta, *habeas corpus*, and dominion status. Yet the threat is real, and the hour late. Our present predicament presents a challenge which it is impossible to ignore.

Index